TWIT PUBLISHING Presents

PULP!

Summer/Fall 2011

I0683119

edited by Chris Gabrysch

The following works are works of fiction. Names, characters, places, and incidents either are the product of the authors' imagination or are used fictitiously. Any resemblance to actual persons, living or dead, events, or locales is entirely coincidental.

Twit Publishing Presents: PULP! 2011 Summer / Fall

Published by
Twit Publishing
Dallas, Texas

Copyright © 2011 by Twit Publishing LLC

Edited by Chris Gabrysch
Cover design by Chris Gabrysch
with special thanks to Brian Rehlander

ISBN-13 978-0-9845477-5-3

Second Edition Paperback 2011

Praise for the
Twit Publishing Presents: PULP! Series

"This collection is a rare gem, and true to its classical pulp form, it gives the reader the feeling of participating in something quite noir-ish that has been cobbled together with simple finesse as well as a touch of disorderly madness. I cannot wait to see what else Twit Publishing has in store for us."

—Debrin Case
Open Heart Publishing

"Each story in the collection is short enough to be enjoyed in a quick moment or two of reading, and all are lively, quick-paced and guaranteed to hold the reader's attention . . . Representing the revival of pulp fiction interest, *Pulp!* is one of the best examples of 21st century pulp yet to be found."

—*Las Vegas Review-Journal*

"It's amazing more people aren't doing this sort of thing."

—*StarNewsOnline.com*

The editor would like to thank Joshua Toon. I would also like to thank the writers from our first two anthologies for all their hard work. Also, a very big thanks to the book stores that carry them: Cliff Notes, Awesome Comics, Paperbacks Plus, and Austin Books & Comics.

Contents

Foreword

By Chris Gabrysch

Really? I have to do a third foreword?

I mean, I enjoy writing them and all. But a third one?

No one cares about any of them besides my mom (she doesn't even read the stories). Who else reads this shit? No, really, let's be serious here, who else reads this shit? All they do is serve as a word speed bump, slowing you down on the drive to the stories for which you actually paid.

So, let's treat this like we're tearing off an old band-aid: quickly and painfully.

First, I'd like to say how excited I am that nine out of fourteen authors in this anthology published stories in our first two volumes.

Returning readers is one thing (a truly great thing), but returning authors is something completely different. That means they're happy with what we produce, which says a lot to me.

Secondly, two stories are continuations of earlier stories and characters from the first two volumes. "The Ball" continues the adventures of Felix and Sa'id, two of the main characters from "Over the Sahara," a dieselpunk story that first appeared in *Summer/Fall 2010*. "Good Fences Make Good" is a Wilder short story. You may remember Wilder from the story "Double Take," which was in *Winter/Fall 2011*. Hopefully both of these stories will become somewhat serialized and appear in future *PULP!* anthologies . . . fingers crossed on that one.

The other seven authors' stories? They just happen to be well written.

Finally, I'd like to address the growth of our company.

I came up with an analogy for our company about a year ago. An analogy, not an anthology.

Imagine: Twit Publishing stands on the top of a mountain (say Kilimanjaro, Everest, or McKinley), and we begin to roll a snowball from the top. It rolls and rolls, picks up snow and becomes larger. It rolls and rolls, picking up speed, traveling down the mountainside. The snowball picks up speed and size as it rolls downhill. It becomes ever larger. It rolls and rolls and keeps on rolling. It becomes bigger and bigger as it rolls down the slope, taking out trees and small woodland creatures.

It gets even bigger, approaching gigantic. Did it just take out a moose? No! That was Sasquatch!

How big is it past fifteen thousand feet above sea level? I don't fucking know. All I know is that it's probably getting pretty fucking big!

It rolls and rolls, until it ceases to be a giant snowball, instead transforming into an avalanche, a tidal wave of ice and slush and impending doom.

There are little fanboys trapped in it now, and squirrels and wolves are attacking them. Look! Sasquatch is reading *Twit Publishing Presents: PULP! Winter/Spring 2014!*

This avalanche continues till it rolls down the hill and takes out a metropolis. Hopefully, it's Dallas. Probably not, though. Dallas is on a plain and there aren't any mountains around.

But one can hope, right?

Chris Gabrysch
5/24/2011
Dallas, Texas

A Stranger in Ferrview

By Frank R Sjodin

It was on the breaking of second dusk of a Sunday night when the stranger came to town. The only transmission the landing terminal got from his ship was: "RECIEVED SOS, WILL NEGOTI-ATE IMMEDIATE AID. RENEGADE, COMBAT RATING ZZ."

Mayor Munthly held a press conference to meet him and announce that we were finally saved, probably to divert attention from the fact that neither the Feds nor AstroDig had responded to the call for help. It had been three months since the SOS transmission was sent out and the people of Ferrview still lived in fear of a dangerous menace that the living had only seen as a dark, distorted shape on a few traffic recorders.

As a nine year old boy, I fully believed that this stranger coming into town was here to save us. His ship was a towering silhouette behind him, peaking between him and the setting sun as he walked the dusty trail into town. He'd removed his helmet but was still wearing his astrosuit, which was covered

5

in lubricant dust and hardened emergency re-sealant. His hair was dark and short, his face hard and cold, and one of his eyes an antiquated cybernetic replacement. He was smoking a fat, white, hand rolled cigarette filled with something I had never smelled before. He wore an antimatter pistol and an electric sidearm, a miniature version of the railguns on the big naval warships, both just below the hip. The awaiting crowd parted as he walked, everyone eying him with a mixture of apprehension, admiration, terror, and disgust. He stopped in the center of the crowd, raised his eyebrows as he scanned the townsfolk, took a deep drag off his space spliff, and smirked.

"You must be the folks put out an SOS, huh? Well, here I am, seems like I'm the only response you got. Take me to your leader and I'll see what I can do about your little problem."

Ferrview town meetings rarely discussed anything important because the colony wasn't a place where important things happened. Back then, Ferrview was a small mining colony on an asteroid one hundred kilometers in diameter short of a dwarf planet. It was populated mostly by Indie war veterans like Pa, who had no love for the Federate Union but had accepted the fact that they had lost the war and looked to settle down peacefully. The nearest settlement was sixteen light years away and the only valuable exports the colony had were common asteroid metals used to make warship armor. Since the Unification War had ended four years ago, there was little demand for armor anymore. The galaxy was so full of leftover warships that even Ferrview used gun-stripped support frigates for mine shuttles.

The meeting that night started early and ended late, and all the kids in town had a meeting of our own to discuss what we thought was going on. Whatever had been devastating the mine shuttles had already been the hot topic of discussion for months, and we all had our own ideas about how the stranger would deal with it. Some kids said it was a Union stealth ship stolen by pirates and refit with fringe tech. A popular belief was that it was an alien scout testing our defenses against an invasion. Giant robot, mutant cyborg space whale, and rogue scientist rumors flew aimlessly, yet I held firmly to the belief that the thing was in fact a dragon, like the ones in the old 3D fantasy videos. I based my theory on the dark shape in the recordings that we had all seen and pure inexperienced imagination.

Pa didn't look too happy when he got home from the meeting. I had a trillion questions for him, but he made me go straight to bed — the only things I found out were that luxury rations were completely cut for the next week and in the morning he was still scheduled to work the mines. I heard him charging his beam pistol as I went to bed, but I had no idea what good it would do him.

The next morning came and the entire town was out to watch the shuttle depart, escorted by the stranger's painted warship. It was half the size of the armored shuttle but teeming with turrets, cannons, sensor disks, and missile racks. I could only clearly read part of the message that was painted on the side of his ship in several languages and there was only one I recognized — "S GEO."

It reminded me of an old code I had seen used in a fictitious war serial. I assumed it stood for "Starship Earth." Luke said that it was a factory mark meaning the stranger's ship was so old it was actually built on planet Earth. Eddy said it was part of a slogan or a protective spell in ancient languages engraved in the hull to ward off ghosts. I think it was the ship's name — like they did in the days of the Grand Old War, before IFF transponders were a standard requirement on warships.

After the ships left sight, Ma said it was okay if I ran to the local info terminal to find out the results of last night's late meeting. I had overheard enough to need to know more. I found out that the stranger had no regular ID, and all the information on him was either classified or useless: combat ratings, blood type, et cetera. He was just a Renegade. One of the war veterans who wasn't able to reinstate himself into society like Pa and Uncle Rainy did. A man with no skills useful to society other than death and destruction. The kind of man we learned about in history videos when we covered the Expansion Decades, but didn't think existed in real life, not after the Unification, and certainly not in Ferrview.

I went to a more reliable source to find out the results of the meeting. Ma told me everything and it was just as I might have guessed. The entire town's luxury rations were cut to pay for him. He was to escort the shuttles to the mines every day, then return and stay in high orbit to defend the city all day in case the dragon approached Ferrview itself, and at day's end he would return to the mines to escort the shuttles back. His contract was to last until the hostile itself was destroyed or it took his life. To ensure his loyalty, the town government had disabled his trans-star drive and paid him an enormous advance from the treasury, with a bonus to arrive if he could bring back remains of the hostile for study after eliminating it. On weekends and evenings he was allowed to dock his ship and stay in town itself, but could never be more than two kilometers from the starport in case he had to rush back to his ship for combat.

It all sounded so exciting, yet so disciplined like Great Grandpa's stories from the Grand Old War. All day in school, I and most of the other boys dreamed about what it must be like to be a Renegade. That evening, Pa and the rest of the miners came home without so much as a blip of the hostile ship on the sensors all day.

As the weeks went on, I learned not to bring up the stranger, the mayor, or what I had been calling "the Dragon" around Pa. He was his normal self most days, but every time he had to board the shuttle, he and Ma acted like it might be the last time. We kids could only barely notice their worry, and I certainly didn't have any concern for Pa's safety. He was the second toughest man I ever knew, under the protection of the toughest man I could ever imagine!

Now although we children of the town idolized the stranger, the business folk hated him. He ignored all minor ordinances concerning curfews, public intoxication, urination, or fornication. On three accounts he was recorded spitting on a constable and he would occasionally atomize a steel-polishing droid for target practice, or miss and scar the buildings when drunk. Although she could never prove it, Mrs. Nonnie claimed that he got all three of her daughters pregnant in one night.

The more we kids heard about him, the more legends we made up. Most of us were kept at home when he roamed the streets or weren't allowed in the districts he frequented, but we all lied about our "frequent" encounters with him.

"Yeah, his name's Ace. Ace Riprockette. He saw me shooting cans with my pneumatic pistol and said he was looking for a kid to be a ball gunner on his rig."

"Shut up, Ernie, you're full of shit."

"Am not!"

"Yeah you are, he never tells *anyone* his name. I know cuz we shared a cig when I snuck out late last night. His cigs have got nerve enhancers in 'em, so he can draw faster, it makes you like all—"

"You're even more full of shit! He wouldn't share a cig with an eight year old!"

"No, but he talked to a thirteen year old — me. He was drunk and needed help loading his pistol while he was shooting buff-and-polish bots. He even let me take a shot at one!"

"James, you're so full of shit we can smell you!"

"Hey James, look, here comes a sewage collector droid. Better look out! You're so full of shit it's gonna carry you off to treatment!"

We laughed and boasted with admiration and complete faith in the stranger. He was our hero.

As weeks passed, the adults in town started having meetings every three days and luckily for me, my best friend Shannon Munthly worked as a junior intern at his uncle's office. To a select few kids, he distributed a virtual live feed of the meetings. This was of course top secret and only kids with the password were those who didn't run the risk of parental interference. Current uncensored news video was becoming harder and harder to access, and, in fact, at this point no more recordings of the hostile ship itself could be found. The first video he distributed wasn't even live and it was only seen by a select few of us. We got about a third through it before a security program caught us and shut down the virtual feed, but it was the most revealing meeting of all — the first town meeting, the stranger's arrival.

"Well, stranger, we have no useful information on the hostile, except that our weapons have been 100 percent ineffective against it. It might have magna plating, a distortion field, or world-class shielding, we don't know. Are you sure you can destroy it?" The Mayor was speaking like I'd never heard him speak. It was as if he really did hold authority, but knew the small thread he held it by.

"Sure. Never seen a ship I couldn't scrap, never met something I couldn't kill. Your 200mm railguns are like crossbows compared to the weaponry I'll unload on it. After one engagement with my ship, you can consider it gone forever. Prolly just pirates who got their hands on some restricted grade equipment."

Pa spoke up: "I don't think it was pirates, there were no bodies of survivors, we have some mass data and a few imag—"

A heavy man in a suit cut him off. "We gave him all the relevant information we have. Now our Renegade says he can kill anything, so I'm sure he can handle it. If he says it's pirates, it probably is. Starships come in all shapes, you know."

"Damn right," the stranger retorted. "I've seen ships shaped like all kinds of things, custom designers think it makes 'em intimidating. And as for missing bodies, I've known no creature of any kind in human history do crueler or stranger things to a body, living or dead, than what humans might do."

The room fell silent.

"Still, by the mass of your warship, you won't be able to

withstand its attack. Our shuttles are former warships with military grade armor—"

"Yeah, Indie made armor," he snorted. "You don't worry about my safety. My ship's fast enough not to get hit and just solid enough to survive when it does."

Kirk said that meant it had to have both a cruiser class distortion field and an entropic deflector, but I always thought it was a boast about his piloting ability. He wasn't the sort to rely on expensive gimmicks and experimental technology. He relied on grit, it was written all over his face, his clothes, his weapons, and his ship. Grit fell from his boots when he walked. It was on his breath when he exhaled smoke, in his blood, in his soul, and I'm sure he left grit in the toilet when he left a men's room.

Pretty soon those of us who were able to watch the meetings became local kid celebs, and I wasn't the only one referring to the unknown terrorizing force as "the Dragon." Younger kids came to me to ask if we were gonna be safe, if the stranger was gonna hurt us or save us, and I felt a great sense of pride as the local Renegade expert. I compared defending his reputation against naysayers to his defending the town from the Dragon.

From watching several meetings, it became clear that not one single adult in town believed that Federal aid was coming anytime soon and few of them had faith in the stranger, either. They said the Feds would only send a warship here if Ferrview discontinued it's regular automated shipment of asteroid ore for a year, and it would just be to pick up refugees. The rich became increasingly angered that luxury rations were paying for the Renegade's wild behavior. There were rumors circulating about him having a "deal with the Dragon," splitting his pay 50/50 with the enemy so it wouldn't attack. But fear kept the adults from cutting off his pay. It always showed in their faces, in their eye movements, in their twitches, and in their sweat.

As we kids saw, it was a simple situation. The Dragon was evil, it ate people, destroyed ore harvests, and crushed ships. Heroes kill bad guys, save the day, and should be allowed to do whatever they want in town. We all wanted to be just like him. I even started rolling my own cigarettes in secret, though I had no idea what to put in them, and my experimentation with what I could steal from the herb garden left me with few tolerable choices.

I woke up to the sirens that night and rushed to the garage, where Pa was busy manning a remote controlled defense satellite. Ma pulled me inside and locked the door, then got busy with her own remote control terminal. I stood where I could see the two HU monitors and stealthily tuned my personal headset to the town defense frequency to listen in.

"That's it all right, hostile has slipped past the first two sensor waves, don't know why we didn't pick it up till now! Must not be radiating standard exhaust—"

"I don't fucking care why we didn't see it, I just want it distracted enough so that Renegade has time to launch and waste the SOB — Deploy the decoy ships!"

I watched on Pa's monitor as the Dragon (for seeing it up close, that became what it was in my mind ever so much more) veered towards the automated decoy ships, closing in as fast as a fighter ship, even though the numbers onscreen indicated it had the mass of a bulk ore hauler. Before it even got to yellow firing range, a magenta-orange flashing beam erupted from what appeared to be its head, and the first decoy ship melted in two. Adjusting its velocity only a fraction, the Dragon nearly collided with the second decoy, there was a flash of sparks and the decoy split — it seemed as if the Dragon had clawed off a portion of the decoy ship's hull. The scanners recalibrated to check for errors and, as I heard the adults spew profanities in disbelief, the monitor displayed the Dragon pulling apart the decoy ship.

Something wasn't right about it, the Dragon pulled from only one direction! How could it pull part of the hull away without pulling the entire ship with it? I remembered the game of handing Ma a chocolate bar in zero-g and holding on so that she pulled me along with it, but pulling the chocolate in opposite directions with two hands could still snap it in half. The Dragon was somehow pulling the ships in two directions for an instant while appearing to pull in only one direction. It was too much for a nine year old high on adrenaline to comprehend.

"Decoys bit it already, open fire! Tell that hotshot fucking cowboy to get outta the atmosphere before that thing attempts entry!"

Aiming lasers activated. Rockets boomed and surface to space missiles began their long, maiden, and final trips. Out in space I could see the Dragon destroy the four automated satellite railgun turrets that fired away helplessly at it. Pa swore like I've never heard him before, and I saw that half the turrets like the ones he and Ma controlled on satellite #3 were trashed. On his monitor I watched his shots, perfectly aimed, veer away from the Dragon as if it had an invisible shell around it that deflected bullets harmlessly. Slowly, the thing landed on the satellite and approached the cameras, as if inspecting a dead rat before tossing it in a rubbish can.

At last I saw a clear image of the Dragon – it had scales of metal, like a real animal, but it moved like a starship or a robot, mechanical and precise. The last I saw of it as the monitor went blank were the teeth inside it's mouth, serrated, buzzing, sparking, and surrounding a cone of white hot flame inside what could only be described as a maw of death. I shouted at Ma and Pa, demanding to know what was happening. Ma callously told me to hold lockdown, and as the lights began to flicker, Pa said we'd better hope the stranger was worth all he'd said he was and more. That's when I felt better, I looked close at Pa and saw the glimmer of hope in his eyes behind the furled brows of worry. Ma kissed him and held me close, and I knew we would last the night.

Unfortunately, the next morning we found out that the east half of town wasn't as lucky as the west. Our neighborhood was fine, but defense satellite #2 had come down like a meteor in the rural zone and destroyed several acres of farmland while covering half the town in dust. Worse yet was the scene on the far east end, where a skyscraper had crumbled to the soil, thanks to a crash landing by our town's very own visiting Renegade. I was in desperate shock and tried to rationalize my incoming tears away. He couldn't be dead. If his ship had crashed, then surely the Dragon must be lying dead, somewhere in orbit or outside the city in a crater, or else it must have split and vaporized in reentry.

Other kids had various reactions, but we all learned the truth almost immediately — not even a disaster of that magnitude could impede the flow of honest and fresh information. Town meetings were no longer private, the mayor was no longer in control of the city, and there was no minor censoring of the press anymore. While Ma and Pa rallied with the fire and health control force, other grown-ups began organizing an evacuation plan, and a small group began to amass what I feared was a lynch mob around the crashed warship, awaiting the hatch to open. Ma and Pa were too busy to keep track of me, so I joined the crowd.

No one dared get too close for fear of radiation leakage, so I crouched around the rubble with binoculars and watched the ship. The mayor, Mrs. Nonnie, and others of the town's affluent society were among those awaiting him as well. I ignored their screaming discussions, met with my friends, and took turns running to get food or water while watching and waiting for the hero to emerge from the wreckage. We exchanged stories from the night before and tried our best not to face the reality that we'd never see some of our friends again.

That reality was the harshest lesson I'd ever learned. I found out that Uncle Rainy and Aunt Denise had been among the dead. Luke and his family were killed as well. I was too hurt to cry, unable to believe that this may have happened because the stranger let us down. I clung that much harder to my hope that he would emerge from the wreckage of *Starship Earth*, raise his antimatter pistol in a rally of hope, strap on a rocket pack, and fly out into space to slay the Dragon one-on-one and return with its head. He was more than just hope to me, I felt as if he was all I had to believe in. He was what I wanted to believe in most.

For nine hours we waited and watched. As soon as his hatch opened, I heard gunfire and jeers. My hero was greeted with bullets and death threats, not applause. The rich men were using their heirloom sporting rifles to snipe shots into the open hatch of the ship. A few repairmen were even aiming modified nail drivers at the hatch. Children screamed for them to stop, the mayor did nothing, and a few miners in the crowd rushed towards the shooters in protest, but were held back at gunpoint. I couldn't even react. How could they attack our hero, our only hope?

I heard a *boom* like I'd never heard before, it was a sound like words I'd seen used to describe explosions with capital letters in the local comics, but never managed to pronounce. Tear gas burst into the crowd. Through the shouts and sobbing, I hit the dirt and crawled away to a low point as the gas lifted upwards. I heard gunshots, but one was a sound that lifted my heart, the sound of an antimatter weapon that I'd only heard simulated in movies, the kind of weapon that only one man the town had ever known would carry. He was alive, he was angry, and he was not going to let a crowd of Ferrview simpletons take him down!

"He can save us, don't fight him!"

I shouted and shouted until I was hoarse. Over the gunfire, over the crying, over the explosions, until finally the gas cleared, I fell to the ground, exhausted, sobbing, and defeated. I felt a hard hand grasp my arm and looked up to see my mother. She embraced me and lifted me up onto the hood of an overturned fuel tanker. I looked down at her and I saw Pa next to her. Then I saw it in both of their faces, the unmistakeable fear. At first I thought it was the tear gas, but they were both wearing facemasks. Masks that stopped the gas but couldn't mask their expressions.

They were more afraid than we children were, but without a hero to hide their fear behind. It wasn't the Dragon they were afraid of, I realized, it was the possibility of losing me.

"Are you alright son? Tell me what's happening, I can't see a thing in this mask."

I held onto Pa's hand as I stared over the gas and described the scene. The stranger was standing at the center of the crowd, holding the mayor up against a street lamp with a gun against the man's bald head. One intact corpse, one pile of meaty mush, and two heirloom rifles sat under his feet. Except for a far off fire siren, the crowd was silent. He spoke: "Did you order these fucks to fire on me or were they just going solo loco on y'all?"

"I, I told them not to, but I've lost my authority here, please don't kill me!"

"Fuck." The mayor was dropped into a pile of former human. "Well who the hell is in charge around here now?"

There was no answer. He closed his false eye and gave one scanning look over the crowd, pulled a sloppy cigarette from a pouch on his utility belt, lit it on a burning car and trudged back towards his ship. I looked from my hero to my parents and begged Pa to do something.

"He's leaving. Should I say anything?"

Pa shook his head.

"No. Let him go, son. Evacuation's a better plan at this point, least that way we'll be together."

I saw that my mother and father were no longer afraid. They had me; they had a plan. I looked back at the Renegade, stomping away through rubble towards the hatch of his ship. He had nothing.

In my eyes, he just wasn't a hero anymore; he was a man to be pitied. A loner without anyone to evacuate with. A failure in every sense; a man who could only destroy and finally met something more destructive than himself. As he turned out to view the crowd one last time, I lifted my binoculars to look closely at his face. I saw no trace of fear.

"Renegade!" I hollered. "You still owe us! Your duty ain't over yet! The Dragon still lives, and we paid you to kill it! We hired you to be a hero and you're bugging out!"

He stopped, looked right at me perhaps with more shame than malice and opened his jaw as if to retort, but had nothing to say. The joint fell to his feet and he swore as he pulled it from a small fire, then trudged back towards the crowd. He searched the faces until he found mine.

"Kid," he said, pointing to the mayor and a few select bodies. "These assholes had recorded images of that thing; they withheld data from me. They thought I'd puss out if I knew what I was up against. Well, if I *had* known what I was up against, it'd be a fuckin' corpse right now! I've killed those things before. It takes preparation!"

He took a long drag on his smoke and blew out a cloud of frustration. Mayor Munthly began to protest, along with several other townspeople.

"Well, you said you could kill anything. We couldn't get a word in to describe it and, if we had, you never would have stayed to fight it!"

"It's an alien monster!" hollered a panicked old lady. "Undocumented, you can't have seen one before!"

A miner gruffly goaded, "You would have fled if you had known, if we'd showed you the images!"

"We needed someone to believe in!" a child cried.

A businessman pointed a finger. "You shot my dog for target practice when you were drunk, asshole!"

Fh-BOAHM! The stranger had hurled some type of grenade into mid-air and blasted it with his antimatter pistol. Now his face was full of malice: eyes small, lips curled, and teeth exposed. He extinguished his joint on the mayor's suit and put the rest into its pouch for later.

"Listen to me, you whiny fuckers," he bellowed. "I ain't one of you, I ain't your friend, and I ain't part of your damn pissant peaceful society. But you paid my price and I *am* your savior.

Now you fucked yourselves by not telling me what I was up against and I stand by my words that I can kill anything when I put my mind to it. I've seen these dragon things before and killed 'em, too. So if you meet my terms, do exactly as I say, and pay what I demand, I will not only kill that son of a bitch out there, but I'll bring back its head for your labs and leave this shit-hole rock. You'll never have to see my crude uncivilized ass again. Do we have a deal?"

There were murmurs, whispers, and I swear I heard a woman sigh, then Pa spoke up.

"We'll do what we need to do for you if you can kill that thing. You just tell us what you need, and we'll make it happen. Right folks?" A cheer started with the children and eventually crescendoed till the whole town was hollering.

"Right." The stranger sat down on the open hood of a taxi. "First of all, I need to make some modifications to my ship and I'm gonna need heavy ore to do it. So I need volunteers to go back to the mine's smelting sector and bring back the densest metal you can make outta those asteroids." He smirked and looked down his nose at the crowd, as if teaching a lesson to a child. "In hand-to-hand, the rule is always pistol-sword-fist; but in ship-to-ship, sometimes you gotta start with the sword," he drew a molecular forged knife out of his boot and stabbed it deep into the engine block next to him, "before you even draw the guns."

A day later, a team of the toughest and bravest miners had returned from the mine, and the most skilled technicians had holed themselves up in the starport with the stranger and his ship. He assured us that the Dragon would be back soon, because it was hungry and didn't get much of a meal out of the defense satellites. All the kids had ideas about how he managed to get it to flee in the first place, but none of us had actually seen the battle take place and none of the adults wanted to talk about it. They just told us to remember the dead and spread the ashes traditionally, and left it at that. To this day I'm not sure if the Dragon ate anyone that day, but I do know that the death toll was higher than the bodies that were accounted for.

It was around four AM when the modifications were complete and I recorded his last launch on our home A/V recorder for posterity. If you want, I can set it up in the basement sometime and we can watch it along with Shannon's old records of the emergency meetings.

It broke the sky in the most beautiful way, the three primary forward cannons had been melted together to form a long, sharp point, and the ship lanced through the cumulus and nimbus almost without leaving a seam. As the ship launched, you could clearly read "ST. GEORGE" on her hull, and it dropped a victory flare before entering the asteroids in hunt of the Dragon.

Pa always said he had little respect for any man who claimed victory before even beginning a fight, but the camera couldn't hide the admiration that even a grown man felt for the departing hero. We waited for seven days before finally launching the evacuation and at that point nobody knew what to think.

Some said he had somehow managed to jury-rig his transstar drive and desert us. Some said the Dragon must of ate him, too. A good portion of the families in town opted to stay behind, but not us. Ma said we couldn't afford to take that risk and we'd still be a family no matter where we went as long as we were together. There were too many memories on that world, too many ghosts. Pa left his pistol there for good. He told me he'd moved out there to turn his warship into an ore ship, not fight for a place to stay. Jobs come and go; death is forever. A Fed gunboat and disaster relief ship showed up to investigate the SOS the day we left. Mayor Munthly and the rich men must have talked the Feds into rebuilding the destroyed half of the colony, because as the years passed Ferrview ev entually prospered into the smelting and shipyard capitol you know it as today.

Mayor Munthly broadcasted a speech as our evac-ship broke out of the atmosphere, but I don't remember a word of it.

Something about regular patrols being on the lookout for both the Renegade or the Dragon, and to consider them both hostiles. Apparently the men who had taken up arms against him were important people with vengeful families.

I thought about him as a human now, not a hero. He must not have had any real family or friends at all. As much as I admired him, I no longer had any desire to be like him. I knew that he wasn't born that tough: hate and hardships had forged him that way.

As we hit escape velocity blazing past the wrecked satellites, past the asteroid field, we passed the most beautiful ship I had ever seen, and I wish to this day I had recorded the image. It was the *St. George*, all right, fully operational and hovering stationary in deep space orbit, polished, pristine, and leaving a tiny trail of gas exhaust that I knew could only be some sort of deeply concentrated cigarette smoke. I pointed it out and the whole family looked to see the severed head of the Dragon placed on the ship's custom, sharpened lance nose cone.

I realized he was stuck, no way to land now that the mayor had declared him hostile, and no trans-star drive. He had drifted the whole time, living off our luxury rations! Probably waiting for a non-Federal vessel to come along so he could trade for parts to make his trans-star repair. I grabbed my binoculars. I was the only one in the family to look right into the cockpit window.

I saw a face with one mechanical eye staring back at me, saluting, smirking crudely, and smoking. His expression was bitter, lips sneering and chin high. It showed grit, anger, pride, jealousy, and even pain; but not a trace of fear.

The Man in the Barn

By D L Chance

Jake didn't see it when whatever it was went over at about treetop level, but he heard its whistling roar and felt the hot wind of its passing. An instant later, he saw a flash of light bounce off one of the massive oak trees in the yard and shoot off in a new direction. Then he heard what sounded like something falling near the barn.

While Jake stood pondering the odd happening, another roar overhead caught his attention, and he looked up in time to see a second streak of light angle toward the east and immediately out of sight over the treetops at the edge of his field.

At an even louder racket from the barn, he dropped the plow handles and, leaving Ol' Doc standing bewildered in the harness, made his painful way across the rough, fresh-plowed part of the field toward the outbuildings where the racket seemed to be settling down.

Past the privy, the smithy, and the chicken coop, he was almost to where the barn doors were standing wide open to allow a breeze to blow through the old structure when another blast of hot air from inside blew past him strong enough to drop him to his knees. Before he could come fully to his feet, the same kind of blast hit him from behind and, shaking the large doors, slammed them shut, nearly breaking one loose from its hinges. Through gaps in the rough board siding, he could see a watermelon-sized pinpoint of light about head-high on a man moving through the inside of the barn. When it glided up to the loft, nowhere near the rickety steps a man would have taken to the upper level, Jake let out the breath he hadn't known he was holding.

"What the hell?" At least the barn hadn't collapsed, he noticed, the way it had sounded like it was doing. Not that it really mattered all that much, he reckoned.

The unmistakable tang of oak wood smoke snapped him out of a momentary puzzled numbness, and he looked around to see fire blazing away in a perfectly round spot on the trunk of one of the massive oaks ringing the house. Vaguely realizing this was where he'd seen the flash of light hit and bounce toward the barn, he ran stiffly to the blacksmith shop and hefted up the full water bucket he kept close to the forge in case of fires and, spilling some of the water down the leg of his overalls, limped back outside. But before he could get to the tree a . . . something — he wasn't sure but it looked like a shaft of light coming from the barn — snuffed out the fire, leaving a perfectly round, smoking ring in the bark that circled what appeared to be an eighteen inch patch of healthy sapwood. Looking closer, the inner surface of the oak didn't even appear to be singed, much less burned by the flames that had just been eating away at it.

Jake dropped the bucket where he was and turned back to stare at the barn. While he watched, the glowing object slowly appeared where the door to the hayloft hung open. Almost as if sensing his eyes on it and not liking it one bit, the ball of light shot away toward the back of the barn while the door slammed shut much as the main doors had done before.

"Much obliged!"

He stood there staring at the barn until Doc's braying drew his attention back to the field and his plowing. Limping after all the exertion, Jake walked back to the field where his old mule looked about ready to run off, dragging the battered double shovel rig behind him.

Fisting the handles and shrugging into the reins, Jake let out a long, slow sigh.

"Doc," he said, slapping the animal into motion once more, "I reckon we got some trouble."

Doc didn't answer, but his long ears did pivot around in Jake's direction. Catching sight of the movement, Jake clucked the mule to a stop and turned to look over his shoulder.

"Now what?"

In the distance, four objects appeared in the sky. They were coming fast and headed directly toward Jake's farm. Almost before he identified them as the military jets that had replaced the prop planes from the war, they roared by overhead and out of sight beyond the tops of his massive oaks.

Just as he and Doc got to the end of the row at the edge of his barnyard, they were back, flying lower and slower. At about where the cornfield ended in thick woods more than the width of ten square acres away, they picked up speed again and were gone with a roar almost as loud as they made going over the first time.

Doc had apparently had enough of this foolishness. He plopped down onto his haunches in the rich Alabama soil, and refused to get up no matter how Jake slapped him with the rein strap.

"All right," Jake said, defeated. He noted the height of the late April sun. With a powdery half moon following not far behind the sun, it was bound to be a dark night, and he knew he really needed to work as long as he could. But with Doc acting up like he was, there wasn't much chance of getting any more plowing done. "It's still a little early, but I guess that's enough for today. What's the difference, anyhow?" He gazed into the field and estimated how much was left to plow before he could finish the fertilizing and plant this year's corn crop, and was disappointed to realize he and Doc had at least three more days of plowing to do. And his leg felt as if it was going to give away at any time. "Let's get you fed and put up, and—"

He turned toward the barn, where the doors were still shut tight.

"Doc, how'd you like to sleep in the cowshed tonight?"

The mule snorted and came to his feet. Jake unhitched the animal from the traces and, leaving the plow where he laid it down, tried to head him toward where the cows bedded down back when he could afford to hire someone to help him keep them. But Doc wouldn't have it. He walked toward the barn, leaving Jake to follow helplessly.

But when he was fifty feet or so from the barn doors, a keening wail started up inside. Doc stopped in his tracks, his ears perked up at the sound, and seemed to listen for a moment. Stiff-legged and braying in protest, the mule turned toward the cowshed on the other side of the barnyard. When the noise in the barn ended abruptly, Doc almost collapsed to the ground as if something had him and suddenly let him go. Whimpering and snorting, the mule allowed Jake to get him into the shed without anymore arguments.

Hay stored in the cowshed didn't make as good a supper for Doc as the measure of oats he'd have gotten in the barn, but the mule tucked into it without complaining while Jake stripped off the plow harness and collar.

With Doc put away for the night, Jake was thinking of firing up the cookstove for his own supper when he heard more airplanes approaching. These were coming directly out of the late afternoon sun, and they were large propeller planes by the familiar drone of the engines.

Moving from under the trees around his house and barnyard, Jake saw what looked like at least a dozen military aircraft flying due east in a spread that stretched from the southern horizon to the northern horizon, and they couldn't have been more than a few hundred feet in the air.

He glanced at the barn, then at the tree where, somehow, the burned circle of bark had shrunk since he first saw it. Less than half of the naked sapwood still showed.

Drawing a deep breath, he waited until one of the airplanes was headed straight at him on a line that would take it directly over the farm. When he thought he could make out the pilot in the cockpit, he smiled and waved as if low-flying military planes were old pals that flew over every day. A slight shudder of the wings told him he'd been spotted.

The planes gone, he gazed at the barn for a long moment. The military might be looking for something else, he thought, but it wasn't likely. They wanted whatever was out there in the barn, and he just couldn't come up with a reason he hadn't motioned toward the old building when the plane flew over. Glancing at the burned spot on the tree trunk before heading inside he noticed that the wound was even smaller now, and it would probably be covered up completely by dark.

"I don't know who you are," he muttered, "but as long as you don't give me reason to regret it, I reckon you can rest up here awhile."

There was no response from the barn and he didn't expect any.

Jake went inside and soon had a fire going in the stove. He put a pan of cold beans on to heat up and set a chunk of cornbread nearby. Even though the sun wouldn't set for another hour or so, he lit a couple of lamps to cut through the gathering gloom in the kitchen. Once, a bright light out at the barn caught his attention, but it dimmed to nothing immediately when he walked over to the large open window for a better look.

It didn't take him long to eat his scant supper and clean up the dishes. It never took very long when there was no one else around to talk with. When he was finished he filled a bowl with the rest of the beans and, taking it and a last piece of cornbread wrapped in a clean cup towel, walked out to the barn. At about the same distance where Doc stopped earlier, he spread an empty flour sack on the sandy dirt and carefully sat the food on it.

"It's not much, I know," he said, laboring to his feet. "But I reckon it'll stick to your ribs. If you got 'em, at least."

Without another word, he turned and walked back to the house. There, he pulled the old banjo his Grandpa Miller left to him from the parlor wall and stepped out onto the front porch. There was still a good half-hour of daylight left, so he eased himself into the porch swing and began softly frailing the melody to a cherished old hymn. After a couple run-throughs, he couldn't help singing for the rare pleasure of it.

"I'll fly away, oh glory. I'll fly away in the morning."

But his voice, once so clear and strong — until some kind of German gas wafted past where his infantry unit lay dug in alongside an obscure French dirt road back in the winter of '45 — wasn't much more than a raspy croak. Still, the words comforted him now every bit as much as they had when he'd sing for Flora, back before . . .

He shook his head and stopped playing. Almost six years later, he still couldn't bring himself to think about those times, and he was glad when a whippoorwill began cooing in a tree somewhere across the road.

Peering through the late day haze, trying to pinpoint where the birdcall originated, he thought he had it zeroed in when from the corner of his eye he caught a slight movement at the far edge of the porch. An icy chill chased itself throughout his upper body and his head jerked in that direction.

But nothing was there.

Snorting at his skittishness, he rubbed his eyes and resumed playing. But instead of the hymn, almost on their own his hands began playing "Devil's Dream." Flora hated that lively old folk melody and he hadn't played it since long before the war. Since right after they'd been married, in fact. But as if to make up for lost time, he played it, and every variation on it he could think of, until after full darkness had fallen. The whippoorwill provided a pleasant, if off key, accompaniment.

With a final furious flourish, he hit a last raucous chord and looked across the road.

"Nice job, sir," he called out to the hidden bird.

This time, he knew he saw something move in his peripheral vision. But instead of turning to look directly at it, he softly strummed a few chords and studied it. On the lawn just off the edge of the porch, it was vaguely man-shaped, and grayish like a cloudy day shadow. If the moon hadn't been chasing the sun all day, effectively backlighting whatever it was, Jake wouldn't have been able to make it out in the dark.

After facing off with what surely must have been at least half the German army, at a time when most men his age were looking forward to welcoming grandkids instead of being called up in the draft, Jake didn't think he could ever be afraid again.

But, turning to look directly at the figure, and knowing he wouldn't see it even as he did so, he drew a deep breath and held it for a long moment, finally releasing it slowly.

"I hope you liked the beans," he said, ignoring the obvious shake in his voice. "They wasn't much, but—"

For some reason he didn't understand, he knew without a doubt that the figure — the . . . the man? It sure looked like a man. Sorta. He knew whatever it was was gone.

"Okay, then. Good night."

Inside, he hung up the banjo, shucked his overalls and, ignoring the radio for tonight, went right to bed. For the first time since he could remember, Jake had the nicest dreams. Usually, the very same images caused him to sweat profusely, and often wake up with his heart thumping heavily in his chest. But this time, the dreams were almost pleasant.

Banjo strings were being clumsily plucked somewhere way off in the distance when he saw the German corporal who threw the funny looking grenade. The man then came apart in a greasy cloud of blood and bone and worse, a second later when

Jake's better thrown hand grenade went off under his feet. This time, Jake didn't even feel any twinges where shrapnel from the ugly Nazi weapon shredded his left thigh.

The awkward banjo noise was replaced by an exuberant rendition of "Devil's Dream" by the time Lester Haines, the president of the county draft board, pulled his new Ford into the driveway and blew the horn. And a moment later, when Flora stepped through the screen door — dressed in her best Sunday clothes and a flashy pair of high heel shoes he'd never seen before, and carrying a suitcase — barely glanced at where Jake sat alone, home unexpectedly early from the war and unable to walk, on the porch swing. Instead, she smiled and waved at Lester, and practically floated across the yard to his car. Flora threw the suitcase into the back seat, and settled in as naturally beside Lester as if she'd been doing it for a long time. Throwing a triumphant leer at Jake, Lester backed out of the driveway, and he and Flora and the Ford disappeared over the hill and out of Jake's life forever. While the sound of radio static whistled softly in the background, Jake felt oddly comforted when the preacher's car stopped in the yard and the Parson joined him on the swing to solemnly tell him that Flora and Lester hadn't survived a run-in with a loaded freight truck down Montgomery way.

He was almost happy for once that he and Flora never had any children. The world was better off with what made her the way she was dying with her instead of being passed on.

The heavenly odor of frying bacon drifting playfully past his nose, it didn't even bother Jake to realize still again just why he, at forty-one, had been drafted into the army in early 1944 when farmers — an occupation necessary to the war effort — were ordinarily supposed to get deferments exempting them from military service.

Refreshed and fully rested for once, Jake opened his eyes an eternity later. Outside, the sun would peek over the tops of the trees momentarily, and inside the house all was quiet and calm.

But it was a different kind of quiet, a different kind of calm, than he'd known in a long, long time.

It was . . . peaceful.

He threw off the covers and gingerly slid from the bed, being careful to ease his weight onto his mangled leg. But, aside from a mild soreness, the pain was gone.

"Naw," he said, the beginnings of a smile playing at the corners of his mouth, "that can't be."

But the more weight he put on his leg, the more the slight soreness faded away. He tried a couple of cautious hops on both legs, then, feeling braver, tried hopping only on his left leg.

"Now, what in the world?"

Laughing out loud, he jumped onto the bed and bounced on the mattress, almost bashing his head against the ceiling at one point.

"Ain't that something!" he laughed, winding down and jumping to the floor to land flatfooted on two sturdy legs. "I don't know how long she'll last, but it's good enough for me right now!"

Then he smelled the bacon again.

Distantly recalling the smell of bacon frying in the night, and knowing he didn't fry it, he crept toward the kitchen. Sitting on the still warm cooktop was the bowl he'd last seen filled with beans which he'd taken out to the man — he was beginning to think of whatever it was out there as a man — in the barn. It was covered with the same cup towel.

He carefully removed the towel and, expecting to find the beans, saw that the bowl was filled with bacon cooked just the way he liked it. Catching another familiar odor, he frowned, puzzled for a moment, and slowly pulled the oven door open. This time he wasn't nearly as surprised to find a pan of warm biscuits. Jake had absolutely no recollection of preparing his favorite breakfast while he slept, but he must have since, after all, here his favorite breakfast sat just waiting for him.

He quickly built himself a couple of bacon sandwiches and, chewing contentedly, Jake passed the window on his way to the ice box for a glass of the buttermilk he could occasionally get in trade for some chores from a dairy down the road a'piece. Out by the barn, he glimpsed what looked like a darker version of the man shadow he'd seen at the edge of the porch. But when he stopped to look closer, it was gone. He tried turning his head and finding it again in his side vision, but he couldn't do it. The man wasn't there anymore.

"'Mornin'," he called out the window. "Sure is a beautiful day, huh?"

Sitting at the table, enjoying his breakfast and sipping the buttermilk, he thought about how since the dairy farmer passed away over the winter, and his right nice-looking widow said she didn't know how long she'd be able to keep the place going — hired help being so expensive these days — he might have to get another cow or two of his own if he wanted to go on having fresh milk around the place. Something to think about at least, he figured.

His meal finished, with plenty of bacon and biscuits left over for a midmorning snack later on, Jake was on his way outside to hitch Doc to the plow and get back to work he was strangely enthusiastic about getting done when someone knocked on the front door.

"I'm coming," he called out, making his way spryly through the bedroom and parlor. He had to rattle the sticky doorknob before he could turn it, but when the front door swung open he saw what appeared to his experienced soldier's eye to be an army captain standing there. "What can I do for you this fine morning, Cap'm?" he asked.

"Are you Jacob Miller?" the officer asked without acknowledging Jake's greeting.

"As a matter of fact, I am," Jake said. "Have you had your breakfast today? I've got some—"

"We're going to search your farm," the man said, jerking a

thumb at an Army truck sitting in the driveway. Armed troops were hitting the dirt and fanning out. "You will come with me and answer any questions I ask, no matter how peculiar they may sound."

"I reckon that's okay," Jake said slowly, as two beefy troops stepped onto the porch. "But ain't you supposed to have some kind of papers, or something, if you mean to look in my house?"

"We're the army, not the sheriff," the officer said, frowning. "Please join me in taking a little walk around your farm while these men do their duty."

Jake wordlessly allowed the soldiers to enter his house, and allowed the officer who had never offered a name to go with his rank to lead him down the front steps and into the yard.

"If this weren't absolutely necessary, we wouldn't be here," the captain said. "I hope that, as a former member of the army yourself, you will understand."

Jake merely snorted. Of course they knew he was ex-army. They probably knew everything about him and everyone else along this road.

While some troops were crawling under the house, others were nosing around the outbuildings before entering them. Jake tried not to look directly at the barn, but he couldn't help it. He also couldn't help noticing that not one of the soldiers was anywhere near it. Even though it was the largest and most obvious building on the farm, not one of the troops had gotten any closer to it than Doc had last night. It was almost as if they all assumed there was nothing out of the ordinary about it, and it wasn't worth searching.

"Did you see anything unusual yesterday afternoon?"

Jake looked back at the officer.

"What?"

"Anything peculiar. Out of the ordinary. Did anything happen that you've never seen before?"

"Peculiar doings?" Jake scratched his chin. "Well," he finally said slowly, "a bunch of jets did fly over the farm while I was plowing. I don't see that every day."

"Is that all?"

"No. Awhile later, a bunch of bombers flew over, too."

"They weren't bombers. They were . . . Mr. Miller, did you see anything happen before you saw the jets and the large planes?"

Instead of lying to the man, Jake shrugged. "What sort of thing would you be talking about?" The soldiers still weren't going anywhere near the barn. He didn't know what the man in the barn was doing to keep them away, but he suddenly wished something would happen to get them completely off the farm. After all, he was almost killed in a foreign country and lost his wife to another man trying to help stop exactly this sort of thing from happening. "You mean like an airplane crash or something?"

"Something like that, yes."

"No, I didn't see no plane crash," Jake said smoothly. "But I can see why you boys would send out search planes looking for one. These woods around here can be mighty thick in places. Hide almost anything. Here 'while back this old boy accidentally drove a car off into the woods trying to miss a cow in the road, and they didn't find him for better'n a week. So you think this plane crashed in my henhouse yonder?" He pointed at where most of the troops were gathering at the small building that hadn't housed chickens in several years. He also saw that, beyond the privy, the entire cornfield was plowed, even though he only had part of it done when he quit working yesterday. "I think I'd have noticed something like that," he went on, stifling a smile. "No offense."

A poker expression shut down all emotion on the captain's face, and he silently motioned for Jake to follow him toward the outbuildings. When they neared the barn, the officer seemed to notice for the first time that the big doors were still closed.

"Has this barn been cleared?" he asked, raising his voice so that the sergeant in charge of the detail would hear him. Another few steps, though, and he was within the invisible limit around the place that Doc had not been able to get past. "Never mind," he said when some of the troops looked over at him. "There's nothing in there worth looking at."

Turning away from the building, he took a few steps toward the cowshed, but he turned back when something banged in the chicken coop. And then he seemed to notice the barn for the first time.

"Who cleared this barn?" he said, raising his voice. "Why are the doors still closed?"

Jake looked from the barn, to the officer, and back to the barn. "It has been cleared," he said, walking toward the building, the officer following closely in tow. "Remember?"

When the captain was within the boundary — Jake couldn't help thinking of it as some kind of invisible fence around the barn — he stopped and blinked a few times.

"Of course," the man said turning back toward the cowshed. "Of course I remember that the barn was cleared. Mr. Miller," he went on, nodding at Doc's temporary house, "what's in that shed there across the yard?"

"Nothing but some hay and my mule, Ol' Doc."

"We'll just see about that."

Doc made it clear that not only was he in no mood for visiting strangers, he had no intentions of allowing Jake to lead him out of the cowshed, either. In fact, to Jake's eye, the mule looked flat out exhausted; which would account for the plowed field. While Jake held his hands over the animal's eyes, two soldiers hastily looked around, careful to stay out of range of Doc's deadly accurate hind legs. Satisfied that there was nothing sinister hidden in the shed, the soldiers seemed happy to look elsewhere for awhile.

They poked into, and under, the various farm buildings for another half-hour before the captain, who still hadn't told Jake his name, decided they had thoroughly searched the place. The little army piled back into the truck. With a final warning to Jake that he had better let an official know about anything unusual happening around the place, the officer climbed into the cab. He ordered the driver to take them to the next farm on the list, and they were soon out of sight down the road.

Jake sat in the porch swing and, smiling at the complete lack of pain in his leg, saw when the shadow figure emerged from around the side of the house to take up station at the far end of the porch.

"Looks like we bamboozled 'em," he said. "For now, at least."

The figure streaked off the way it came from.

"But I 'spect they'll be back," Jake muttered.

He sat in silence for another few minutes, but he couldn't stay down long. He wanted to walk. To use his leg, now that he could, and move around the way he hadn't been able to in years.

Since most of the morning was already gone and he didn't have any pressing chores to attend to now that the plowing was done, Jake decided to do some fishing. He loved fishing, but usually by the time he got the buckboard hitched up for the quarter-mile or so ride down to the creek his leg was bothering him so much that he couldn't take any pleasure from the simple act of pulling in a few hungry cats. But now he could walk it without bothering Doc.

He carefully placed the last of the bacon biscuits in a clean sugar sack, grabbed a handful of cane poles and his small tackle kit off the back porch and, humming contentedly to himself, took off walking toward the edge of the woods.

"Going fishing," he called out as he passed the barn. "Be back later. Hold the fort, now. Or you can come along if you want to."

The familiar old logging trail he once used to bring in firewood was already a little overgrown, so he grabbed up a handy deadfall stick about as big around as his wrist just in case any rattlers or copperheads were also using the trail.

At the creek, he rigged up four poles and soon had lines stretched a dozen yards down the sun-dappled surface. Reaching in the sack for a biscuit, he settled back on the bank to enjoy the day and the fact that his leg still didn't pain him any.

After thirty minutes or so, although he didn't hear it, he sensed a definite question in his mind.

"Huh?"

He looked around and didn't see anyone, so he checked to make sure one of the grasshoppers he'd caught on the way in was still firmly impaled on one of the hooks, and settled back again.

"*Why?*"

Jake drew a deep breath and let it out slowly.

"For food," he finally said. "I'm trying to catch fish so's I can eat 'em."

A longish silence later, he sensed another question.

"*Death?*"

Jake took a long time in answering. He didn't want to say the wrong thing to . . . someone? . . . someone he didn't know all that well, and who obviously wasn't exactly from around these parts.

"The fish will die, yes," he said slowly. "But they will keep me alive. Everything alive has to eat food, and that means killing some other living thing. For everything to live, something else has to die. That's just the way nature set it up here."

The image of the German corporal he'd killed, in the second after Jake's hand grenade went off, welled up unbidden in Jake's mind.

"No," he said quickly, hoping the mental image wouldn't last long. "That was different. That was kill or be killed. And besides, we don't eat other people, we just have to kill 'em sometimes."

There was a heavy sadness about the next question and Jake was tempted to lie, but he knew he couldn't possibly get away with it.

"*War?*"

"That was a war, yes," he said, sharing the being's sadness. "And sometimes, like when the army came by this morning, the trickiest part about war is being able to tell your friends from your enemies. But it's over now and the right side won."

Jake suddenly sat upright as another image filled his mind. But it wasn't from anything he'd ever personally experienced.

He was encased in some kind of flying vehicle and peering at the Earth, far below, through a small window. He knew he was traveling fast, and he flinched when two sun-bright streaks of light shot past the window to explode directly in what he instantly knew was his flight path.

Something abruptly erupted in a flurry of activity behind him, but he couldn't tear his eyes from the window, and the still expanding fireball of the blast. He knew this craft was going to fly directly into the flak and there was nothing he could do about it.

But to his surprise, the blasts were suddenly overhead as the vehicle turned at an impossible angle and, picking up even more speed, flew directly at the Earth. Lights began blinking inside the vehicle, and what he knew beyond a doubt to be warning bells began clanging and buzzing, but whoever controlled the craft leveled it out just above the surface, and kept on a straight course that would take it north across the Gulf of Mexico to the Alabama coast and beyond.

Jake's body jerked involuntarily. The vision gone, he blinked and realized he wasn't breathing. His fists clenched involuntarily, and he had to will his lungs to start working again and his heart to stop thumping dangerously in his chest. In a few moments, he wiped an eye and drew a long, deep breath.

"*War,*" the not-voice said in his mind.

"So that was the other streak of light I saw yesterday," Jake whispered, knowing the man in the barn could hear. "It chased you to my place because whoever was flying it wanted to kill you."

"*War.*"

"I reckon so."

Jake sat quietly for an hour or so, but none of the poles so much as twitched. After swapping war stories with the man in the barn, he wasn't sure he was still hungry anyway. But when he realized it was getting along toward late afternoon, he came to his feet.

"*Food.*"

All four poles began jumping at the same time, and Jake had four hefty catfish hanging from his stringer a few minutes later.

"Much obliged," he said, gathering up his fishing tackle and poles for the walk home.

Jake made sure Doc was comfortable for the night before heading in for his own supper of fried catfish. When he sat swinging and playing the banjo later, the shadow figure didn't run away the one time Jake spoke directly to it. But there were no more words in his mind, either. An hour or so after sundown, Jake went inside to bed and thoroughly enjoyed a dream-free night.

In the morning, he brewed a fresh pot of coffee, figuring he'd eat later after watching the sun come up. He took his hefty mug and walked through the house. He fidgeted with the stubborn front doorknob, and then pulled it open and looked into the face of a nightmare creature come to life.

Some kind of man-tall insect-like thing with huge black eyes, and at least four skinny arms, was standing upright on spindly hind legs.

Before he knew what he was doing, Jake threw the hot coffee in the thing's face and slammed the door shut. Out on the porch, the creature let out the most horrifying noise Jake had ever heard a living thing make. While one part of his mind reminded him that he didn't actually know if the ugly bastard was properly alive or not, another part of it sensed another word.

"*Come!*"

Jake burst out the back door and slammed into another of the creatures. Its body was hard and slick, but he felt something belonging to it break when they both hit hard in the dirt. The nightmarish thing stopped moving, but it did duplicate the first creature's hideous cry.

Instantly, Jake was on his feet again and running across the yard toward the barn when a commotion at the cowshed caught his attention. Doc's distressed braying sounded a lot like the two . . . whatever they were . . . he'd already made acquaintance with, and then the shed door shattered when a third bug creature flew backwards through it.

That one didn't make any noise when Doc appeared in the shed door and, running right over it and causing pieces of it to fly across the yard, galloped toward the barn alongside Jake.

The barn door was swinging open, and Jake was already through it and in the gloomy interior when he realized that Doc had been able to run past the invisible barrier that had stopped him the day before yesterday. The doors were swinging shut when he saw another three of the repulsive figures emerge from behind his house and, raising their spindly arms, point something at him.

"*War!*" he heard in his mind.

Three bright flashes lashed out from the objects. The last thing Jake saw through the doors before they closed tight were three immense fireballs spreading out over what must be the invisible fence fifty feet or so beyond the barn. But he still felt their heat through gaps in the barn siding.

Doc found his familiar stall and backed into it. Lowering his head, he flinched when another three blasts hit the barrier and lit up the inside of the barn again.

In the temporarily increased light, Jake glanced up and saw a solid man-shaped figure dressed in shiny blue coveralls standing on the edge of the hayloft and fiddling with some kind of small machine in its hands.

Then Jake's eyes were pulled to the front wall when a perfectly round hole opened just to the right of the hayloft door.

Guessing the barrier had failed, he hoped the insect nightmares would make his end quick and clean when they came for him.

Without warning, he was thrown to the dirt floor when a familiar *boom* smashed the corner of the barn to his right, splintering the aged old wood and raining whistling shards of shrapnel around where he lay. The remaining timbers groaned as if the entire loft was about to fall.

He could hear shots outside — actual gunfire from familiar-sounding small arms — going off all over the farm, but none of the bullets opened up light-winking holes in the thin barn walls.

Jake looked up, and through a thick mist of dust still hanging in the air from the ruined wall, he watched as the man in the barn first turned dark, then light gray, then faded out completely.

But in the eerie silence that followed, he began hearing what sounded like familiar voices out in the barnyard. Human voices. It took him a moment to realize he was hearing the constant shouting of military orders. So that's what the explosion was, he realized — an American-style army hand grenade going off!

Suddenly, the barn doors were jerked open. Jake looked up, squinting through the dust, directly into the rising sun.

"There's someone in here!"

Three figures appeared in the doorway, and it took Jake a moment to realize they were soldiers. People, not nightmare insects.

"Are you okay, Mr. Miller?"

Jake recognized the voice as belonging to the army officer he'd met yesterday.

"Is . . . is this what you meant about peculiar doings, Cap'm?" he croaked, trying to lever himself upright. "Damn'dest thing I ever seen."

"Yeah." While two soldiers helped Jake to his feet, the captain said, "We'd better get out of this barn. It looks like it could collapse."

In the barnyard, Jake saw what was left of at least a half-dozen broken bug creatures, and troops standing guard over the unmoving insect forms.

"What the hell happened?" Jake shook his head. "What are those things?"

"Nothing happened," the officer said slowly and firmly. "Mr. Miller, there is nothing here that doesn't belong here and nothing involving the United States Army happened here this morning. Do you understand me?"

"But—"

"But nothing, Mr. Miller. Please believe me when I say that if something unusual did happen here today, I can't guarantee your continued freedom or safety." He let that sink in for a moment. "Now, do you understand me?"

Jake met the officer's eye and held it for a short eternity.

"I understand, Captain," he said softly. "But someone damn sure better fix my barn."

That evening, as Jake sat swinging and playing "Devil's Dream," the man in the barn appeared, and sat on the far edge of the porch.

"*Why?*"

"I'm afraid I don't know—"

"*And sometimes, like when the army came by this morning,*" Jake heard himself say in his mind, "*the trickiest part about war is being able to tell your friends from your enemies.*"

"Oh, I see."

"*Why?*"

"Because you put out that fire on the tree." Jake stopped playing. "The easiest thing you could have done was to just lay low and let it burn, and maybe let it set the other trees, and all the buildings, afire. But you broke cover and put it out. That showed me you didn't have any hard feelings again' me."

The whippoorwill started singing across the road, and Jake went back to playing his banjo as the sun went down. Awhile later, he set the instrument aside and just enjoyed the cool night breezes.

"*Come?*"

"Come where?"

"*I'll fly away, oh glory. I'll fly away in the morning.*"

"Oh. What about Doc?"

"*Food?*"

"Naw." Jake couldn't help chuckling. "Doc is my friend. I couldn't ever eat him."

"*Come.*"

Jake stood up and looked around. At the house, at the yard, at the woods. At where the whippoorwill across the road had stopped cooing. At the moon just appearing over the trees.

If he'd gotten the same offer right after Flora left, he would definitely have taken it. Hell, if he'd have gotten the offer last week he'd have jumped on it like a possum on peach pits. Now, though, after meeting the man in the barn — and even with everything else that happened because of it — he just didn't know.

Now, he . . . he cared again.

About his leg, about his farm, about his life. After merely existing day by day in an open grave of soul-numbing melancholy for so long, the caring felt good to him. He wanted to go on caring.

He gazed down the road and wondered if the dairyman's widow might need some chores done tomorrow. His own plowing already finished, he had a couple days of free time on his hands. Might just be worth walking over there to see. She was, after all, a right fine-looking woman,

"I appreciate the offer," he said softly. "But I reckon not. You're sure welcome to stay on, though. If you want to."

An almost overwhelming sorrow flowed into Jake's mind.

"*War.*"

"I understand." Jake nodded, sighing. "Them bug things. They'll keep coming back as long as you're here."

Neither said anything for a long time. Eventually, the man in the barn began fading away.

"You're welcome to come back whenever you want," Jake said before the entity was completely gone. "Next time, you can stay in the house instead of that filthy old barn, too."

"Much obliged . . . Jake."

Jake resumed his seat on the swing and, frailing the melody to "I'll Fly Away," said his silent goodbyes. He never asked the name of the man in the barn, and he never introduced himself by name, but it didn't surprise him that the stranger knew it anyway.

He also wasn't too surprised to see a bright streak flash past the house and into the southern sky a few minutes later. Within seconds, it was just another point of light among the stars.

Jake sat there another half-hour before going inside to bed.

Darmok and the Mermaids of the Sea

By Ethan Nahté

A bright morning sun floated on the gentle waves of the Skarlan, reflecting off the market walls of the seaside city of Amphere. The market was alive with merchants in their booths throughout the mall hawking fresh fruits and vegetables, housewares, clothing, and jewelry. Along the docks fishermen filleted fresh sea bass, flounder, and shark next to traps filled with lobster and crab.

Lady Daphenia and her two escorts were looking at a strand of black pearls, each beautiful lady taking a turn holding the luminous beads up to their throats for the others to comment. So caught up in their shopping, they failed to notice the young Phalankian sneaking through the crowd. He leapt with the litheness of a jungle cat from behind a portly man, slashing the air and cutting through the strap of Daphenia's purse with one hand while snatching it with the other in one practiced move, all without pause. He rushed through the crowded mall, dodging in and out of unwary citizens.

43

"Thief! Thief!" Lady Daphenia cried out with no real expectations that anyone would or could stop the blue-skinned boy with four eyes, two of the eyes being on either side of his head above the large ears. Phalankians were naturally built to be wary of predators and quick on their feet, making them some of the best thieves in the entire known world. In Amphere his odds were even better because most people of the port city, especially along the docks and in the mall, minded their own business. Robberies and murder happened everyday; best not to be one of the poor or the dead.

Lady Daphenia cried out once more, echoed by her two escorts. People looked on to see the path being cut by the blur of the blue figure, but none made a move. The Phalankian turned his head ninety degrees and looked back over his shoulder to make sure he wasn't being pursued. From the side, the back of his head now facing that direction, a large sun-bronzed fist came lashing out and crashed into his skull. Crimson broke through the blue skin as the culprit went smashing into three bystanders. All four crumpled into the dust in a tangle of robes and sundries.

Before any could rise, the giant of a man with the sun-bronzed fist and an equally bronzed body made his way to the dogpile in two quick strides, lifting the Phalankian off the ground by the back of his neck. He carried the would-be thief with one hand while clutching the female belongings with the other and made his way through the parting crowd back to the three ladies. As he strode towards them, all three noticed the stiffness of his windblown, sea-crusted dark hair and the supple muscles of his arms. His broad chest expanded from a piece of white cloth meant to be a shirt, held only partly closed by a belt of black material wrapped about his waist. His breeches were loose and billowing. He wore no shoes. It was obvious he was a sailor fresh off a ship.

As he got within an arm's length of them they noticed his light hazel eye distinctly set in a deeply tanned face on the right side, but the left, which had been shadowed as it faced away from the rising sun, was covered in an ornately carved onyx mask, the eye behind it a cold ice-blue. The design was curious but represented no culture or cult which most that saw it could designate or recognize. The mask didn't seem to be attached by bands of any sort. It was as if the mask was melded to his face — as if he were born with it. And yet this did not take away from his masculine good looks or appall in any manner.

"I take it you are looking for this," said the man, handing the purse to Daphenia as he lowered the culprit to the ground, just allowing his feet to touch.

"Why, yes, thank you. I am Lady Daphenia and these are Lorlana and Gysella," she said, introducing the two beauties beside her. "And whom may I have the pleasure to be showing my gratitude?"

"I am Darmok."

Out of the crowd two guards appeared, one grabbing the Phalankian and the other grabbing Darmok from behind. Darmok looked down at the grimy hand over his shoulder. Without turning he said, "If you prefer not to draw back a stump, you need to remove that dirty paw."

"Listen here you sea scavenger. You do not threaten—"

"—a man who wants to live," Darmok interrupted.

Daphenia intervened, not wanting to see her rescuer wrongly accused, nor wanting to explain to the magistrate why one of the royal guards was severely, if not mortally, injured. "Sergeant, this man is not the guilty party. He caught the thief, which your companion has in his possession."

The sergeant looked at her, then at Darmok. He reluctantly let him loose. "Yes, Lady Daphenia. Just trying to protect you from heathens such as this."

Darmok turned and looked down on the sergeant who stood at five foot six, nearly a foot shorter than himself. He glared into the guard's eyes. The sergeant placed his hand on his short sword but Darmok never flinched or made a move for his own weapon. He knew the guard wasn't looking to fight him as much as the fact that he was simply intimidated by Darmok.

"Just be warned, pirate, I'll be keeping my eyes on you."

"Count yourself fortunate if you never see me again, for it may be the last thing you ever see. That is not a threat, but a promise you heel-licking lackey."

From behind Darmok a sharp cry of pain was followed by an astounded gasp from the crowd and the sound of leather armor hitting the ground. Darmok turned to see the other guard clutching his bleeding side, lying on the ground. The blue youth was bounding at full speed through the onlookers waving a bloodied dagger and clearing a path. While the sergeant bellowed, ordering the man to stop in the name of the law, Darmok took flight, chasing down the scoundrel.

They dodged people, horses, dogs, and camels. They rounded the corner of one merchant's booth, the Phalankian spilling a bushel of melons to try and slow Darmok's long legs which were gaining quickly. Darmok leapt the baskets, grabbing a clay vessel in midair hanging from the booth. As he landed he followed with three more running steps and hurled the pot. It smashed into the back of the already bleeding blue scalp. The thief staggered, crashing into a stand of swords in front of the blacksmith's booth. Dazed, he rolled over to face Darmok, attempting to grasp a sword. He turned to meet a huge set of knuckles. The crunching sound of his cheek and orbital bone could be heard above the din of the crowd. The violence was quick and sudden. Then it was over.

Those nearby gathered closer for a better look at the unconscious thug, his face partially caved in. Darmok called for a towel from the smith to dry his hand after tipping a barrel of water to wash the blood and snot off his knuckles. He could hear the sergeant trying to clear a path to get to them.

"You are under arrest for aiding this murderer!"

"Aiding, hell! You mangy cur, I stopped the man because you were too busy crying for help while standing back there soiling yourself."

"Well . . . well . . . then I am charging you with murder."

"I didn't murder that guard. I was facing you."

"I meant the murder of the Phalankian."

"He's not dead, you dolt. I simply made it easier for you to handle him. With him being unconscious maybe you won't be so inept." With that, Darmok shoved the sergeant out of his way and stormed past him. He almost hoped the imbecile would draw his sword and give Darmok good reason to run him through. He listened for the sound of a sword sliding free of its scabbard but heard none as he stalked back to the booth where all of this had begun.

There he saw the ladies and the merchant being questioned by four new guards while two others carried away their dead friend. The captain turned to Darmok as he approached, no malice in his gaze, only questions.

"The murderer is unconscious by the blacksmith's booth. Assuming that baboon's butt of a sergeant doesn't slip up and lose him, he's yours for attempted theft and murder."

"Ummm . . . yes, that would be Sgt. Xitor. You two," he commanded, "go assist the sergeant. You must be the Darmok that Lady Daphenia was just telling me about. I am Capt. Brasov. I thank you for your assistance. I cannot officially reward you as our new regent does not recognize the, how shall I say, collaboration of a citizen. Personally, I am happy that you have aided us in getting the wretch off our streets. I also apologize for any lip that the sergeant may have given you."

"The lady told you of that, as well?"

"She needn't. I know the sergeant. He means well but he has the personality of a small dog — a lot of bark and teeth, but stands back when danger approaches." The captain shook Darmok's hand before ordering his remaining guards to wrap up their reports and go back on patrol.

"I, on the other hand, am fully capable of thanking you," Lady Daphenia chimed, reaching a hand up into his dark, curly hair and pulling him to her for a kiss on the lips which tasted of honeysuckle. "I operate The Mermaids of the Sea, if you get my drift."

"A whorehouse, huh?"

"Quite more than a common whorehouse."

"I meant no offense."

"None taken. In this city my establishment is one of the most respected and prosperous businesses. If you come by this evening I will make sure that you have the pick of your choice."

Darmok looked at the trio and smiled. "I think the three of you will do nicely."

Lorlana and Gysella giggled, giving him a wink and coy looks. Lady Daphenia blushed. "Generally I don't *participate* in the activities, but tonight I am willing to make an exception. That is, if you are not simply boasting and can handle all three of us."

"I'll either raise a hot molten volcano from the sea or die trying," he said with a wry smile.

"Just follow the market to the west. Once you've reached the end you'll find one path that is bordered by rose bushes along the way. You can't miss us."

Darmok chuckled to himself as he watched the evening's entertainment sashay down the dusty path. A mug of ale was thrust into his hand by the pearl merchant, toasting him with his own mug in honor of his heroics this morning and for those to come in the bedroom later tonight.

Darmok finished the tasks and dealings he originally had set before him after disembarking *The Stalwart* earlier that morning. He made his way back into the market area and proceeded to make his way west as the rays of the sun bounced off the bottom of the cirrus clouds that were making their way in from the Skarlan. The sun itself was hidden by a small chain of mountains which served as a border for Amphere, giving the city a long, yet narrow, occupancy along the coast.

Safely nestled low upon the mountains were the abodes of the wealthy, including Amphere's sovereign, Prince Nelanth 'Tu. From what Darmok could gather throughout his conversations and by overhearing the locals it seemed that the sovereign had mysteriously disappeared almost three months ago. A regent ruled in his place while a search took place within the country of Meulansk and its neighboring countries. Being a port city, a case of abduction could be even more of a task if the sovereign had been snuck upon a vessel and taken out to sea. He could be anywhere, assuming he still breathed.

At the edge of the market he saw a handful of paths, but only one was paved with cobblestone and lined by gorgeous rows of brilliantly colored rose bushes growing up its winding path. At the top of the path, about three arrow shots in distance, sat a glorious building lit with oil lamps on sconces hanging from its many columns. Darmok, impressed by how regal The Mermaids of the Sea appeared, at least from without, set forth for a night of wenching and drinking.

Within a few minutes he reached the front entry gate. He noticed a side entry as well. He assessed that the middle class, soldiers, and sailors who could afford some form of service, entered through the side and were walled off from the front entrance. If it were like other whorehouses he had seen in well-to-do cities then the odds were that the house had a lower level for entertaining those guests and kept them segregated from the high-ranking officials and the social elite. It was obvious that the gate he was standing before at the front of the house was for those with money and power. To maintain that segregation there stood a small group of guards, all carrying pikes and a short sword, dressed in their finest armor, spit-polished and shined so that the rising moon reflected like a burning sphere off their metal chests.

Darmok sighed, *Might as well get it over with.* He attempted to just move forward through the gates as if he had no reason to be stopped, but he knew deep down that nothing was ever that easy when he had to mix with high society. As if his clothing and mannerisms didn't already say "I am a warrior who bows to no man," then the onyx mask that covered half of his face gave cause enough for suspicion.

A pair of pikes crossed before him, blocking his advance. "Halt! You need to enter from the side, rogue. Assuming you have enough coin for even that."

"I have enough coin, if my coin were needed. I am a guest of Lady Daphenia. As a cordially invited guest I shall enter through the front and not from the side entrance like some common beggar."

The guards laughed. The commander who first spoke replied, "A guest? You? We have heard it all before, you masked freak. Be gone with you."

Darmok silently counted to five before speaking, trying not to cause a row for the lady and her establishment. "I spoke with your captain today after saving the lady's purse and capturing the Phalankian who struck down one of your members when that poor excuse for a sergeant was incapable of handling the situation. I am sure that you would not want me to report you to your captain. But if I must, then please call for him."

"The captain is a married man. He neither comes here for entertainment nor does he bother with guarding The Mermaid . . ."

"Yes, why would he do such a simple job when a small gathering of mice would suffice?" Darmok struck out, quicker than an adder, lifting the commander off the ground and swinging him forward to block any attempts at a quick thrust from a pike. The man's own pike clattered to the stone steps.

His cohorts looked at the fallen pike and saw that their commander was being lifted high enough that he couldn't touch the ground. Logic would dictate that the commander should reach for his short sword and attempt to stab his attacker, but logic didn't prevail as he grasped Darmok's muscular hand and arm, trying to wring himself free of his deathgrip.

"Now, as I was saying, I am a guest of the Lady Daphenia. I believe you will find my invitation is in order."

"Ummm . . . yes, sir," said one of the other guards. "I believe everything is as you say. Please enjoy your evening."

With that, Darmok lowered the man back to the ground. Despite the rudeness he understood that the lowly paid soldier was just doing a job. He saw no reason to give a further show of strength by tossing the bastard headfirst down the flagstone. That would only rile the other guards and start a fight that he had no desire for when there were ladies of the night to be wrestling with in the sheets for the next few hours.

He didn't wait to see how the guard would react but moved casually up to the front doors which two eunuchs rushed to open and welcome him into the luxurious and opulent mansion. The setting was surreal: the marble floor was highlighted by a design of a mermaid created by glittering diamonds, rubies, sapphires, and emeralds; an alabaster staircase spiraled up to a landing which obviously led to the rooms, yet opposite of the landing was a balcony containing a four-piece string ensemble performing to perfection; a series of stained glass windows depicted a story of a ship torn asunder by a storm and gorgeous mermaids swimming to the rescue of the sailors and taking them to a desert island, the favor being returned as the men made love to the beautiful goddess-like creatures.

If the concubines can live up to this grandeur, he thought to himself, *then tonight will be one that might take a day or two to recover from for all parties involved.* He smiled and stepped into the colorfully lit room.

"There's the man of the hour." Lady Daphenia looked and smiled from the top of the staircase. She was escorted down in a tight-fitting dress of brocaded silk by a man with a fat belly and a jingling bag of gold at his belt. She paid no heed to him as she moved across the floor and right up to Darmok. In her heels she managed to come to his collarbone. She extended her hand which he gracefully took and placed a kiss.

"If you do not mind, I would like to introduce you to a few of Amphere's notables. But first, Glascon," she said, motioning to a servant. "Bring us two Blasgaal Bourbons. That seems like a strong enough drink to start the evening, don't you agree?"

"Quite," he replied, happy to know he wouldn't be relegated to fruity wine. This was his type of woman, powerful and strong with a good head on her shoulders for business and some common sense.

Lorlana and Gysella approached from a room off to the side, grabbing Darmok's arms on either side and leading him to the main ballroom behind Lady Daphenia as the servant bowed and rushed away to retrieve the drinks. Each lady was dressed in an elegant evening gown also of brocaded silks, a different color with a similar pattern motif for all three. Obviously they had put much thought into this evening's activities. Before Darmok could think anymore on the situation he was brought into proximity with the owner of the most ships in the harbor; a silk trader with the most exotic and largest selection of wholesale material this side of the Skarlan; an envoy from Misalaran and another from Tavarel; followed by Amphere's new regent.

"Darmok, may I introduce our regent, Lord T'Lan Ahklu." Darmok extended his hand in greeting but wavered a bit. His face tingled beneath the mask, the hairs on his arm standing up. No one noticed these minute sensations as Darmok kept his composure.

"So, Darmok, let me first thank you for saving these three beautiful ladies."

"It was only a purse stolen by an inexperienced thief."

"A murderous thief."

"A nervous young man who saw an opportunity to escape which took a turn for the worst. I have traveled to many locales and climes. The poor and oppressed are the same in all, regardless of their color, language, or the clothes they wear. The rich and powerful tend to be the same as well."

The crowded ballroom stood aghast that this foreigner would be so discourteous to the same people whom he was now sharing drinks with since the return of the servant. Lord Ahklu didn't seem taken aback.

"Yes, man is a predictable beast who preys upon the weak and enjoys the spoils. But never mind all that. The city of Amphere would like to reward you for your heroics this morning."

"And of the guard who was killed?"

"Why, he has been replaced."

"And his family?"

"They have been notified," Lord Ahklu said in a definitive manner, curious as to where the conversation was leading.

"Then give my reward," said Darmok, "to the guard's family." With that, he turned to Lady Daphenia. "Shall we seek more private company," he asked with a charming smile.

"Lead on girls. I'll have this rugged beast-of-a-man escort me up the stairs. But before I go," she raised her drink to the guests, "may you all have an enjoyable evening which allows you to forget your worries but not forget the great time you had. Until the morn, my friends."

Darmok and Lady Daphenia followed Gysella and Lorlana up to the second floor and down a long, plush carpeted hallway to a door located at the very end. A large, pink pearl doorknob set it apart from all the other doors. They entered into a room decorated in aqua and shut the rest of the world out.

As the morning sun rose above the horizon, bedazzling the stained glass mermaid atop a rock out at sea, beckoning to the captain of a magnificent ship, Darmok awakened. His head was a bit groggy but he was aware enough to remember the events of the evening. Seeing the three lithe forms strewn across the massive bed, an arm or leg lying across his muscled body and Lady Daphenia's head nuzzling his chest, Darmok smiled. The evening had been one of mutual pleasure.

Good thing the bed was as large and sturdy as it was or we would've been using it for kindling, he thought.

He reached for a vessel of bourbon and a silver chalice, pouring himself a drink. He didn't generally start his day off with alcohol, but it was the closest thing to him and his tongue was a bit dry from last night's activities.

While replacing the vessel, Lady Daphenia shifted, her eyes opening dreamily. "So, you weren't kidding about your capabilities. Such a rare feat."

"What, satisfying three gorgeous women?"

"No, putting your money where your mouth is."

Darmok smiled then took a swig of bourbon. He caressed her hair with his other hand. "Tell me, what do you know of this T'Lan Ahklu?"

"Lord Ahklu? What would you like to know?"

"For one, I would never consider him my lord, ruler, or any other position of honor."

"What do you mean?"

"When did he arise to power?"

Lady Daphenia thought a moment, raising her head from his chest to sit up and look at Darmok. "He arrived probably within a fortnight of Prince Nelanth 'Tu's disappearance."

"He arrived from where? How did he gain the power?"

"I'm not really for certain. I have heard it said that there is something in Amphere's laws that state the order of office and protocol. He came from the northern mountain pass with a thrall of men, claiming that he had been requested to fulfill the position by Amphere's members of council until the prince could be found and rightfully returned to his throne."

"So he takes up position as a thrall. Has there been any proof that a search is ongoing for Nelanth 'Tu?"

"They say there is but I'm not certain."

"Have any of your key military clientele been missing, possibly off on the search?"

"Come to think of it, no. All the regular officers are still coming to visit on a regular basis. All but the captain, he's married."

"Yes, I've heard. He may be the only man in this town I can trust based on his morals and the feeling I got when I met him yesterday."

"Why, what's the matter?"

"I don't want to say anything that will frighten you or possibly put you in danger. Just be careful of what you do or say around Ahklu. Tell me where I can find the captain."

"Let's have breakfast brought up first," she said with a smile. "You must be ravished after last night."

"Well maybe a quick bite . . . and some breakfast as well."

Darmok found his way to the garrison and approached the gate. Once again he prepared himself for the sentries. This time instead of trying to walk past with his usual manner he stopped and asked, "Has Capt. Brasov arrived yet? I have something of an urgent matter I must discuss with him."

"Wait one moment . . ."

"Darmok, he will remember me."

The sentry ran off to find the captain while the other sentry stood his post, wondering what he would do if he had to take on this giant on his own. A few minutes later the other sentry returned with a private in tow. Darmok was told to follow the private to the captain's office.

The headquarters was much like the surrounding rock walled garrison, a building made from the large rocks from the surrounding mountains. It would withstand the raging winds from the sea or off the mountain and, being this close to the beach, would weather the wetness much better than if it was constructed of wood. It had windows on three of the four sides with two sentries at each window and at the door.

The private led Darmok in past a couple of small offices and to the middle of the building where Capt. Brasov was looking over a map. "The visitor, sir," the private announced, snapping to attention. The captain saluted back and dismissed the man.

"So, I see you survived the night at The Mermaid. Enjoy yourself?"

"Quite so. A lovely place with a lovely hostess and entourage."

"Glad to hear it. I've never been but my men seem to enjoy it. Keeps them out of trouble and the establishment brings a lot of business to Amphere. Its reputation precedes itself and there is rarely any trouble."

"That could all change. I have some news that might be of importance to you but is not for anyone else's ears at this time."

"Hmmm . . . Let me take you down into the armory. I believe you will find our weaponry and the solid construction of it to your liking." With that the captain and Darmok went through a door just down the hall and made their way down a staircase lit by torches. At the foot of the staircase was a short tunnel that came to a steel door. The captain ordered the man on guard to open the door. On the other side was a much longer tunnel with a steel door at the far end and another door half the length on the left side.

"The troops can access the armory from the far door in times of emergency or battle. Of course we have to protect headquarters with another door but it saves my officers from having to run clear across the compound if the need for getting into the armory should arise." He pulled a key from within his uniform and proceeded to unlock the armory door. A vast array of weapons was neatly organized throughout with plenty of room to walk the aisles without fear of knocking anything over.

"Now we can talk without fear of being overheard. The nearest two guards are at each of the steel doors at either end of the tunnel, and the ground is over twenty paces thick between us and the soldiers that walk the surface."

"Most impressive, Capt. Brasov. I am glad that you are not only taking me seriously but feel secure enough to take me privately into such a well-fortified area."

"I pride myself at being pretty good at sizing a man up within a few seconds of meeting him and a handshake. Despite your appearance, which I'm sure intimidates or biases others, I believe you are a man of honor."

"Then what does your handshake with T'Lan Ahklu tell you?"

Brasov's friendly demeanor turned sour. "That is one hand that I have shaken once and intend to shake no more. There is something odd about him but I cannot determine what it is. Is he the *trouble* that you have come to tell me of?"

Darmok grabbed a nearby torch and brought it closer to his mask, the flames reflecting off the smooth polish. "Captain, are you familiar with Zartroethians?"

"I have heard of the country, a far-away land beyond the farthest sea, hidden in a veil of fog."

"Very impressive, most have never heard of Zartroethia and those that venture out that far at sea believe that the world ends at the fog and entering it is entering the mouth of Hell. They fear demons and devils, and rightfully so."

A glimmer of fear passed through Brasov's eyes. Darmok gently clasped a hand on his shoulder. "It is not the Zartroethians that are the devils and demons," he assured the captain. "We are the beings that seek them out to destroy them. You mentioned my mask. Yes, it causes fear and prejudice, primarily by stupid men who allow their fear to get the best of them. Occasionally I have to set someone in their place, but the mask is not ornamental. Those of us born to the purpose of seeking out these demons are born with a mark."

"So it is to hide the mark? Is it so grotesque?"

"Not necessarily. It is more to hide the magic that allows us to sense a demon or devil. When I touch a being that is made of this evil, certain reactions and sensations, which I will not bore you with, occur and allow me to *size up* the being. It does not deceive and it does not fail."

"And you got one of these sensations meeting Ahklu last night at The Mermaid, didn't you?"

"How I love working with a perceptive and intelligent man. I really mean that. Most humans try my patience as they ask questions not important to the matter at hand. To answer your question, yes, Ahklu caused a strong sensation. Lady Daphenia told me what little she knew of his coming from the mountain pass and assuming power, but she knew little. She did say that most of your troops who normally visit her still visit, which tells me that no search must be actually happening for your prince."

"To be honest, I was looking over a map of places a select group of men have secretly searched. Ahklu has said that of the hundred he brought with him that the majority of them would take charge of the search party. Since I do not know his men and I do not see where they are at all times, I am not sure if he has actually sent anyone to look for the prince. That is why I have put together my men without his knowledge."

"Did you work closely with the prince?"

"On a daily basis."

"Anything unusual happen, an event or a message perhaps, before his disappearance?"

"Only an envoy from a mountain tribe is the only thing I can think of. We get various people in court on a regular basis, most from within the city but an outlander on occasion. Generally they are looking either for trade or assistance after a bitter winter. Otherwise it's normally someone being tried for highway robbery."

"So how was this man different?"

"I can't quite say. He was a dark, little man wearing a tattered robe. What skin and hair that could be seen was dirty and gray, as if he was not only old but his skin was possibly moldy.

"He presented a rolled piece of parchment bound in some sort of leather, handing it to the chamberlain, whom would normally read the contents, but the prince took it upon himself to open the letter. When the prince unrolled the parchment a cloud of dust filled the air. The odd little man quickly approached the throne, quicker than the guards or anyone else would've surmised him capable of moving, and brushed away the dust from the prince's vestments, apologizing profusely. He also began muttering something indiscernible while looking the prince in the eyes."

"A spell," Darmok breathed through pursed lips.

"I'm not sure. All I know is that the prince read the letter out loud, nothing of import, and said that he would look into it. Then he called the next appointment."

"What was the mountain man's reaction?"

"He simply smiled, bowed, and gave thanks for the prince's time. Then he left the chamber and was escorted back out."

"How long after that did the prince go missing?"

"No one is for certain but my guards that were on duty that evening are accustomed to Prince Nelanth 'Tu waking due to a chronic symptom with his back and legs. They generally accompany him on a short walk in the gardens on pleasant evenings such as the one in question. When an hour had passed from the general time the prince awakes, one of the guards took it upon himself to lightly knock on the door. Hearing no answer, he decided to peek in and assure the prince's safety. Not seeing the prince, both guards entered the bed chamber calling for him and lighting the candles and torches. They called out the alarm and we have been without him ever since."

"But they did see him enter the room that evening?"

"Yes, and as usual they checked the room and outside the windows before exiting and allowing him to bed down."

"I must see this room for myself," Darmok urged. With that, he and Brasov exited the armory and headquarters, pulling a couple of officers, one being Sgt. Xitor, along with them to the modest keep of the missing prince.

"Ahklu will be seeing the local people about trade, problems, requests, and such," stated Brasov. "He will not be in this part of the castle this time of day. His men are of no concern in regards to blocking our passage, but they will quickly send a report to him that we are within the castle walls."

"Then you may want to have more men on hand. Once he discovers what I am, and he will, then odds are we will have a battle at hand, assuming his guards are loyal to him and not just mercs."

Brasov gave orders to the officer, who ran back to the last checkpoint that one of his own men was stationed, before running to an opposite checkpoint to bring guards quickly from both sides of the city. Brasov and Darmok walked to the door with Xitor following close behind, his hand ready to draw his sword.

"We are here on official business," said Brasov to Ahklu's men standing guard. The men stood aside, not offering to challenge the captain's authority. Once inside, Darmok could hear the steady pounding of feet running away from the castle door and probably to wherever Ahklu might be. Although he knew not which direction the bed chamber sat, Darmok increased his pace, forcing Brasov to speed up and get them there with haste.

When they reached the door, Darmok first inspected it, lightly passing his hand over the exterior. Satisfied, he pushed the door open, surveying the scene before him. Nothing seemed out of the ordinary. He stepped forward, reaching the bed. A soft glow appeared before his eyes and the tingling beneath his mask sent tendrils of shock rippling across his face. He reached his hand up and held it just over the bed, moving it back and forth as if sensing something. As he brought his hand up to the jeweled wall at the head of the bed, a bolt of light flashed between a black stone and the palm of his hand, sending him staggering back against a padded leather chair.

"Darmok?" shouted Brasov.

The masked man rose, his face full of fury, his hand clutched tightly in his other hand. "Damnation! Ahklu has managed to pull your prince into that stone."

Xitor reached for his short sword, moving forward to pry the stone from the wall.

"Touch nothing. If you break the stone free, then your prince is lost in another realm for all time."

The mocking clap of Ahklu came from behind the trio. They turned to find Ahklu and five well-armed men standing just inside the room. Outside the window they could hear the beginning of the skirmish between Brasov's soldiers and what Darmok hoped were simply Ahklu's men. He could tell by the aura in the room that though the creatures before him appeared as men, they were definitely not human.

"Demons," he said, and then moved forward so quickly that the first two were caught off guard as twin swords pierced through their chests. From the back a bluish-orange flame rolled off each blade and black blood dripped to the floor in a sulfurous boil.

Two of the remaining demons each advanced with a flail upon Xitor and Brasov. The third took a fighting stance in front of Ahklu, a sharpened glaive on one arm and a scourge in the other hand.

Brasov just barely blocked the flail with his short sword, extracting the sword from his sheath and quickly raising it into the air. The force of impact spun the chain around the blade, breaking it almost to the hilt guard. The demon smiled. Brasov noticed that the teeth were extremely jagged — there were a lot more of them than should be able to fit into a human mouth. He spun and ducked all at once, whipping his other arm around and slicing a dirk through the creature's midsection. The demon's smile changed to surprise and then dropped to a grimace as he realized that he had been seriously injured. Looking down, he saw the broken short sword blade's jagged remnants coming from knee-high and thrusting into the air just below his chin before slamming his jaws shut. The blood gushed, burning Brasov wherever it landed before he could jump clear.

Xitor had managed to get a knick across his opponent's face but all that had done was anger the demon. He was now being bludgeoned with the haft of the flail across the crown of his skull.

He tried to thrust his sword into the demon but there were multiples of him as far as Xitor was concerned, his vision getting blurrier blow-by-blow. Brasov grabbed the flail off the floor and rolled behind the demon. He swung the flail from his knees, catching the beast behind the knee. The demon went down with the battered remains of the sergeant landing on top of him. The corpse was cast aside as the demon attempted to roll and get back to his feet, only to be met with a dirk piercing his right eye and going straight into his brain.

He backhanded Brasov, sending him flying into the demon with the scourge that Darmok was fighting. Brasov bounced off of him and to the floor, right at the feet of Ahklu. Darmok spun with a kick and shoved the dirk the rest of the way home, killing the foul beast. He gave up a bit of his form which allowed the remaining fighter's glaive to come sweeping in and swipe a path of crimson across his broad chest. Darmok returned the favor, raising both swords into the air and slicing down and across from shoulder to hip.

The demon howled, his head tilted back and his jaws extending as the vicious teeth came tearing through the façade of human skin. The howl was cut short by the removal of his head, both swords brandished with a fury and blood spurting throughout the room. Brasov was the only mortal to suffer from the boiling darkness that bathed them all, screaming in agony as the back of his neck was held by Ahklu.

Tiring of the yelling man, Ahklu threw Brasov across the room and into a wall, breaking his shoulder and arm with a resounding crack. He turned his anger on Darmok, shoving his hand into his face and grabbing for the mask. Pain like no other he had ever felt drove through his fingertips, up his arm and burned into his head. The intensity dropped him to the floor. He attempted to clutch his head with both hands, but one hand no longer existed. It had disappeared into a smoldering ash after contacting the black mask. It was eating its way up Ahklu's arm, not just dissolving but burning and grinding away at the flesh and bone which was quickly changing to its natural hellion form.

"Shouldn't have done that," Darmok said with a smile.

"You . . . you are Zartroethian?"

"Very good. A little late, but nonetheless."

"That is how you knew of the spell and to leave the stone be."

"And very soon, once you are destroyed, it is how the spell will be broken."

"How did you know what I am?"

"Call it an innate power, a sixth sense, or maybe you just reek." Darmok kicked Ahklu hard in the ribs. The entire arm was gone and the destructive energy was eating at his neck. Ahklu tried to cry out for mercy, but his vocal chords were deteriorating and the muscles that formed his mouth were burning away.

Darmok had no mercy, not for demon-kin. He picked up the scourge and raised it high. "This is for The Mermaids of the Sea," he growled as he pierced the demon with an underhand swing between the legs and ripped upwards, allowing him to feel the torturous pain just before his head combusted and black ash covered the floor.

The sounds of battle began to cease outside the window. Darmok strode over and looked out to see that Ahklu's men really were men. They seemed to be in a daze and coming out from under a spell.

"Allow them mercy, men of Amphere," he yelled down. Darmok could be vicious, but he was not unjust. Ahklu's men were simply pawns in a game of evil.

He heard a crackling sound coming from the black stone. He grabbed the fallen captain and carried him out into the hall, closing the door behind him. An explosion burst forth, the sounds of tinkling crystal shattering across the stone floor and embedding into the wooden door and turning to dust against the stone walls. He gently sat Brasov down so as to not hurt him. The captain would be recovering for some time but he would live.

Darmok reached for the door and shoved it open, sword in hand in case something besides Prince Nelanth 'Tu returned through the portal that had imprisoned him. Yet there stood the prince, no worse for wear, although a bit confused.

"Brasov, your sovereign lives." With that he moved out of the doorway to allow the prince to step through. Seeing the captain with multiple burns and an obviously broken and mis-shapen arm brought alarm, but Brasov had the clarity of mind to speak up, announcing the man before them as a brother-in-arms and the hero of the day.

Darmok had no interest in being the hero of the day. He was going to clean up and return to Lady Daphenia as the god of the night.

Darwin's Demons

By S C Hayden

I'll start by saying this: fact is stranger than fiction. Mother Nature is the architect of creatures more fantastic than any mythic beast of lore.

Consider the lancet fluke, a parasite who, in a stunning feat of telepathic mind control, commands its host as thoroughly as a puppeteer commands a marionette. An ant, infected by *Dicrocoelium lanceolatum*, will eventually be overcome by an inexplicable and overwhelming urge to find a field where sheep are grazing, climb to the top of a tall blade of grass, and wait. The infected insect will forgo food, shelter, and all of its antly duties until at last it is devoured by one of the grazing animals. Why? Because the parasite can only grow to maturity and lay its eggs in the belly of a ruminant, and hijacking an ant's mind is a convenient way to get there.

If evolution can produce something as baffling as the lancet fluke, as tender and ethereal as the orchid, as majestic and humbling as the blue whale, why then should a werewolf, or Bigfoot, or the Loch Ness Monster be any more improbable?

Ah, now I have your attention.

My name is Doctor Wolfgang Horst and I am a cryptozoologist. I have hunted the creatures that reside in the shadows of science for most of my adult life. I have tracked the Yeti through the Himalayas, collected the droppings of the Sasquatch in the forests of the American Pacific Northwest, and studied beneath a microscope the hair of the lycanthrope.

Learn this, good reader, if you learn nothing else. The creatures I chase around the globe are no more supernatural than you or I. They are nothing more than the products of that most fantastic process, evolution.

Three weeks ago today I was contacted by a colleague in Ireland regarding a mermaid sighting near Galway Bay. A fisherman from the Aran Islands claimed that he and his brother had spotted the creature while returning home one evening with their catch. The story had been vetted through a trusted source and so, without hesitation, I traveled to the fisherman's hometown on the island of Inishmaan. We met in a small pub called, fittingly enough, The Merrow. He was a salt-haired gentleman with a weathered and honest face. I liked him instantly. He said his name was Declan and told me his story over a pint of ale.

"I have been a fisherman my entire life. I have seen strange things in the sea over the years, but the thing I saw that day I have never seen before and hope to never see again."

I was intrigued. Why, I wondered, would anyone who had seen something as rare and as fantastic as a mermaid wish never to see one again?

"It was near sunset. My brother and I were hauling in the nets and getting ready to head in with our catch when we heard a strange sound. We turned towards the sound and saw a pale skinned woman floating in the water. My first thought was that she had fallen from a boat. I readied a line and buoy, but as she drew closer, it was clear that she wasn't human at all."

"How can you be sure she wasn't human?" I asked.

"I only saw her from the waist up, but her skin was aglow with some sort of devil's light. Her hair moved as though caught in a breeze, but the air was still. And she was nude. No one could survive for long in that icy water, but she swum along as relaxed and as lazy as you like."

"You mentioned a sound. Was the sound still present?"

"Indeed, the sound was coming from her. She was singing, but not with words. It was like a bird's song, but not quite."

He paused, seemingly searching for words to describe the melody, but I bade him continue.

"It was a beautiful haunting song and I was lost in it. I did not know who or where I was. I was in a trance. After a few minutes, the singing stopped and she disappeared beneath the waves. It made me terribly sad to see her go. I wiped a tear from my eye and turned to my brother just in time to see him leap over the side of the boat and plunge head first into the frigid water. All at once I came to my senses. I leapt in after him but it was useless. I could not find him. The water was icy cold and black as the devil's own sin."

Declan shivered as he recounted the incident.

"Is it possible," I asked, "that it was suicide?"

"I know my brother as well as I know myself. It was no suicide, it was that devil fish. She captured his mind with her song and lured him to his death. I'm as certain of it as I am of my name."

Declan gave me the exact coordinates of the encounter. It was clear that our conversation was over. I offered him my deepest condolences, promised him I would investigate the matter, thanked him for his time, and wished him farewell.

He seemed not to hear me.

Walking back through cobbled lanes, then graveled roads, then winding footpaths to the small seaside cottage I'd rented, I considered the fisherman's tale. Fantastic? Perhaps. Unprecedented? No. There is abundant historical evidence for those who have eyes to see it. In 1493 Christopher Columbus reported seeing three mermaids near the coast of Haiti on his first voyage to the Americas. In 1608 Henry Hudson reported seeing a mermaid near the Arctic coast of Russia while seeking a northeast route to the spice markets of China. In 1614 John Smith wrote elegantly of a mermaid he and his crew encountered in the Caribbean. But they were hardly the first. There are endless accounts of sailors, throughout the ages, telling tales of long-haired maidens gazing from the waves. The idea is as old as antiquity.

But there is, more importantly, an evolutionary argument. The aquatic ape theory proposes that human beings are direct descendents of a semi-aquatic ape that lived between five and seven million years ago. The theory explains some notable differences between modern humans and our primate cousins.

We, unlike chimpanzees, are nearly hairless. For the most part, only aquatic or semi-aquatic mammals, whales, dolphins, hippos, et cetera, are hairless. We, like other aquatic mammals, have an insulating layer of subcutaneous fat, making us ideally suited for cold water environments. We have hooded noses, perfect for diving. And, less scientific but no less relevant, human beings across the globe share a deep and heartfelt love of the sea that is as old as humanity itself.

If the aquatic ape theory is true, and I suspect that it is, is it not possible that some of our semi-aquatic prehuman ancestors remained in the sea, evolved there, and can be found there still? The implications of an aquatic hominid, a distant cousin fully adapted to an ocean environment, are simply staggering.

The next morning I purchased a small but seaworthy skiff and readied a day's provisions. I spent several hours exploring the island's eastern coast, familiarizing myself with the area. At midday I maneuvered the skiff to the spot where Declan and his brother had encountered the Mermaid. I dropped anchor and waited.

Lulled by the boats gentle rocking and the far off gull cries, I drifted into sleep. It was, I admit, unprofessional, but the travel, the lack of sleep, and the excitement of the quest had finally caught up with me. When I woke, the sun was setting in the west. The clouds over Inishmaan turned first a fiery orange then a blood soaked red. As I came to my senses, I heard a sound unlike any I'd heard before. It was a strange sort of humming, like cicadas in June, but deeper and more rhythmic. The sound lulled me and I looked out across the sun burnished water as though in a trance.

I saw a pale white woman, completely nude, swimming lazily through the placid water. She moved with the fluid grace of a seal, as though she were at home in the sea, as though she were a part of it.

She righted herself and floated vertically, exposed from the waist up. Her cheeks puckered as though she was blowing kisses and I understood that the unearthly sound was coming from her.

Like a drunkard I stumbled towards the apparition and nearly fell over the gunwale. It was only the ring of my satellite phone that brought me back to my senses. I paused and looked askance. When I looked up again she was gone.

I do not know who called me that day but whoever it was probably saved my life. I had been completely ready to dive into the water and follow that woman beneath the waves.

It had been exceedingly foolhardy to begin my investigation so unprepared. Declan had been clear about the hypnotic nature of the mermaid's song, yet I'd taken no precautions. Scolding myself for my impudence, I buckled down and devised a plan.

When I returned on the following sunset, I was ready. With diving gear at hand and a pair of wax earplugs suspended from a cord around my neck, I threw my anchor and waited. I did not wait for long. As the setting sun steeped the sea in copper, the mesmerizing music washed over me.

Only with enormous will power was I able to press the wax plugs into my ears. Immediately, my senses returned. I could still hear the music, muffled and far off, but it held no power over me.

With a smooth and practiced speed, I donned the diving gear and plunged into the frigid spume. I righted myself and spotted her bobbing in the choppy waves. For a heart stopping moment, just before she dove beneath the surface, we locked eyes. She was devastatingly beautiful. I emptied my buoyancy compensation vest and followed her into the gloom.

Her skin, pale and waxy white on the surface, was an incandescent green beneath the waves. She pulsed with an eerie inner light that was both beautiful and haunting. Slowly, she slipped deeper, arms outstretched and beckoning.

I descended and followed the emerald glow into the depths. She moved quickly and purposefully but I did not feel that she was trying to elude me. Rather, I had the distinct impression that she was leading me. I followed as fast as I was able, but as we neared thirty-three feet, I had to slow my descent.

To my delight, she paused. Was she waiting for me? She seemed to pulse brighter still and I felt I had my answer. She hovered seductively beneath me, her skin translucent, her body lithe and shimmering, her sea green hair undulating and radiant. She waited as I sank slowly to her depth. Why had she led me here, I wondered, what did she want to show me?

Slowly, gracefully, she came to me. As she approached, I felt an icy chill run through me. Somehow, she was different. Her eyes, once deep and mysterious seemed now empty and dead. The light that had pulsed from someplace deep within her was gone. I noticed, for the first time, a long fleshy cord growing from her back and disappearing into the darkness beneath her. How had I not seen it before?

Something was wrong. My heart thundered in my chest. I was overcome by an urge to get away from the dead-eyed creature bobbing before me like a piece of bait on the end of a line, but my scientific curiosity was stronger than my fear.

Suddenly, the white fleshy cord snapped taught and the woman was pulled downwards, at incredible speed, into the inky black. In her place, I saw a giant tooth-filled mouth rushing towards me.

There was no time to think, no time to react. In a flash, my world was surrounded by tooth and jaw. I was being swallowed by something of leviathan proportion. As the peristaltic action of the esophagus pulled my body toward the great fish's stomach and hence my doom, I felt something pulse beneath the spongy flesh of the monster's throat. At last, my wits returned to me. I quickly deduced that the pulsing object was not the beast's heart, but its swim bladder. Although my body was being compressed and contorted, I was able to reach my waist and pull my diving knife from its sheath. I sliced through the fish's gullet, plunged my arm in to the elbow, and penetrated the bladder. After taking one last breath of air, I cut my air hose and pushed the severed end into the hole.

The monster's swim bladder filled with compressed air. The fish became a living balloon, rocketing toward the surface and taking me along for the ride. As we rose, I exhaled that last life sustaining breath. When we crested the waves, the bladder burst. I barely had time to unhook my tank and vest and slither from the monster's mouth before it sank, lifeless, back into depths from whence it came.

Floating face down in the water, I peered through my facemask, eager to behold the thing that had nearly devoured me. What I saw shocked me to my core. It was a gargantuan anglerfish, an ugly brute wielding a lure unlike any known to science.

All at once I understood. I watched and marveled as the dead beast sank into the briny blackness. The long fleshy cord protruding from its head spooled out around its body. Last to disappear, at the cord's end, was the form of the mermaid. She fell from sight, ghostly in the gloom, arms outstretched as though still beckoning, hair fanned medusa like, eyes cold and dead.

Anglerfish, over the years, have evolved their glowing fleshy lures to attract their prey. But what if your food of choice was human flesh? Throughout history, sailors have been predominantly men. Naturally, this beast of the deep had evolved the perfect appendage to lure lonely sailors to their death. Rather than a fleshy luminous orb, this leviathan dangled the form of a beautiful woman, a mermaid, before its toothy maw.

As the sea swallowed the beast, it occurred to me that I had no proof of my discovery. I would, of course, publish an article detailing my adventure, and my article would, like all of my articles, be ridiculed and scorned by the majority of the scientific community.

I pay them no mind. My work goes on. Such is the fate of the cryptozoologist.

A Reason for Living

By David M DeMar

"So how d'ya like this story, folks? That lunatic is still skulking around Scottsbluff, slicing people up. Seems this freak ties up his victims with duct tape before going to work with some heavy, long-bladed knife, if what the police say is true. They're calling him the Scottsbluff Butcher. Late last night was the third fatal attack in the last—"

Dan finished tying off his apron and flicked off the radio. "That's enough of that," he said. "Only so much media nonsense I can deal with in one day."

The short, middle-aged man on the other side of the counter smiled politely back at him. "Yeah, I'm just glad I'm going out of town for a couple weeks."

Dan sliced carefully into a kaiser roll. He then began covering it with deli mustard. "Oh yeah? Where you headed?"

"I've got family down in Arizona. I had some vacation time coming to me so I decided to go someplace warm for a change."

"Lucky you." Dan began building the rest of the man's sandwich. "I can't remember my last vacation. I haven't been able to get a hold of my boss for a couple of days, actually. That Butcher better not have gotten him. I've got to pay my heating bill next week."

"Yeah, it's been cold this autumn, hasn't it?"

"Sure has. So much for global warming." Dan set a neatly wrapped package down on the counter. "Anything else?" he asked.

"No, just the sandwich." The man checked his watch. "I hope I get home before the weather gets bad. It's been threatening to rain all day."

Dan rang the customer up. As he did so the little string of bells that were hung on the door to the deli jingled. *Church bells,* Dan thought. *Little wedding bells.* He looked up as he handed the man's lunch to him.

A slightly built blonde haired girl was wandering down the deli's single aisle. She was looking through the long, tall drinks cooler that every deli and convenience store use to market their beer and soda.

The wedding bells tinkled again, and he raised a mute hand in farewell to his previous customer without looking. *Neither fish nor fowl,* he thought, watching the new girl with curiosity. *Well I guess I can't put her in with the Kosher products.*

His new customer was not one of his regulars. She was scarecrow-thin; her boot cut jeans looked like they had been airbrushed on to her petite frame. Her dirty blonde hair had been gathered up in tufts across her scalp with hair ties; the tips of each had been dyed cobalt blue. The shade of her hair clashed horribly with her shaggy woolen coat which featured an eye-watering rainbow pattern. It was almost comically large on her.

He stepped up to the counter. "Hey, how you doing?"

She nodded at him, still looking through the cooler. "Mmph."

Oh boy, here we go. "Well, let me know if you need anything." *Like a ride back to the circus.*

She grunted again, then reached into the cooler and pulled out a six-pack of Natural Ice and placed it on the counter. She then unzipped her hideously bright jacket to reveal a black v-neck tee shirt underneath that was emblazoned with the logo for some band Dan didn't recognize. "This and a pack of Reds," she said, dipping her hand into the plastic fishbowl next to the register and pulling out a fistful of matchbooks. Her black lacquered fingernails gleamed under the fluorescent lights.

The girl's skin looked pallid and pale against her black shirt, like the flesh of a freshly butchered pig. Dan looked up and met her eyes. There was a single silver ring through her left eyebrow. "Sorry kid, I need to see some ID if you're gonna buy that today. Nebraska state law."

The girl looked away for a moment before turning back. Her movements were quick and jerky as if impatient. She sighed sharply. "I don't have it on me," she finally said.

"Then I can't sell you Reds or that beer either. I could get fined pretty bad if anyone found out." He slid the six-pack over to the right to reveal a large yellow and black sticker on the counter. It read YOU MUST BE 18 TO PURCHASE TOBACCO PRODUCTS in big block letters. Right next to it was another highly visible sticker that stated in no uncertain terms that IT IS ILLEGAL TO SELL ALCOHOL TO MINORS.

The girl's eyebrows shot up. "You really think I'm underage?" She laughed and leaned over the counter, looking down at the two notices. Doing so gave Dan what would have been a fine view of her cleavage — if she'd had any. She looked back up at him through her eyelashes.

"Doesn't matter what I think," he said, raising his hands up in the universal sign for *don't blame me, I just work here.* "If I get caught not carding any customer under the age of forty I could lose my job. No ID, no beer and smokes."

"But I already told you, I have ID. I just don't have it on me." She frowned petulantly. "Hey, if you let me off the hook just this once I'll come back and show you my license, I promise."

He arched an eyebrow at the girl. "You drove down here without your license on you?"

"No, I walked." She hitched up the blue denim sausage skin she was using for pants. Her tee shirt rode up to expose a pale patch of midriff at her waist. The belt she was wearing had a buckle in the shape of a rhinestone-studded skull and crossbones. The skull had a pink bow on its head. "Listen, I've got a party to go to tonight," she said. "You can't just do me a favor just this once?" She gave him what must have passed for a coy grin.

Yeah, whatever, Dan thought. *Where were you when I was in high school?* She wasn't bad looking under all that make-up and bizarre hair, even if it looked like she needed a training bra. *From the look of her, she was probably in about the fifth grade.*

Dan stifled a yawn, casting a glance over at the wall clock. Gathering up a clump of his now slightly soiled apron at his midsection, he began cleaning his hands on it methodically. "I'm sorry, miss, but I don't make the policies. Listen, it's starting to get late, and I was about to close out — do you want a sandwich or something?"

"Hmph." The coquettish grin on the girl's face vanished in a flash. She wrinkled her nose and leaned back, folding her arms across her chest. "No, I don't want a sandwich." She spat the word out violently, like a piece of rotten meat. "I'm vegan," she barked, her teeth bared in a belligerent rictus.

Meet Mr. Hyde, Dan thought. He stopped kneading his hands as he forced a smile. "Well, I'm a Gemini."

The girl snorted and rolled her eyes before spinning on her heel. She stormed down the aisle and Dan looked down to see she was wearing silver painted platform shoes. Her angry footsteps left hollow reverberations in his ears.

Dan suppressed a smirk and then reached over to flick the radio back on. He immediately grimaced as that damn song came on again, performed by some latter-day mook with the keys to Marilyn Manson's wardrobe. He couldn't remember the name of the song, since the pretentious little shit liked to give them all names in Latin like *Futue Te Ipsum* or something. It seemed that every station he could get on the radio had been playing it nonstop for the past month.

You know some people kind of deserve to be carved up with a butcher knife, Dan thought. He changed the station before walking over to clean up the meat slicer. It was a mess after he'd made that sandwich for his last customer and the reek of cut flesh was cloying in the air. Even after all the time he'd been working with raw meat, the smell could still make him gag sometimes.

He methodically picked all the little bits of meat and skin from the slicer before wiping it down. The radio droned on in the background as he took the time to wash his gore steeped hands in the sink, careful to get everything out from underneath his fingernails. The feeling of dead meat in his nail beds always made him shiver.

Dan turned around when he heard something thump down on the checkout counter behind him. His little vegan party girl was glaring back at him. Her long, black fingernails were tapping an irritated tattoo against the plastic of a twenty ounce bottle of Coke. Her hands looked pale and gaunt under the fluorescent lights, and he noticed how delicate and fragile they looked.

Dan stifled a sigh. He rang up the soft drink methodically. "Do you need a bag?" he asked.

"No," she growled. "I want the Natural Ice and a pack of Reds, but I obviously can't get that here from a sheep like you."

Dan blinked. "What?"

"I said you're a mindless corporate sheep," she said, "being led by the nose to the slaughterhouse of individuality and free will." She held a crumpled greenback out to him, disdain dripping from every word. "You're just another low class nine-to-five conformist breathing my air. Hurry up and gimme my change back. Just being in the same room as you is making my skin crawl like you wouldn't believe."

Dan stared at her for a moment, dumbstruck. *What the Hell is she going on about?* He opened his mouth, then just shook his head and took the money from her claw-like hands. *Fuck it,* he thought. *Crazy bitch.* He looked down to the crumpled up bill she'd practically thrown at him. He smoothed it out; Ben Franklin peered owlishly back up at him.

"Well?" the girl demanded. Dan looked up. The bottle of Coke was still on the counter, and she had put her hands on her hips and thrust her chin out at him defiantly. "You going to give me the smokes and beer or what, man? You can keep the change if it makes you happy."

Is she trying to fucking bribe me? He waved the hundred at her. "Don't you have anything smaller? Like a five or a ten?"

She sneered at him. "What's wrong?" she asked, her tone mocking. "Can't you count that high without someone holding your hand? Or do you have to go look up the store's policy on making change for its customers? Do you need to call your boss?"

Dan squeezed his eyes shut tightly for a moment. He shook his head as if clearing cobwebs from his brain and took a deep breath. He had to let go of the sudden urge to grab the girl by the scruff of her neck and stick her in the meat slicer. *Maybe if I shaved off a couple of slices it would wipe that look off her face,* he thought.

Instead he took another deep breath and silently punched in "1, 0, 0," into his register. It popped open with an audible DING. After fishing out ninety-eight dollars in change, he handed it to her. "Here, honey," he said, his voice dripping venom. "Don't spend it all in one place. Better yet, buy a personality transplant." The girl took the money and shot him a smug look before stuffing the wad of cash into one tight blue denim hip pocket. "Do you want a straw," he went on, "or are you just going to bite it on the neck and suck the life right out of it?"

She reached out to grab the bottle. "Fuck you."

"Yeah, I love you too, baby," Dan growled. Dan rolled his eyes as that damn song came on the radio again. "Christ," he muttered and reflexively reached out to change the station again.

The girl shrieked. "Don't you dare!" she yelled.

Dan jumped, his hand recoiling from the radio as if it was a spitting cobra. The song continued playing. "What? Don't do what!?" She was glaring at him, sulky and unresponsive. "What the hell is your problem, lady?"

"That's *Solus Ipse*, it's an amazing song. That man is a *god*," she said, pointing at the radio. "Don't you dare turn that off! You could learn something from him, all his songs are about striking out against raging conformity and being the beautifully flawed individual that he is. His message is too important to deny!"

"What?" Dan's brows knitted together. "That moron with the Alice Cooper wig? You're kidding, right?" She glared at him furiously, but didn't answer him. "Tell me you're kidding." Nothing but stony silence greeted him in response.

Dan began to grind his teeth. "Better yet, tell me this whole thing has just been some sort of practical joke or something. Is there a webcam in your belt buckle or something?" He looked down, confused. "You're for real, aren't you? Jesus Christ. You'd better go home to Mommy and Daddy and tell them to up your Ritalin prescription or something. How old *are* you, anyway? What are you, like an A-cup? Hell, isn't it a school night?"

The girl opened her mouth and sputtered, but Dan cut her off and steamrolled right over her. "You know I see all kinds of people come in here every day. All kinds of people. And I gotta tell you that it's lunatics like you who give fucking psychotics like that Butcher guy a reason for living. Hell, you make what they do a public service! He deserves the key to the city for grinding up people like you and turning them into hamburger meat."

"Shut up!" she shouted back at him, indignant and snarling. "Who the fuck do you think you are?"

Dan pulled himself out of his slouch and glowered at the girl. Now that his blood was up he couldn't stop himself. "Oh, give it a rest. You think you're such a fucking trendsetter? How many assholes at that party you're going to are going to be drinking Natural Light or PBR or some other hipster bullshit? You walk in here with your glow-in-the-dark retard porcupine hairdo, and your fashion felony jacket, and your holier-than-thou ultra-trendy vegan lifestyle, and *I'm* the one with the problem? Gimme a goddamn break, kid. You'll probably grab at the next fad to come along like . . . I dunno, like a drowning sailor clutching a life preserver. I don't know. You know nobody would miss you if you died tonight? People like you are a dime a dozen. Some other toolbox would come along that looks just like you and your little friends wouldn't even know you were gone."

The girl snarled back at him, her hands balled up into fists. "How the fuck would you know, asshole? You don't know the first thing about me. You just stand there with your rules and your policies, with that apron all covered with the blood and filth from all those murdered animals. They should lock you up, you fucking shithead. Don't you judge me!"

The anger drained out of Dan. All he felt now was tired. "Kid, get out of my shop already. I ain't the one being judgmental here. And this conversation is all I ever wanna know about you. I've really got no desire to get to know you better, ever."

"Shut up," she cried. "I'm better than you. I'm *better* than you!"

Dan sighed heavily. His hands itched for the handle of a nice long sharp knife. *I'd only have to clean up afterwards,* he thought. Finally he broke his silence. "Miss, I'm afraid I'm going to have to ask you to leave the store," he said. She grabbed her bottle of Coke with a sneer and began stomping her way towards the door. "And don't come back without some Prozac," he muttered under his breath. She yanked the door open violently and stalked out. As she did so the little church bells jingled one last time. *Wedding bells my ass,* Dan thought.

Dan pinched the bridge of his nose. A wicked headache had blossomed right between his eyes and it seemed to be growing by the second. The radio was still vomiting forth its vapid payload, so he turned it off. Immediately he began to feel better.

With a visible effort Dan stopped clenching his jaws together. He looked out across the counter; it was strewn with the remnants of the countless meals he had prepared for the day's customers. He shifted his gaze downward for a moment and he realized that once again he had been wringing his hands with his apron. Only this time he was simply smearing more blood and slime all over himself.

"Dammit," he said, forcibly dropping his hands. He turned back to wash up again. Then he stripped off his bloody apron and tossed it through the open doorway into the back room, where the laundry basket was. Finally he got to work cleaning up the countertop with a spray bottle and a clean rag.

After a minute or so he heard the deli's wedding bells chime again. Dan continued wiping down the counter. "We're just about closed," he said, his back still to the door. He heard loud, echoing footsteps coming towards him, squelching on the linoleum. "Hey, did it finally start to rain out there?" he asked, still without turning around.

His new customer cleared their throat and he turned around. The girl he'd just thrown out of his store was standing there, dripping water all over the floor and looking like a cat that was just fished out of the river. "Is that your car in the lot out there?" she asked. Her skin was pallid and clammy, like a movie zombie, and her hair was plastered down to her forehead. "It started coming down hard," she went on. "I have to get home and it's way too far to walk in the rain. Plus, it's cold." Both her shaggy jacket and her black tee shirt had been soaked through. She suddenly looked to be about twelve years old.

Dan stared at her. Seconds ticked by as an uncomfortable silence unfurled between them like a piece of greasy paper parchment. "Let me get this right," he began haltingly. "First, you come in here and try to scam beer and cigarettes off of me. Then you go all schizoid on me, essentially calling me some sort of Nazi Hitler Youth member or something because I won't break the law and sell them to you without ID. Not to mention you started howling like a meth-fueled banshee when I go to turn my radio off because I don't want to listen to some androgynous no-talent halfwit pretend to 'perform' a song. *My* radio, mind you!" He pointed up at it. "Is there some sign that says, 'Property of Psycho Bitch, Do Not Touch' on there?" She was sullenly silent. "Well, *is there?*"

"No," she finally said.

"That's right. And now, you want me to drive you home like we'd just gone out on a date or something. Are you deranged? What the hell makes you think I'd ever give a ride to you after the way you completely flipped the fuck out on me?"

"Because it's raining. And you've got a car. And . . ." She looked down. "And it's getting dark and I'm far from home. So are you going to give me a ride or not?"

Dan looked down to notice once more he'd been wringing his hands. This time he'd been doing it with the cleaning rag he had just used to wipe up the last messy leftovers of the day. As a result he was covered in filth. Again. "Yeah, sure," he said slowly. He looked up at the girl, who was standing there and shivering. He felt strangely detached, like he was hearing someone else agree to drive her home. It reminded him of how his voice sounded on his voice mail greeting, tinny and artificial. "I'll give you a ride." He blinked a couple of times, clearing his head. "Let me go wash up, and then I'll lock the store up for the night."

Dan walked into the back room in a daze. He dropped the dirty cleaning rag into the laundry basket. It was already filled to the brim with dirty aprons, at least a dozen. Dan stopped counting when he hit ten. He usually went through two or three every hour, more if the deli was busy. His boss always gave him shit for it, the cheap bastard.

He moved over to the sink and began to once more wash his hands. He washed and he washed; he scrubbed his fingertips until his cuticles began to sting from the soap. He barely noticed it when he went to shut off the faucet, though he did see that the water escaping down the drain was tinged with red. He looked down at his hands to see how inflamed and raw his fingertips had become.

Dan turned the water off and gingerly dried his sore hands with a clean paper towel. He looked down at it — it was wilted and damp, and cross-hatched with tiny rust-colored half-moons of blood. He crumpled the paper towel up in his hands and tossed it in the garbage can before walking over to retrieve his winter jacket from its peg on the wall. He slowly slid his arms into the sleeves, wincing as his fingers caught on the rough flannel lining.

"Hey, you still there?" the girl called out from the other side of the counter. Dan stuck his head out of the back room. She was hugging herself and shivering. There was a puddle of water accumulating at her feet. "Are you ready to go yet? The heat in your car isn't broken, is it?"

"No, it works just fine," he said. He began shutting off the lights inside the deli. "Come on, I'll give you a ride. You're right, it's not fair to make you walk home in rain like this. Besides, it's not exactly safe to go anywhere by yourself with that crazy Butcher around here. It gets dark fast this time of year." He hazarded a polite smile at the girl. "I'm giving you fair warning, though. If you even so much as think about breathing on my car stereo, I am going to murder you."

"Okay, whatever. Just could we go please? I'm fucking freezing." She turned and walked away. Dan heard the bells hanging on the door ring, just like miniature church bells at a wedding. *Or a funeral,* he thought. They rattled against the frame as the door slammed shut.

"Okay," he said to the dark, empty room. He stuck his hands deep inside his coat pockets and recoiled sharply. He held his hand up in the dim light. There he saw a tiny dark spot welling up on the ball of his thumb.

Dan reflexively stuck his thumb into his mouth. He sucked on it a moment, much like he did as a child. The coppery tang of his own blood filled his mouth. The taste coated his tongue, leaving it feeling syrupy and thick. He spared a moment to look out through the front window of the deli where he could see the girl in the amber light given off by the single sodium lamp in the parking lot. She was standing forlornly in the rain as she waited for him.

"Never can seem to get the stuff off my hands," he murmured as he reached more carefully into his pocket. He brushed past the long wooden handle of the knife and picked out the keys to the shop before walking outside. The bells jingled as the door closed behind him.

Good Fences Make Good

By Chris O'Grady

Wilder was a few minutes early. He locked his car, left it in the parking field, and crossed to the public park between the parking area and Main Street. Going in under the trees, he got out of the afternoon sun and cut across the park to a bus stop. Drogo the fence wasn't in front of the drugstore across the way.

Wilder waited on the nearest park bench. When Drogo didn't show after five minutes, Wilder changed benches. This time he sat on one back under the trees a ways. When Drogo finally turned up, he was half an hour late.

Wilder stayed where he was, watching Drogo and looking over everyone in the vicinity. If Drogo had been on time, Wilder would have gone right over to him, collected his cut for the hot ice, and been on his way. But Drogo hadn't been on time.

Warily, Wilder checked out the scene, trying to see if anything looked out of line. It wouldn't be the first time a scared fence turned a client over to the law, and Drogo was the kind who scared easily.

Traffic passed both ways in the sunny roadway. Afternoon shoppers kept the opposite sidewalk busy. Drogo looked up and down the street and across at the park, where Wilder sat concealed, back under the trees. He looked jumpy. Drogo couldn't seem to stand in the same place for more than a couple of seconds at a time.

Drogo wore a dark brown straw fedora with a narrow brim and a wide band of a lighter shade of brown. Under his gray sharkskin suit he had on an open at the neck Hawaiian sport shirt that showed a white T-shirt tucked in close to his plump tanned neck. His pointed brown and white shoes kept shifting on the sidewalk as he turned to look this way, then that way. Finally he walked over to the drug store entrance and peered in at whoever was inside to see if Wilder was in there. He was still bending into the doorway out of the hot sidewalk sun, squinting in at the people at the lunch counter, when Wilder came up behind him.

"All set?" Wilder asked quietly.

Drogo jumped, turned, saw who it was, and looked relieved. Trying to smile, he stammered, "Jeez, you surprised me."

"Yeah," Wilder said absently, "slip me the take."

Drogo's eyes shifted.

"Not here," he murmured. "Let's get around the corner." He turned and walked off, taking quick steps.

Annoyed, Wilder stared after him. Following Drogo, he caught up with him as he turned the nearby corner.

"Why? What's the big production? If you peddled the ice, you've got my part. If you didn't, hand it over and I'll fade and try someone else."

Drogo kept walking swiftly along the quiet sunny street. Reaching out, Wilder took Drogo's arm, stopped him, and spun him around.

"What's with you, man?"

"Don't, don't," Drogo said, looking down at Wilder's big hands. His eyes blinked rapidly, as if he were already closing them just before he got hit.

"Drogo," Wilder murmured, "I don't like this."

Drogo swallowed, realized that Wilder wasn't going to hit him, and calmed down some. Sighing, he hesitated, looking past Wilder at Main Street.

"Wilder, I'm sorry. They made me do it this way."

"Who made you do it what way?" Wilder growled irritably. "This graft is between you and me, nobody else."

Drogo edged back a little. Wilder heard a step on the sidewalk behind him and turned.

"Easy!" the man said.

Wilder thought it was a nice quiet spot. They were just far enough from the busier street for anything to happen, and for Drogo and this pale, thin-faced specimen to get clear afterward.

"Easy it is," Wilder said, thinking this was why Drogo had delayed the contact for a half-hour. This gun type had wanted to eyeball Wilder before closing in on him.

"They just want to see you," the pale man said.

"Who's they? And who are you?" Wilder asked, keeping his voice polite.

"This is Mr. Raney," Drogo said, off to one side now.

Wilder nodded. "Mr. Raney."

The pale man nodded. His lips were thin, his eyes lashless, his face without expression, his hat yellow straw, his shirt white, and his tie mauve. The rest of him was neat and easily forgotten.

"Who *just* wants to see me?" Wilder asked.

Raney shrugged. "The people who run things here."

Wilder glanced at Drogo. Wilder's eyes and face didn't reveal a thing. He looked away from Drogo and back at Raney.

"Why?"

"They like to know who they're doing business with," Raney replied. His words were spoken softly, lazily, as if he were being patient, but his muddy eyes were beginning to appear not so patient. His face had a look of concealed contempt, not too well concealed now.

Raney's right hand was in the side pocket of his suitcoat, but the pocket held more than his hand. Wilder wondered if it held knucks or a handgun. He decided not to find out, yet.

"They just want to see me?" Wilder asked. "And then I can go?"

"That's it."

"Sure," Drogo put in. "I told them you don't work that way, but they insisted."

Wilder didn't look at Drogo, just nodded slowly, making himself look as if he was thinking it over. Then he shrugged and grinned.

"Okay," he said, "no problem."

"That's the way, Wilder," Drogo said, looking relieved. "They're all right. You'll see."

"This way," Raney said, nodding back toward Main Street. "The car's across in the lot, there."

Wilder didn't hang back. He went past Raney. Drogo came up and walked on Wilder's left. Raney stayed a little behind, on Wilder's right. Wilder knew he would.

They crossed Main Street with the traffic light, Drogo chattering away, Wilder occasionally responding, Raney silent. Traversing the little park, they emerged onto the path skirting the far side of the park, next to the public parking area.

"Over this way," Raney said, turning toward the distant railroad station at the south end of the park.

They walked halfway to the station in pleasant tree shade before Drogo turned into the parking field and went up to a dark green Chrysler. Raney handed him car keys. Drogo went around the front of the car to the driver's side, opened the door there, slid behind the wheel, and leaned across to open the front door on the other side. Then he reached over the seatback and pulled up the lock-knob on the back door of the passenger side.

"Sit in front," Raney said, "next to him."

Wilder nodded, went between the Chrysler and the car parked beside it, got in, slammed the door shut behind him and ran the window down. Raney stayed close behind him, waited until Wilder closed his door, and started past, reaching with his free hand for the back door handle. Wilder shoved his door open as Raney went past.

The door walloped Raney's right side and shoulder.

Reaching through the open car window, Wilder grabbed Raney's tie, and hauled him into the window opening. Raney hit the door, slamming it shut. His eyes looked enormous. His face was as white as paper. He spat words in a spittle-whisper, strangling from the tie Wilder was pulling tighter around his neck.

Wilder clipped him with his left fist. Raney's head snapped up. Wilder gave him another one.

Raney's right hand stuck a short-barrelled .38 revolver through the window. Wilder had to grab it with his hitting hand. Raney hadn't cocked the gun, so Wilder just clamped his hand over the top of the thing, held the cylinder to keep it from turning, and prevented Raney from getting off a shot.

Hooking his thumb behind the hammer before Raney's thumb could pull it back and fire, Wilder pulled harder on Raney's tie, twisted it around his head, and pulled Raney farther in through the window.

Raney's face wasn't white anymore. It was thickening up, turning red, then purple. Raney kept moving his lips, snarling, trying to spit words, but the tie was too tight now for him to speak.

Wilder slid away a little to keep Raney from getting any teeth into him. Drogo plucked at Wilder's sleeve.

"Don't, Wilder," he begged. "They'll find both of us."

Wilder shook the hand off. "Shut up."

He heard Drogo opening the back door.

"Stay here, Drogo, or I'll find you myself."

Drogo got out of the car, slammed the door shut, ran one way, found himself blocked by one of the cars parked in back, turned, and ran the other way, around the front end of the Chrysler. He disappeared into the park.

Wilder returned his attention to Raney, holding onto the .38 and ramming Raney's wrist and forearm against the dashboard until he let go of the gun. Dropping it onto the seat beside him, Wilder belted him again and was grabbing for Raney's other hand when Raney slumped and was quiet.

Wilder held onto Raney's wrist and tie a moment more, to make sure. Then he loosened the tie choking Raney's neck and shoved Raney back out through the car window. He heard Raney hit the pavement as he was sliding behind the steering wheel.

Good, at least Drogo had left the keys in the ignition!

Starting the engine, he moved the Chrysler forward a foot or two so there would be room behind it and the car parked there. Putting it in neutral, he braked, took the keys out of the ignition, slid across the seat, and got out.

For the moment, there was no one in sight. All right, that was a plus.

Wilder tried to keep the car door open, but it kept swinging shut by itself. He wanted it open to hide what he had to do next, in case anyone passed while he was in the middle of it. He jammed the edge of the car door into the side of the next car.

Watching it a moment, he decided it would hold that way for as long as he needed. He went back to where Raney lay and hauled him behind the car, opened the trunk, and tumbled Raney in beside the spare tire.

He couldn't tell if Raney was dead or not, and he didn't have time to bother finding out.

Driving slowly, he left the parking lot, turned left at the end of the park, and waited for the traffic light on Main Street. He couldn't see Drogo. When the light changed, he turned left, drove along the street, back the way he'd just come but on the opposite side of the long narrow park.

Wilder figured Drogo would have cut through the park, but he couldn't be sure he would stay on the main drag or keep going. If Drogo was smart, he'd be on a phone now to "the people who ran things around here." Wilder chuckled, thinking that. Drogo would be trying to cover himself for whatever happened to Raney.

All right, Wilder decided. Drogo would be phoning. He wouldn't be trying for distance, not yet. The people he phoned would tell him to stay put. That meant Drogo would be in some store along the drag, here, waiting for reinforcements.

Checking for side streets, Wilder saw that none ran into Main Street for the entire length of the business block opposite the park, so he decided to stop and wait at the first cross street, down by the railroad overpass. Drogo should then be somewhere behind him.

Finding a parking spot at the curb, he checked the .38, slipped it into his pocket, got out of the Chrysler, and put some change in the parking meter. Standing close to the buildings, he looked over the heads of strollers and shoppers, back the way he'd just come.

He waited five minutes before he spotted Drogo.

There wasn't much traffic on Main Street. A car coming toward Wilder double-parked at the curb about the length of a regular block away. Drogo appeared, scuttling across the sidewalk, where he leaned down and spoke into the car, waving his arms, pointing over the roof of the car to the park across the way.

Three men got out and started across. The last one beckoned to Drogo, went on, glanced back, and saw Drogo still standing on the sidewalk, unwilling to follow. The man called something, beckoned again angrily, and Drogo started across after them, not going too fast.

Wilder grinned, got back in the Chrysler, made a U-turn, and cruised back toward them. The park slid past on his right. The three men went in among the trees on a path through the park.

Drogo was almost across the street.

Wilder sped up. When Drogo reached the opposite side-walk, Wilder drove past him, stopped, and swung the door open nearest the curb.

"Drogo!" he called.

Drogo turned and saw whom it was. He skittered sideways a step or two, peered in through the trees, and looked back at Wilder.

"Get in," Wilder told him, pointing the .38 at him. "Get in or I'll pump you right here."

Drogo stared at the gun, licked his lips, looked into the park once more, and came over to the Chrysler.

"In!" Wilder ordered. "Quick!"

Drogo climbed in and slammed the door shut, still staring at the gun.

"Wilder," he whispered, "I didn't know they were . . ."

"You can talk later," Wilder growled.

Putting the .38 away, he swung the Chrysler out into the center lane and drove off. In the rearview mirror he saw one of the three men come plunging out of the park and across the sidewalk. He stopped in the road, staring after the Chrysler for a long moment before turning and going back in among the trees again.

"Is this Raney's car?" Wilder asked.

"What? This . . . ?"

"Who owns this car?" Wilder snapped. "Answer me."

"Oh, the car. Yes, it's Raney's. What did you do with him?"

"Then they've spotted us," Wilder said, ignoring Drogo's question.

Driving the length of the park, he passed the drugstore, caught a break in oncoming traffic up near the corner with the traffic light in his favor, and made the turn down the side street where Drogo had fingered him for Raney. Driving along for several blocks, he got off it, did some zigzagging, and finally stopped in a lonely stretch of road leading up to a highway that skirted the western edge of town.

"Wilder, what did you do with Raney?"

"Raney's out of this," Wilder told him.

"Where'd you leave him?"

"Back there in the park." Wilder grinned at Drogo. "He was out like a light. Maybe he's dead by now."

Drogo's eyes grew sick.

"Wilder," he whispered, "they won't forget. They'll kill the both of us now. Why didn't you leave me back there? You drag me along like this, they'll think I'm in it with you . . ."

Wilder slapped him.

"You dragged me into this," he snarled. "Don't forget that, you little creep."

He slapped Drogo again, harder this time. Drogo's head snapped to the side and stayed that way. For a second, Wilder was afraid he'd hit Drogo too hard. Grabbing the front of his coat, he pulled him nearer.

Drogo's eyes opened, looking vague, then his gaze sharpened as he came out of it.

"Keep quiet," Wilder told him. "Understand? Keep quiet."

Drogo nodded.

"Sure," he whispered. "Sure, Wilder. I only . . ."

"Keep quiet," Wilder told him again. "All the way quiet."

He stared into Drogo's eyes until he was sure Drogo realized what all the way quiet meant. Then he released Drogo's coat front.

Drogo fell back, staring at him, his hands making clumsy movements trying to straighten the lapels of his suit coat.

"You answer me, and you tell me only what I ask you, understand? Drogo, do you understand?"

"Yes, I understa—"

"Just yes is enough," Wilder interrupted him.

Drogo swallowed, nodded, and said bitterly, "Yes."

"Now tell me about it," Wilder ordered. "And keep it short. Who's got my plunder?"

The first words burst from Drogo's mouth in a rush: "Wilder,

I was peddling the stuff like I always do. Then they told me they were gonna hold onto it . . ."

"Who? Who's got my goods? A name!"

Drogo gulped, then murmured, "A man named Harris. He's got this town sewed up."

Drogo realized he was talking too much again. He muttered, "Sorry, Wilder . . ."

"I know," Wilder said absently. "You just can't keep your mouth shut."

Wilder thought about it a moment before saying: "Drogo, I turned the stuff over to you. You got a recommend. I deal with you. Not with any Harris or any Raney. Just you. And you turned me over to them."

"You don't understand," Drogo said desperately. "They run things here, the whole town, even some of the cops."

"They don't run me," Wilder said quietly.

Drogo stared at him, his mouth hanging open.

"They may run this town and they may run you," Wilder said evenly. "But they don't run me. They aren't getting any organization's hooks into me. If they had you working your grift with their say-so, you shoulda told me before I handed over the ice. You didn't tell me. So that means I was still dealing with you. Only with you."

"What . . .?" Drogo's voice was a dry croak. He licked his lips, swallowed and tried again: "What're you gonna do, Wilder?"

Wilder took out Raney's .38 and held it loosely in his lap.

"You turned me over to them," he said, "so I'm gonna leave you on your face in those woods behind you."

"Wilder, you don't know!" Drogo screamed. "I just thought they was customers. They never tried nothing like this before. I've pushed stuff through them plenty times. Just this time they start with this wanting to see the guys like you, that pull jobs. Freeze off your market, Harris said. Around here, anyway."

Wilder shrugged.

"There's plenty of other places. They can do anything they like with you and their market here, but I don't want any of them seeing me. I don't work with scum like that. I don't deal with them."

"I know, I know," Drogo groaned, "but they want it that way. They want to know who's got a grift going, what you look like. They want everything organized. Wilder, don't you see? I had to go along. I'm here every day. I don't just blow on out of town tonight like you. I got to deal with these people."

"I don't," Wilder said. "I deal with whoever I want to deal with."

Drogo's shoulders slumped. He sighed and his eyes dropped. His head shook wearily from side to side.

"All right, where is he?"

Drogo stared at him, eyes wide. "Where's who?"

"This Harris. The big organizer."

Drogo blinked. Slowly he shook his head.

"Wilder," he whispered, "they'd cut you in pieces if you showed."

"Where is he?" Wilder asked again, staring up the hill at the late afternoon sunlight turning the clouds orange.

A big semi roared past on the highway. He could see only the top half of the rig and the exhaust stack streaming thin gray fumes.

"I don't know where he is," Drogo finally said. Wrinkles cut dark gullies across his wide forehead with the effort he was making to think. "It's hard to say where Harris would be. With this rumble you started he could be any—"

"Save the lecture, Drogo," Wilder warned. "Where can I get my hands on Harris. Where does he live? Where's his business, his operation?"

Drogo turned in the passenger seat and pointed through the rear window of the Chrysler. "Harris lives on South Valley Drive, on that ridge, the other side of town. That's where all the money people live."

"What's the house number?" Wilder insisted. "Never mind the status part."

"One-seven-oh-seven. There's a sign in front with his name on it, Harris."

"I know his name. Where does he work?"

"Mainly he operates out of the big bowling alley, the Olympia, corner of Walnut and Melrose. You can find Melrose easy. It's the big boulevard—"

"I'll find it," Wilder interrupted. "Look at me, Drogo."

Startled, Drogo turned on the seat and stared down at the gun. He didn't see what Wilder's other hand was doing, but he felt it.

One punch was enough. Drogo settled limply against the door.

Reaching around him, Wilder opened the car door. Drogo tilted, fell out, slid loosely down the sun-yellowed weed-slope beside the road and came to a stop at the bottom of the roadside ditch.

Pulling the car door shut, Wilder drove away.

It wasn't as dark as he would have liked when he ditched the Chrysler on Walnut Avenue and walked toward the Melrose Boulevard intersection. Under the last shade tree, he stopped and examined the Olympia bowling alley standing in the middle of its wide asphalt parking area on the adjacent corner. Off in the west, the sky was a long orange-red smear. The sun was setting behind roofs. Everything looked clear but blurred in the early evening light. Street lights went on. They didn't throw much illumination. It wasn't dark enough yet.

Wilder went out from beneath the trees and along the sidewalk to the corner. A cool breeze that smelled like nighttime blew against his face. He stood on the corner, studying the bowling alley. A wide entrance with a concrete patio apron in front of it was one step up from the asphalt that surrounded the entire building. A long row of windows stretched along the front wall on the second floor.

Crossing over, Wilder went inside through the front entrance. He saw that the row of windows faced out from a dining balcony which also overlooked about twenty alleys. Only two of them were busy this early in the evening. Three fat sweating men were using the alley opposite the front entrance. To the right, five kids were working the far alley next to the wall. Near the entrance was a long bar.

The other way, on Wilder's left, the niche that rented bowling shoes stuck out toward the alleys. He headed toward that, passed it, went around its far corner, and along behind the rows of seats behind each alley. He kept looking at the alleys, but he noticed a closed door in the wall as he strolled past it.

Near the last alley at that end, he stopped, turned, started back, and stopped when he came to the door in the wall.

Both the fat guys and the kids were busy with their bowling and the bartender couldn't see him behind the out-thrust of the bowling shoe kiosk, so he tried the door. It was locked. He went around to the front of the kiosk and asked the girl who rented the shoes, "Is Mr. Harris around yet?"

"I think he went home for supper," she said.

"Thanks."

Wilder went back outside and strolled around the north side of the building to the back. Only a couple of cars were parked there. A concrete platform railed by silver-painted iron pipes was built out from the blank back wall of the building. A single window high up the white-painted wall showed a faint light

Climbing the platform steps, he tried the door opening onto the platform. It didn't open. He went back down the steps and tried the doors of one of the parked cars. Its doors were all locked. The doors of the second car weren't. Wilder climbed in back.

He watched the platform door for ten minutes before it opened. A dark-haired man stepped quickly out onto the platform, closed the door behind him, made sure it was locked, and came down the steps, pulling out some keys on the end of a chain. He headed toward the other car, glancing at the one

Wilder was in. He took a second look, turned in his stride and came over, stooping to see who was inside.

Wilder opened the back door. The man stopped, stared at him a moment, and started to back away. Getting out of the car, Wilder went over to him.

The man reached behind his hip.

"No," Wilder said softly, taking out the .38.

The man brought his hand back around front. He watched Wilder warily. He had startling light-blue eyes in a bronze tanned face.

"You Harris?" Wilder asked him.

"No."

"Who then?"

"Al Belton."

"Is Harris inside?"

Belton shook his head. "No, he isn't."

"Let's go in anyway," Wilder said.

"Listen, what the hell are you trying to . . .?"

Wilder shoved him toward the concrete steps. "Let's go inside," he repeated.

Belton started to say something else, but Wilder pushed him again harder. He tripped on the bottom step and had to grab the iron railing to keep from falling.

"Stay that way," Wilder ordered. He frisked Belton, found a long-barrelled .32 automatic in a tooled leather hip holster, took it, and stuck it inside his belt.

"Mister," Belton said through teeth that gleamed in his dark face, "you can still walk around but you're dead. You won't even see tomorrow."

Wilder stood over him and said quietly, "Maybe you won't even see tonight."

For a moment, Belton stared up at him as if he hadn't heard a word. Then something he saw in Wilder's eyes brought a flicker of uncertainty to his own. He squinted, looking closer at Wilder, then he looked away.

Wilder could hear the man's breathing.

"Look, man, you haven't got a prayer," Belton said. "This is our town." His dark face swung up, his light eyes flashing angrily again. "Harris will see you get . . ."

"No," Wilder said evenly. "It's my town. I took it away from you when you people tried shortstopping me. It'll be your town again when I decide to give it back to you and that'll be when I'm through with it, not before."

Belton started to say something. His voice was pitched higher than before, partly with rage, partly with something else, something he didn't like hearing in his own voice, something too close to panic.

Wilder didn't bother listening to it.

"Shut the guff," he growled. "Open this door. We're going in."

Belton took a long time finding the right key in the bunch at the end of his chain. Inside, a flight of steps led upward along the rear wall of the building. At the top was a box-like vestibule with a single ceiling bulb and the window that faced out onto the two cars parked below.

Belton worked even longer trying to find the key for the vestibule's only door.

"Snap it up," Wilder told him.

"I'm trying," Belton replied.

"You're trying too hard," Wilder said. "Relax."

Droplets of sweat were on Belton's leather brown forehead. His hands were shaking.

"What's in there?" Wilder asked him, to calm him down a bit. "Just offices?"

"Yes. Two rooms. Mr. Harris's, and the office where the help work."

"How you coming with that key?"

Belton didn't say anything. He dropped the keys. They swung at the end of the chain. Reaching out, Belton put one hand against the wall beside the door to support himself. Wilder smiled.

When Belton's hand came away from the wall, Wilder could see the spot had smudges from being touched often.

"Quit stalling," he said, as if he hadn't noticed anything.

"Yeah, yeah," Belton said softly, under his breath.

Recovering the keys, he found the right one without any more trouble and used it on the door lock.

Reaching out, Wilder took a fistful of Belton's suitcoat in his left hand, up near the collar. He braced his left forearm against Belton's back, straight up and down, his elbow gouging a little into the man's lower back.

"Now open it," he murmured.

Belton turned the knob and started to push the door open. Wilder slugged him behind the ear with the .38, bracing himself to take Belton's weight and at the same time shouting, "Harris!"

He heard movement behind the door. He pushed the unconscious man against it, swinging it abruptly inward into darkness.

Still holding Belton upright, he again shouted, "Harris!"

The shout echoed loudly in the vestibule and stairway.

Wilder shoved his decoy partway through the open doorway, keeping himself to the right, close to the wall, out of the line of fire.

"Harris!" he roared. "Come out of there or I'll give you what Raney got."

Then the shooting started. He felt the impact of the bullets ripping into Belton. Again and again he shouted Harris's name, just to keep the uproar going.

More shots flashed out of the dark room. Belton twitched. A moan escaped him. Wilder dropped him, took the .38 and smashed the vestibule's ceiling light. Darkness was immediate.

Crouching, Wilder peered carefully through the doorway into the darkness, saw movement, and fired at it.

Another couple of shots came at him. He waited until they stopped, then went through the doorway in a dive. Hitting the floor, he kept rolling. He heard another shot rip into the floor back where he'd landed.

Vaguely in the gun-flash he glimpsed a face, snapped a shot that way, heard a grunt, and went on rolling until he thudded up against something hard. His fingertips explored and told him it was a steel desk. He lay on the floor beside the desk, listening and waiting.

He could hear small clicking reloading sounds. Over by the doorway were other sounds from the wounded man, like gargling. Wilder wondered how Belton could still be alive with all the slugs he'd taken.

Another shot cracked. Harris, or whoever it was, had his gun reloaded.

For an instant, the flash lit the room. Wilder saw the shooter stretched out on the floor, like himself, in a room beyond the one he was in. Wilder shot him in the darkness after the flash was gone.

Giving it a minute, he got up, crossed the room and slipped into the next, moving silently. He could hear harsh breathing and he approached the sounds from the side. With careful fingertips, he traced along the man's coat sleeve. When his fingertips came to where the wrist should be, he lifted his left leg and stepped down hard on it.

Thrashing, the man cried out. Keeping his left foot on top of the twisting wrist, he kicked the man with his other foot. The thrashing stopped. Now there was only a hoarse gasp.

Reaching down and probing, Wilder found the man's gun, and then turned, found a light, and switched it on.

On the floor lay a big-shouldered gray-haired man in a spreading pool of his own blood. His right arm was extended along the floor, the fingers of the hand curled as if they still held the gun. Wilder used a foot to roll him over onto his back. Angry black eyes steadied on Wilder.

"You Harris?" Wilder asked him.

The man cursed at him.

Wilder leaned down and clipped his cheekbone with the gun he'd taken from him. The man's mouth twisted with pain. A high nasal "Aaaah!" escaped his lips before he could stop it.

"Are you Harris?" Wilder asked again.

"Yeah," the man gasped, "and I'll see that you get—"

"Where's my stuff?" Wilder interrupted. "That ice you shortstopped on me. Where'd you stash it?"

Harris began cursing again. Wilder rapped him with the gun again on the same cheekbone, not too hard. Harris stopped cursing.

"You're shot twice," Wilder told him evenly. "This one's through your shoulder. Looks like it just got the meat. The other one might be worse. You want me to walk out of here?"

"Hell with you!" Harris gasped. His face was white and twisted in fury.

Wilder shook his head, turned away and started to search the place.

Every so often, from what sounded like a great distance, he could hear sudden *clocking* noises, followed by ringing roars. The bowling was still going on down below, so they hadn't been able to hear any of the shots.

It took him ten minutes to find the little felt sack of jewels he had turned over to Drogo for conversion to cash. He checked to make sure the ice was inside. It was. He put the little sack into his pocket.

Harris was staring at the ceiling, looking white and sweaty. His lips whispered words Wilder couldn't make out. Wilder looked down at him while he wiped his own fingerprints off the gun he'd taken from Harris. Then he stopped, slapped the gun into Harris's right hand, pressed the cold fingers around the butt, and dropped the gun a foot away on the floor.

Harris was muttering, "My town. I'll handle . . ."

Wilder grinned.

"Sure it's your town. You're welcome to it. I'm through with it myself."

Going over to the other man out in the vestibule, he found him dead and put the .38 he'd gotten from Raney in Belton's hand, after wiping all his own prints off it. He nudged Belton's trigger finger against the trigger. The shot hit the opposite wall, near the doorway to the inner office. That was in case the police gave Belton a paraffin test.

Wiping the .32 automatic clean, he stuck it back into Belton's hip holster and left the place.

No one was out back. He walked across town and found his car where he'd left it in the parking field beyond the Main Street park.

He was a hundred miles away before the news on the car radio started telling about the two prominent businessmen who had apparently shot each other to death. When he heard that, Wilder grinned, then grimaced in disgust.

"Did the bastards think I'd pay them dues every month?" he muttered to himself.

Wonderboy

By Charles Martin and Will Weinke

It's depressing when you realize that your entire life can be summed up in one sentence: "Anne Fredrick is the bastard daughter of Wonderboy."

That's all anyone really needs to know about me. That one statement pretty much tracks my life from birth nineteen years ago, where a brutal delivery left my mother gasping her last breath, all the way to me landing a job with the anointed one's publicity firm. It was a convenient way to funnel me some of that sweet, sweet hush money.

Not everyone's life is so conveniently folded up into a tight, easy to carry package. You can't just say: "Bob was a father of four in suburban Philadelphia." Or: "Ronald Reagan was a US president in the 1980's." Or even: "The Mamas and the Papas produced the best pop song of the 1960's."

That just doesn't cover it, does it? There's more to the story. There is context you need to provide; tragic story arches of mental deterioration and Free Love gone terribly wrong. But for me, everything in my life can be summed up by those seven words. How sad.

I like to fool myself that this little autobiographical writing exercise will change all that. I will instead become: "Anne Fredrick is the bastard daughter of Wonderboy. Her elegant and witty memoir became the definitive account of Clint Solh's complicated personal life." Hell, let's just tack on: "Which she then followed up by marrying into the royal family of some fabulously wealthy European nation." That's not so bad, three sentences. I bet most people would love three rock solid sentences to sum them up as a figure of great significance in human history.

Of course, I know that better accounts have been and will be written about my father, but this one is mine and I will do everything in my power to make it so unbelievably kickass that you will want to put the book down, walk into your living room and hit your own dad right in the mouth. Not because you are mad at him or I'm turning you into a sociopath, but because you want him to feel the soul shocking impact of my brilliant insight and charmingly self-effacing narrative.

Yeah, that's what's about to happen. So buckle in, folks.

Since this is going to be a literary document of great import, I'm assuming at least thirty million kids in the distant future will be forced to read this in brightly lit classrooms while a hawknosed teacher with frizzy hair diligently watches to ensure the children are adequately absorbing the text. Maybe she'll even have them take turns reading out loud, just to demonstrate how perfectly my sharp, spot-on snarkiness communicates my generation's growing cynicism with the cult of Wonderboy.

At any rate, let's go over the basics so you snot-nosed brats who aren't paying enough attention to the subtle nuances will at least be able to pass the impending pop quiz.

Clint Sohl is Wonderboy, but not a secret identity like Peter Parker or Clark Kent. Everyone knew Wonderboy's real name, but no one called him that because, where's the zip? There were actually a ton of names at the start of the Wonderboy Era such as Superboy, the Red Storm, Swarm or Justin Case (my favorite). The feminists, human rights groups, and libertarians called him the Red Menace and the Crimson Wave. His enemies called him the Scourge. From the first headlines popping up about a real deal superhero, editors grappled at finding the perfect moniker, something with pizzazz. There were nickname contests, novelty songs, billboard campaigns, but the general public seemed to respond to "Wonderboy" the most since it fit the perpetually young superhero. *National Enquirer* even tried trademarking the name, but by that point, "Wonderboy" had fallen into common usage.

In everyday life, I called him "Clint." Even after I graduated high school and he decided it was time to connect with his only offspring. He tried to get me to do that whole "dad" thing, but I still called him "Clint," just to twist the knife a little.

Clint had this incredible arsenal of unnatural abilities. Some believed Wonderboy had hundreds of individual powers, but others insisted there were only three or four really significant powers that he kind of tweaked from time to time to keep evil-doers on their toes. Sort of like a juggler shifting from tennis balls to bowling balls and pretending it's a whole new thing. You're still just juggling balls, buddy.

So, maybe once a year, when the public started growing bored of eye lasers, explosive spitballs, or what-have-you, he'd switch up his outfit a little and then suddenly get this new power. It usually popped up during a tussle with a bad guy, which then gave an aura of a divine benefactor with a bag full of tricks that he was carefully rationing out to Wonderboy.

Regardless, those powers ushered in two decades of global peace and the Golden Age of humanity. Oh shit — before we get too far, you need to know that my father had a run-in with a woman named Wendy Werthington. What actually happened is up for debate. Some people think it's no big deal, more of a misunderstanding. Others are trying to make Clint out to be some kind of creep, which is a tough sell to the general public when he is saving lives on a daily basis. Regardless of the validity of Ms. Werthington's claim, that little nugget will inform other aspects of my father's character.

So, now you ask, "Do you think Wonderboy did it?"

Clint is a horndog, but he's no rapist. The guy's got skeletons in his closet as would any man as influential as Wonderboy. And I know these skeletons intimately as part of my job at his publicity firm, IMagemaker. But nothing that dark. He's a world leader, you know? Sometimes shit happens.

But, Christ. Does any of that matter anymore? I don't want to seem callous, but my father just unloaded a big secret on me. You know which one, nothing about startled feminists or sketchy dealings with banking institutions. The secret that, once it comes out, will doom our entire way of life.

Clint just sort of blurted it out to me while we were watching old kung fu movies, our Tuesday night ritual. It was like he was tired of holding it in all alone and figured he'd put some of that weight on his bastard daughter's shoulders.

So, consequently, here I am, furiously writing my memoir because I know that once the world finds out . . . well, I can almost taste that fat book advance.

Now, future kids, you may not realize just how earth-shattering this confession will be. That's the problem with history: you really never get a sense of the emotional context. "How could Time Magazine make Hitler Man of the Year? Didn't they know he was an asshole?"

"New Kids on the Block? Really?"

"How could you be so surprised about Wonderboy? Didn't you see the signs?"

But you don't realize how naïve we all were — well, are. And we are for good reason. Watching the shimmering red cloud sweeping across the sky, we knew he was protecting us. When we saw his boyish and brimming smile greeting adoring fans, we felt that he was one of us. When we saw him inhale the firestorm of a nuclear blast in Southern California, we believed that he was a constant and infallible king-god that would deliver us from evil.

Twenty years with no wars and crime rates so low that they were almost nonexistent. We lived in a utopia that one man had made possible. That is why we trusted him completely and why the world will be so completely unprepared for the truth, once it finally comes out.

And it will.

But not from me. I'm good with secrets. You have to be when you are the child of a superhero that the world could never know about. That said, when someone finally flaps their lips, my manuscript will be on every editor's desk the next morning.

I do feel a little bad for the world. And for my dad, I guess. I'm not just a bitter little twat. I know I have the benefit of knowing, since I was four years old, that Wonderboy had no problem lying to the world and telling a little girl that she had to lie too.

"I have a reputation," he said while I sat on his lap and ran my fingers over the satiny fabric of his cape. "The world just won't understand, but I will be here for you as much as I possibly can. I love you, do you understand that?"

I nodded enthusiastically.

"Do you understand that you cannot tell anyone about me?"

I nodded.

"Do you really understand? Do you understand why?"

I nodded, but I didn't understand why. I just knew that he'd fly me around once a week and bring me presents from all around the world as long as I never told a soul.

"But why don't you get a little more exercise, honey, you don't want Wonderboy throwing his back out lifting you up, right?"

"No, Daddy."

"Cause who will save the world then?"

"No one, Daddy."

"That's right, no one."

And yet, it is still very hard for me, the most cynical girl in the world, to process the mother of all secrets Clint told me tonight. I can't imagine what it will be like for the rest of the world when they find out Wonderboy had been lying to us all along. The Wendy Werthington scandal is nothing compared to this. That little flap did little to diminish the shine on Wonderboy's persona when she came forward last year. It was easy for men to shrug off "rape" as a misunderstanding and for women to guess at Werthington's ulterior motives.

To my father's credit, he offered to apologize to Werthington in person, which she refused, but settled the case quietly out of court. My father didn't have to, of course, since no judicial system on Earth would ever dare to put him on trial and no prison could ever hold him. He knew he'd screwed up, though, and it appeared that he was making earnest attempts to mend his ways.

Okay, so a little extra context to the Wonderboy phenomenon: Werthington wasn't even the first controversy in his superhero career. They started almost immediately after he got his powers, hence the need for IMagemaker.

First, there were the difficult legal ramifications of having an omnipresent and borderless vigilante. Then there were conflicts of interest and market manipulation hearings during the energy crisis fifteen years ago when he set out to clean up corruption at oil and natural gas companies. There have been accusations of corruption at his various charities as well as the many, many conspiracy theories surrounding his criminal rehabilitation center in McAlester, Oklahoma. Internet conspiracy theorists have even gone back to examine the darker mysteries surrounding the North Korean War.

Officially, I am appalled by the ridiculous and libelous accusations against a good, decent citizen just trying to do what he can to make the world a better place. Privately, I'm riveted by each and every little shred of gossip, even those that I know are just bullshit. Long ago, I had disassociated the Wonderboy in the papers from Clint, my father. I could spend all day reading lurid stories from Hollywood starlets and then meet my dad for dinner and not even arch an eyebrow.

Come to think of it, that's really creepy. Maybe I should take that bit out.

Well, anyway, most of the scandals are ridiculous. Opportunists mostly, since there is no quicker way to the top of *The New York Times* bestseller list than writing a bawdy Wonderboy tell-all.

That's why IMagemaker was founded twenty years ago by Clint's friends, Tim and Mandy Berchum. For damage control when starfuckers, badgering journalists, and professional litigants come trolling after Clint. Along with my foster parents, Tim and Mandy were the only other people on the planet that knew I was Wonderboy's daughter. They hired me after I dropped out of college "as a favor to Clint," but I knew they were hoping that I would keep their golden boy from jumping ship after the fallout from the Werthington fiasco.

They were alright to work with. Just a nice, old couple that had sticky hard candy they insisted on pushing on me, didn't approve of me dating "below my station," and were brutal when it came to defaming Wonderboy's detractors. The work was boring, but I got to meet plenty of famous people. I even bagged two guys from last year's "Sexiest Men Alive" list after insisting I would put a good word in with producers working on *Wonderboy: The Movie.*

There was no movie, of course.

So IMagemaker was better than drinking stale beer at keggers on the lawn of some lame frat house with rich boys trying to make it seem like they were doing me a favor by sleeping with me.

Motherfucker, my dad's Wonderboy! Your Porsche does not impress me!

Where was I? Ah, yes, a handler. Part of the job meant I was very familiar with Wonderboy's dirty laundry. On top of that, my dad was a bit chatty when he got drunk and he only ever drank around people he trusted, hence our weekly kung fu night. So whatever I didn't read in reports or confidential dossiers, I found out after a fifth of Jim Beam. That's how I got to know about the one big lie, the lie that will change everything, the lie that will untangle everything Clint had worked to build in the past twenty years.

And, before you ask, no. I do not have any of Clint's superpowers. I didn't even get to inherit his name. The only thing I got from my dad were his blue eyes and hair that's brittle and unmanageable in the summer. I most definitely did not get his amazing good looks and slim, athletic build. I've always been a little on the bigger side. Not scooter and muumuu fat, mind you, just fifty pounds off hot. I'm the girl with "such a pretty face." If my life were a movie, I would be the chubby, wise-cracking best friend of the beautiful and improbably single lead actress.

Don't think it didn't bother Clint, either. He would always frown a little when he saw me and he never failed to promise me some fabulous present if I "just slimmed down a little." Oh, and he brought apples and oranges on my birthday instead of cake. Because clearly that was the problem: just too much damn birthday cake.

"Anne Fredrick is the fat bastard daughter of Wonderboy." *Le sigh*.

At least I don't have to worry about hordes of other bastard children coming out of the woodwork and diluting my leverage when it comes contract time for *Behind the Suit: The Bastard- Daughter of Wonderboy Tells All*.

Is that a good title? Doesn't come off as . . . incest-y, does it?

Well, regardless of the title, I'm fairly certain I am one in eight billion. I guess there is no way to know since he's slept with so many women. Perhaps it's just a numbers game. Clint did tell me that he was much more careful after I was born, but he didn't tell me what that meant. Maybe he found a way to sterilize himself or maybe he was just using the rhythm method like millions of other dumbass men and I would soon be stumbling across a rainbow coalition of brothers and sisters.

Jesus, nine pages already? I need to focus before I lose Miss Hawknose's tenth grade class.

So, Wonderboy. I'm sure you've seen pictures, but all through my life, he retained the same easy good looks of an eighteen year old holding the world by its ear, the bright-eyed cockiness of a young man still unafraid of death and probably still terrified of vaginas.

He never lost his love of being the world's only true superhero. He liked "discovering" a brand new superpower which he would then roll out to the general public as part of fan contests.

"Be the first to have Wonderboy levitate you over the Grand Canyon!"

"Have Wonderboy take apart your car with his mind, change the oil, and then reassemble it again like new!"

Publicity events were an everyday occurrence. He chuckled with groups of delighted schoolchildren as they teased him about his well-publicized fear of the dark. Then he shrugged bashfully as the children's mothers teased him about his even more publicized fear of commitment.

The only thing he actually feared was becoming irrelevant. Well, that and commitment.

Wonderboy loved the media, he loved adoring fans and he loved, loved, loved swooning women, which is how I happened.

He tolerated Roger Beam, the self-appointed defender of all things Wonderboy. The fiery man with pasty, freckled skin and a receding hairline was a failing newsman twenty years ago when he clutched onto this new rising star, the freak from Oklahoma that had quickly become the country's protector. As my father's powers grew and his sphere of influence extended beyond national borders, Beam declared himself a champion of Wonderboy, protecting the poor superhero against "incendiary elements in the cynical media looking to tarnish the image of my friend, Clint Sohl, and soil the good work he does in bringing democracy and justice to our planet."

Sure, nearly everybody loved Wonderboy during those first years when he was stopping genocide or foiling terrorist plots, but it soon became clear to dictators and crime syndicates that violence was a sure way to ping on Wonderboy's radar. With no violent crime to stop anymore, Wonderboy turned to the world's economies, busting up monopolies and rooting out white collar crime. That's when the fit hit the shan.

Later, charges of misogyny and harassment emerged from feminist groups claiming Wonderboy was setting the clock back on a hundred years of women's rights.

"You are an overeducated insurgent looking to incite unrest among the uninformed masses!" Beam declared during an interview with the president of the National Organization for Women, one of the first groups to start speaking out against Wonderboy.

Then there were the handful of nations that, two years ago, tried to enact sovereignty laws to keep Wonderboy at bay. The German chancellor said that "as much as we appreciated Mr. Sohl's egalitarian endeavors, there are domestic issues that he does not understand and a people must have the right to rule themselves without outside intervention."

I thought the chancellor had a point, but Beam called the woman a "Nazi" and suggested there might be dark motives behind these "rogue nations' efforts to outlaw Wonderboy."

Of course, Beam wasn't the only person defending Wonderboy at every step, just the loudest and the most self-righteous. And then came Werthington, the only true black eye my father suffered in the media. In this fight, Beam stood alone in my father's corner. IMagemaker even put together Wonderboy's official written apology. I have no idea if Clint actually signed off on it.

My father always told me he resented Beam for being a polarizing blowhard, hated when Wonderboy was used as a pawn in petty politicking and would never do anything to legitimize any of the talking heads.

And yet, two weeks ago, there was Wonderboy on *Your Nation, Your World, Your Rights with Roger Beam.*

Wonderboy had entered the studio, like always, in a swirling cloud of red mist that enveloped the room completely as the crowd gasped in fear and delight. I'd seen the entrance many, many times in my life and it seemed to me like watching ocean waves from underneath, just swirls of motion, all formless and indistinct while his massive cape flapped, cracked, and whistled.

If you looked closely, sometimes you could see Clint's face appearing in the storm of red, peeking out along the crowd as he passed through the studio to his chair. One woman boasted that he'd appeared before her while she sat in the crowd and gave her a kiss on the lips. She was five foot nine inches, blonde, and thin as a tent pole, so it was possible. Perhaps even likely.

Roger Beam met the red storm at the edge of the stage, hopping and clapping like a hyperactive child. He'd been working on getting my father on his show for twenty years. It was the culmination of an entire career spent riding another man's coat tails.

Cape tails . . .?

The cloud swept past and settled over a chair next to Beam's desk and trademark ten foot touchscreen monitor he used like a chalkboard when villainizing the enemies of Wonderboy. The red storm settled and floated down like mist around the chair, revealing my father. He was wearing his new red on red suit, skin-tight to show off his chiseled physique with the iconic logo of an infinity symbol merged with an atomic energy symbol printed on the chest. Even I don't know what the logo meant, but the rumor I liked best was that Tim drew it up to hint that Wonderboy had been created in a lab just to rattle the Chinese and whatever other nation might try to stand up to the American superweapon.

After all, my father was to the Golden Age what nuclear missiles were to the Cold War.

Wonderboy's clever grin was cautious and skeptical as Beam scampered toward my father, jutting out a small, eager hand. Wonderboy reached out and shook it without bothering to stand.

I was relieved that Clint didn't appear to be excited to be there, then confused as to why he would show up at all. Wonderboy didn't need Beam. Wonderboy didn't need anyone. Sure, Clint's public image had taken a few hits over the years, but Beam wasn't going to be of any use in winning over the hearts Clint lost in the Werthington scandal.

I should have been there with my father. As his agency escort, I was supposed to be by his side. If I had been backstage at the Beam appearance, perhaps it would have gone differently and the rumors wouldn't have started.

I was a natural at helping Clint deflect questions. And really, if you didn't already know the truth like I do now, the interview just comes off as a rather strained and uncomfortable conversation between a superhero and the man who worshipped him too much to ask a single probing, worthwhile question.

It was only until a couple days after the interview had aired when the conspiracy mills started humming. Wonderboy was always so good at interviews, but Clint paused on a couple questions as if they'd caught him off guard. Nothing should catch him off guard. He's fucking psychic after all! Or kinda psychic. I dunno. He explained it to me once but it just left me more confused.

"What is the future of Wonderboy?"

A simple, easy question. Clint should have had an answer prepared. And yet he started to talk, paused, gave a chuckle and then shrugged.

Then Beam asked, "Any regrets?"

A sigh, a bite of the lip.

"I suppose I am human, after all."

Crowds don't want that kind of reaction. They want Wonderboy to be boyish and playful, they want a flirtatious wink out into the crowd, maybe a self-deprecating joke. Appear human, but never appear weak.

The interview was capped off with technical difficulties that cut the program thirty seconds short. Any other celebrity and it would have been written off as a bad night, a hack interview by a hack journalist with an interviewee that didn't want to be there in the first place.

But it was Wonderboy, so the curiosity became a sore that was picked at until it became infected. It was the public's insatiable curiosity into the enigma of Clint Sohl. Something was happening. Something was wrong. Something big was coming and maybe, just maybe, Wonderboy wouldn't be strong enough to protect us this time.

And then Roger Beam disappeared without a trace. No goodbye letter, no sign off on a farewell episode of *Your Nation*. No one seemed to know where he went, but everyone had a strong suspicion. And yet, even the most twisted conspiracies that emerged on the internet didn't come close to the truth.

Where was I when my father was bombing on national television? At home, in my apartment, the TV providing the only light in my small bedroom, a naked stranger providing the only warmth in my bed.

Ben? Barry? I was pretty sure his name started with a "B." Daddy wasn't the only person in the family with sexual addiction issues.

I was sidelined by the agency because there were concerns raised by Beam's producers that a confrontation a year ago at a promotional event for the Shriners Hospital might be repeated.

Beam's story: I accosted him when he was simply approaching Wonderboy for an interview.

My story: Clint had already politely brushed Beam away three times that day in favor of spending more time with sick kids. Beam got his feelings hurt, was getting more aggressive and, in my opinion, smelled like alcohol, so I shoved him into a side room before he could make any more of an ass out of himself.

And I might have hit him in the face with my clipboard.

Watching my father struggle for answers during the Beam interview, it struck me how young Clint looked. I would soon start looking older than him. The others at the agency who had no idea I was Clint's daughter joked that we looked like brother and sister, or we were already an old, bickering married couple. Tim tried to squash the teasing as best he could. I suspect he felt sorry for me.

Interesting side note: Tim had actually been declared dead once after a massive coronary before Clint revived him. Even without the impending shitstorm, Tim's time at the firm is coming to a close. He was losing interest in playing the games necessary to protect Wonderboy's image. He probably stayed too long, but felt an obligation to stick with Clint as long as he could. I guess I was supposed to be his replacement, but, well, we see how that went.

Second interesting side note: A few months before the interview, I walked in on a nasty argument between the two of them, but at that point, I had no idea what they were fighting about. Tim was my dad's only real friend and was also the only person willing to call Clint out on his bullshit.

And during that fateful interview, I was sure Tim was on the edge of a second coronary from the very first question out of Beam's stupid grinning face:

"So, how about that banshee, Wendy Werthington?" Beam exclaimed, giving the crowd a second to dutifully boo. "Can you believe the nerve of some people? How are you holding up under such vile and shameless character assassination?"

"Wonderboy" was originally published as "The Wonderboy Serials: Issue One" by Literati Press. The Wonderboy Serials is an ongoing project to adopt the dime novel style to a modern retelling of the superhero mythos. Each chapter is told from a different perspective offering a wide-ranging view of a world tragically dependent on one all-powerful man. The digital series is available in all major eBook stores including iBooks, Nook, Kindle or at www.Smashwords.com. More information can be found at www.LiteratiPressOK.com.

James and the Gentry

By Kevin Lauderdale

"Yes, oh, yes! Of course I'll marry you, Reggie! Kiss me!"

How on earth was I supposed to explain to Serena Wessox that not only had I *not* meant to ask her to marry me, but that I was, in fact, already engaged to Galia, First Princess of the Lande of Faerie?

Hang on! I'm not sure that's the place to begin with — Serena canoodling and my double jeopardy. Naturally, I remember Homer's *Iliad* from my days at school. Beginning *in media res* and all that. But I think I'd better, as those Hollywood chappies put it, rewind the reel. It began two days earlier.

Let's see . . . I was at home having a whisky and soda . . . Oh, yes, that's much better. Note to self: Whenever possible begin with a whisky and soda — a *large* whisky and soda.

I was relaxing at home in my zebra striped armchair enjoying a rather large whisky and soda when James entered.

"Telegram, sir." My trusted valet proffered the yellow paper on a silver tray.

"It's from Flippy," I said after I had perused the missive.

"Sir?"

"Frederick Lidd-Jones. 'Flippy.' You remember the Lidd-Jones estate, James. Huge pile down Hastings-way. The scene of last New Year's Eve's revels."

"Ahh, Liddston Hall. Of course, sir."

"I bet you remember. Didn't I see you chatting up that very pretty redhead of a lady's maid? Ummm . . . Molly, eh?"

"Miss Margaret is a devotee of the German metaphysicians, sir. We passed the time discussing Schopenhauer."

"I bet you did."

James cleared his throat. "I take it that we are leaving for Liddston Hall, sir?"

"Yes indeedy. ASAP. 'Come at once,' reads the epistle. 'Life or Death. Weather remains charming. Flippy.' Seven . . . eight . . . nine . . . that's Flippy for you. Ten words for a shilling and he's not going to waste a single one."

"I shall commence packing, sir."

I gave a nod of approval and set to work on the old *W* and *S*. It was a lengthy and arduous task, but I muddled through.

Is there anything more restorative to the soul than a picnic? To relax in the shade of a willow tree while your gentleman's gentleman unpacks salmon and watercress sandwiches from a hamper . . . to cool your feet in a babbling brook while sipping Chateau Peyraguey as your man peels your apple . . . to stroll about the verdant green of the countryside secure in the knowledge that all will be cleaned and packed away when you return from the old bucolic perambulations . . .

I heartily recommend it to one and all.

True, Flippy had said, "Come at once," but, even in this brave new world where mankind races about in two-seaters at the harrowing speed of thirty mph, the niceties must still be observed. The sandwich is all that separates us from the animals. That and detachable collars.

While lunching, I had noticed a low fence not too far off in the distance. After handing my napkin to James, I set off to investigate in the hope that it might provide an amusing anecdote for use during dinner that evening. The fence was a typical country corral, about chest-high and made of rough-hewn wooden rails. A crudely lettered sign was nailed to it:

Do NOT cross this
Field unless You can
Do it in 23 seconds.
Our Bull can do it in 24.

Sure enough there was a bull. You know the type: ring through nose, sharp horns, and about the size of my sofa.

I was appreciating him from humanity's side of the fence when I heard a soft cry of "Oh!" and then saw a flutter of pink at the opposite end of the corral. Something vaguely young-lady-sized and young-lady-shaped appeared to have fallen into the bull's domain.

This was a lady fair in trouble and that clearly came under the Rule of the Brubakers. And I, Reggie Brubaker, never shirk from the R of the B. Although I personally find women to be more trouble than they're worth, I feared the wrath of thirty-two generations of ancestors going all the way back to the Norman Conquest if I did not behave chivalrously.

I will draw the curtain of discretion over the ensuing twenty-five seconds. Suffice it to say that the bull acquitted himself in the best tradition of his breed, and that later that evening James did yeoman's work cleaning my wingtips and repairing the seat of my pants with such tiny stitches that even my own tailor would not have known that they had gone adventuring.

The young lady and I soon both stood safely outside the bull's domain.

"Are you . . ." I panted, quite out of breath. "Are you hurt at all?"

She was about five feet tall and ten years younger than my three decades, and she seemed to glow with an inner light. Her hair, chic and short, could only be called "titian" in color. Her eyes were the gray of the finest top hat ever seen at the Ascot races, and her ears slightly pointed at the tips. Her pink dress was gauzelike and unaccountably spotless. As I said, I've never really had much use for women, but this one was, in the words of the chaps down at my club, "A bit of all right." She was the very embodiment of glamorous.

"You saved me!" she said, throwing her arms around me.

"Um," I said, and then, as politely as one can in such circumstances, slowly extracted myself and took a step back. "Reginald Brubaker at your service."

"Oh, Reggie, I owe you my life, my everything . . ." she stepped forward, arms outstretched.

I took another step back and found my back up against the corral's rails.

She continued. "I will be yours forever and ever."

"Um, Miss . . ."

"I am Galia, First—"

"Miss First—"

"No, I—"

An "Ahem" came from my right. I turned to find James standing at my side, boar bristle clothes brush in hand.

James has that way about him, of being where he's needed at all times. Just when you think he's in the kitchen polishing up the long-spouted Georgian silver coffee pot, and you yourself decide that you'd like a gin fizz, suddenly there he *is*, bearing same. He just sort of manifests.

"Oh, thank you, James. The young lady . . ." I turned back to Galia, but she was gone.

I scanned the immediate vicinity. No Miss First. I stood on tiptoe to gain the advantage of higher ground. No Miss First.

Where she had stood, there was now a small swarm — if swarm is the word I'm looking for — of butterflies. Little pink coves with red streaks. Quite nice. They hovered for a moment and then simply dispersed into the firmament (and I *know* firmament is the word I'm looking for).

"The young lady . . ." I croaked.

"Young lady, sir?"

Point to James. Not only was there no young lady, but there was nowhere to which a young lady could have dashed off.

James began delicately dusting my shoulders. "Perhaps your head, sir. I did not see a young lady, but I did see you make contact with the ground rather forcefully."

"Shook up the old bean, eh?"

"Quite possibly, sir."

I turned to my left. The bull was there sure enough and he almost looked like he was laughing. Prime rib was certain to be served for dinner at Flippy's and I decided that I would have double helpings.

Flippy was not, as I had expected, waiting for me like a spaniel, tail and whiskers all aquiver with anticipation. I steered the two-seater up the gravel drive in front of the hall (four stories of butter-coloured stone accented with more leaded glass than, well, as the sixteenth century ditty runs: "Liddston Hall, More glass than bloody all") to find only the family *major domo*, Cliveson, in attendance.

"Welcome, Mr. Brubaker." He turned and exchanged barely perceptible nods with James.

"Flippy about?" I asked.

"Mr. Lidd-Jones is down by the folly, sir."

Just as anyone can go from "crazy" to "eccentric" by the infusion of enough ready cash, an eyesore may be elevated to "folly" if the estate it adorns is large enough.

I sighed. My *raison d'être* for biffing down from London was that this was a supposedly urgent matter. To learn that Flippy was at that marble construction built by the fourth Baron Liddston with the dome of a mini-Parthenon and the columns of a mini-Acropolis when he should be here filling me in on the *R D* did not warm the Brubaker heart.

Nonetheless, I set off across the manicured lawns. The Rule of the Brubakers requires that I never turn down a friend in need. This I repeated to myself as I strode over the hill and down into the valley (both also constructs of the fourth Baron) and soon arrived at the folly.

There were two figures leaning against the columns and talking.

"What ho!" cried one of them, waving to me. Flippy.

The other I could not quite make out in the shadows cast by the dome until—

"Hawr! Hawr! It's Reggie!"

Serena Wessox! The very byword of the horsey set for two seasons now. A girl whose slaps on the back had dislocated more than one shoulder. Not that she was particularly large, but she was *solid*. And, while her splendid profile was admired by all who saw it, her cries of "Tally Ho!" at the start of a fox hunt were known to temporarily deafen her party and her hounds. I simply found her to be . . . too much.

That we had been briefly engaged a while back I will chalk up to misplaced youthful exuberance. She had called it off after I had expressed reluctance to wear the traditional "hunting pink" coat while foxing.

"Reggie!" she exploded. "Flippy said you'd be stopping by." She let me have one of the best on my back and I lurched forward a yard. "What brings you down? A spot of fishing? I know a capital pool. Brought home three brown trout only last week. One was a ten pounder!"

"Flippy called me down," I wheezed.

"Did you, dearest?" she asked Flippy.

Dearest? This was an innovation.

I said, "Yes. Said it was a matter of life or death."

"Really, sweetness?"

Sweetness? I was beginning to detect a trend.

"Um." Flippy stepped back and was jerking his head in the direction of Serena. "Um."

"Had it something to do with your neck?" I asked. "Seems to be all right now."

Before he could reply, Serena put both hands on my shoulders, spun me round to face her, and said, "Been a long time. Been a dashed long time."

"Oh, surely not that long."

"Long enough." She looked me up and down. "Well, Reggie . . ."

"Yes," I said.

She looked at me more intently. "Well, well, Reggie."

"Yes, yes, indeed," I replied.

"Well, well, *well*, Reggie." Now she smiled broadly at me.

"Yes . . . um indeed."

Her eyes took on a certain sparkle. I knew that look. Her eyes had sparkled like that in the early days of our engagement.

Another flicker of light caught the corner of my eye.

"What's that on your hand?" I asked.

Her left hand shot behind her back. "Oh," she looked away and then back at me with resignation. "Flippy and I are . . . engaged." She slowly dragged out the hand in question and I saw that it was adorned by a very respectable solitaire accented with emeralds.

"Are you? Oh, good show!" I breathed the proverbial inner sigh of relief. The Brubaker charm being not inconsiderable, those looks of hers were beginning to make me wonder exactly who exactly "dearest" and "sweetness" were. But no. My presence was not rekindling what the poets call the "Flame of Love." An engagement ring was a sealed deal. Flippy was *D* and *S* and that was all there was to it. I need not ask for whom the eyes sparkled; they sparkled for Flippy.

"Ah," I said, turning to Flippy. "That must be why you wired me. To come on down and hear the good news in person."

Flippy was standing just behind Serena and shook his head rapidly. When she turned to face him, his head froze and his visage took the grin of a lad who, when caught with his hand in the biscuit tin, is about to pretend that he was actually putting something in.

But what he said was, "Oh, yes, of course. Engagement. What else? Now I really must dash. Must see Cliveson about . . ." Whatever he meant to say was lost to the ages as he took off like a roman candle towards the hall.

Serena said, "Well, I've simply got to go down to the boat house and . . . uh. Say, Reggie, I don't suppose you'd like to . . . come with me?"

"No, I'd better go see what room Cliveson has given me. Last time it was too far from the kitchen. James complained mightily. Something about hot water bottles and the cooling effect of travel time."

She touched the lapel of my tweed coat with what can only be called a lingering caress. "We're dressing for dinner. See you then." She winked and trotted off.

I had trudged about halfway back to the Hall when out of nowhere: "Strawberries, Reggie?"

Now, as I said, James has a habit of just sort of suddenly being there. While I hadn't exactly grown used to it, it no longer startled me.

But I was nearly knocked nadir over apex by the instantaneous arrival of Galia First bearing an ebony bowl full of strawberries. Huge, luscious examples they were, some nearly as big as a fist.

"Strawberries?" she entreated.

I took a bite of one. It was de-lish and I said so.

"Anything," she said, "to please my fiancé."

"Fiancé?"

She nodded enthusiastically and smiled beatifically up at me.

I said, "You appear to be laboring under a misapprehension, Miss First."

"My name is Galia, First Princess of the Lande of Faerie. And you, Reggie, are my betrothed. We shall wed upon the next full moon . . . um, a week Tuesday."

"When exactly did this engagement take place?" I certainly had no recollection of it.

"You saved my life. Of course we're engaged."

I had stopped walking after the first use of the word fiancé. The sun was just setting and its rays shooting out behind Galia gave her a shimmering halo. She was lovely, and for half a moment I was tempted. But, although I am descended from a long line of Brubakers who did marry, I had long ago put the notion behind me. I much prefer my carefree bachelor life: bopping down to Monte Carlo on a moment's notice, no one to tell me what not to eat or drink.

"But," I said, "I'm so much older than you. Surely you wouldn't want—"

She lifted her nose in the air. "I am one hundred and twelve. I am of age and I am old enough to know my own mind on such matters." Galia surveyed the acreage. "What a funny little place," she said. "Is this yours?"

"I—"

"You know, Reggie, it took me a long time to find you. You have a very difficult ethereal essence to follow. I've been looking for you all afternoon."

Over the hill came a tall, slim figure bearing a tray.

"Ah, James," I said.

"James?" Galia asked.

"My valet. I'm sure he'll be able to straighten this out."

She gave a superior sniff and then twisted, like a Christmas cracker's wrapping, off into nothingness.

James and his tray proved to be bearing a gin and tonic.

"Did you see that, James?"

"Yes, sir."

"What do you make of it?"

"Magic, sir."

"Not a trick of the light? Mirage?"

"No, sir. That was, I venture to assume, the young lady of whom you spoke after your luncheon adventure?"

"Yes."

"Most intriguing."

"Serena's here too."

"Miss Wessox?"

"Yes. James?"

"Yes, sir?"

"I may be engaged, but I'm certainly not getting married."

"Indeed, sir."

After a very good meal (prime rib, as presaged; Serena in a gown positively bedecked with décolletage) and the port having been passed, Flippy and I repaired to the billiards room. I called in James. Whenever a situation grows sticky, I always take it to James. You can trust his melon to steer you through the fog.

"Now, Flippy," I said. "We need to batten down a few facts. Item: you are engaged to Serena."

"Yes."

"Query: why did you call me down here?"

"I don't want to be engaged to Serena."

I nodded sagely. It was yet another example of the eternal triangle that would confound even Pythagoras himself: man, woman, and R. Brubaker, called in to set things right.

"That's very fine for you," I said. "Or rather, not so very fine. But in the course of coming to your aid, I seem to have become engaged myself." I described the "Mysterious Affair of the Bull Pen and the Strawberries" and ended with, "James believes that the mystical is involved."

Flippy walked to the sideboard and poured himself a large one. "Were her ears pointed?" he asked.

"Now that you mention it, yes, slightly."

"The Gentry," he muttered. "Of course it's magic, Reggie. The ears. How could you not see she was a faerie?"

"But I know so little of fashion. I simply assumed that's how girls were wearing them this season."

"'Wearing' their ears . . .?"

I shrugged. "I quite agree. I don't understand the rage for those bell-shaped hats either." I turned to James for validation and he nodded in agreement. "But by faerie, do you mean like leprechauns? The little people? That spotlight effect in that play? 'Clap your hands if you believe—'"

"That's the stuff of the past, Reggie. Everyone 'round these parts knows about the *real* . . . well, we call them 'the Fair Folk', or just 'the Gentry'. And they're not little. They're as big as any of us. They look more or less like us except that the women are always beautiful and the men handsome. They show up every generation or so."

He knocked back his drink, then poured another and continued.

"They always cause some kind of trouble. They're the reason my Aunt Matilda's hair is dark. She was born blonde, you know. But a pair of the Gentry turned up at her wedding back before the war, and the lady of the two said she thought Matilda would look better as a brunette. Suddenly she was. And no amount of peroxide or anything else has been able to restore it." He took another sip. "Now it looks as if they are venturing out again. Or at least one is."

"So, we're both in the soup without a paddle. Dash it, there must be a million ways to get unengaged to a girl."

"Name one."

"Well, there's . . . Yes, you're right. It's impossible." I turned to James. "Two engagements to be ended. What do you say, James? Grab the old grey matter and give it a squeeze."

"With Mr. Lidd-Jones's permission, I will address your predicament first, sir. It is the more complex."

Flippy nodded.

"Beginning with first principles," began James, "if you save a faerie's life, it is then indebted to you."

"Ah," I said, "so all I have to do is make it clear I'd rather have a pot of gold instead of her hand. That should square the deal. Oh, wait, faerie gold isn't worth anything. It turns to dew on the morn or some such."

"So we are told, sir. But I do not think that the young . . . *person* to whom you are affianced possesses any gold. In the case of faerie princesses, they have only one gift to bestow: themselves. Any mortal man saving a princess is rewarded with a betrothal."

"Why would anyone want that?"

"It is my understanding, sir, that Princesses of Faerie are unparalleled in loveliness and all that any man might desire."

"Well, I don't desire Galia."

"You, sir, are not just any man."

I nodded emphatically. We Brubakers are made of sterner stuff.

"But why," I asked, "would *they* want us? I mean, a betrothal is a beast with *two* backs and all that."

Flippy said, "Yes, I've never understood why a lady of the Gentry would want — no offense, Reggie — *you*, or for that matter any village blacksmith who just happened to save her from a bull when she could have a Prince of Faerie.

"The Gentry," said James, "are immortal. We are not."

"Ah," I said. "Even a blacksmith with muscles as strong as iron bands must eventually age and perish."

"Or be killed off," said Flippy. "I think I get it. We're toys to them. They grab one of us, have a few decades of fun, and then move on to another."

"Rather like keeping goldfish, eh?" I said.

"A trenchant simile, sir," said James. "History is rife with men in entanglements such as yours."

"And how did they get out of it?"

James arched an eyebrow.

"Or didn't they?" I asked, the proverbial sinking feeling gathering in my tum.

"They are simply never heard from again, sir. They go off with their princess to the Land of Faerie and . . ."

"And what, James? What, what?"

"Nothing, sir."

"Well, I'm not going to have nothing. I'll just have to break the engagement, that's all. It goes against the Rule of the Brubakers, but better a Brubaker with no rule than a rule with no Brubaker. Though I don't relish the thought of hurting Galia's feelings." I looked over in the mirror across the room. Poor girl. She never really had a chance. A devastating face like mine doesn't grow on trees. And it is not unknown for members of the fair sex to turn my way while I am strolling the Strand in order to get a second look. Especially when I am wearing my periwinkle tie.

"That might not be advisable, sir."

"Why not?"

"History does not recount any instance of a — you will excuse the use of the phrase, sir — mere mortal successfully breaking with one of the Gentry. Their anger at being rejected is, I understand, legendary."

"'A woman scorned' sort of thing, eh?"

"To the utmost degree, sir."

"Possible lawsuit for breach of promise and all that?"

"More likely being torn to pieces by golden stags, sir."

I swallowed hard. I'd once been nipped in the ankle by my Aunt Gladys' Pekingese. The pain had kept me in bed for a week. This, I imagined, would be much worse.

"If, however—" James began.

"Yes, yes!" I was champing at the bit like any blue ribbon bit-champer you care to name.

"If *she* were to break the engagement, sir—"

"Yes, yes! Then what?"

"That might make your position more tenable, sir."

"Ahhh. Good old James. Knew you wouldn't let me down. How do we go about arranging that?"

"I do not know, sir."

Enter the sinking feeling for an encore.

Flippy said, "All of this is very fascinating, Reggie, but it doesn't go anywhere near solving *my* problem. I'm engaged to Serena. And I need to . . . disengage."

"You could try my method," I suggested.

"Serena already told me about that. Too late. I've already been foxing with her twice. In full dress hunting pink."

"Indeed . . . " said James as he turned his head in thought. It is upon such turns that my world continues to spin.

"Yes, James," I said. "Have you a thought? An inspiration? Is the spark of the divine about to leap from your lips?"

"I believe so, sir."

The sun rose again in my heart, spreading rosy-fingered dawn to all the bluebirds.

"Good old James!" I said. "Never doubted you for a nonce. Let's have it."

"I believe that we should seek out the feminine view pertaining to this matter."

I was nonplussed, but Flippy saw the angle at once.

"Of course!" he said. "*We* don't know how to break up with a gal, but *another gal* would. A stroke of genius, James. Reggie asks Serena how best to break it off. Pose it as a hypoth- . . . um, hypno- . . . um, 'Merely-A-Question' sort of question. Then we do it."

"You mean," I asked, "that if Serena says that no young lady would stay engaged to a chap who wears a check-patterned waistcoat with evening dress, we dash out and both buy half a dozen of the things to wear at every meal?"

"Precisely, sir," said James.

"Do you really think that whatever shocks La Wessox would apply to a princess as well?"

"All the more so, sir. A member of the Gentry would have even more refined sensibilities."

I nodded. "Very well then. Tomorrow morning I'll speak with her. I shall be discrete."

I found Serena strolling through the rose garden. It was one of those plots of land populated by several species of the ol' red, reds and surrounded by a waist-high hedge.

"Hello, Reggie," she said, putting both hands behind her and leaning in towards me.

"Ah, morning, Serena. Look, I've got something to ask you."

"Oh, really?" The sun must have been in her eyes because she batted them fiercely.

"Yes. Dashed important," I said. "Before it's too late and all that."

"Yes, Reggie." She kept her lips slightly parted in a most disconcerting way.

"There are times when a chap has to say certain things to a girl—"

"Yes, Reggie." She was swaying back and forth very lightly.

"And it can be difficult to know exactly how to ask—"

"Yes, Reggie." She had a look in her eyes — a faraway look that led me to wonder if she was even listening to anything I was saying. Still, replace the word "Reggie" with "sir" and it could have been a conversation with James. And he always catches the drift. I trudged onwards.

"Um, Serena, now. Could you — or, rather, *would* you—?" She stepped forward.

"Yes, oh, yes! Of course I'll marry you, Reggie! Kiss me!"

How on earth was I supposed to explain to Serena Wessox that not only had I *not* meant to ask her to marry me, but that I was, in fact, already engaged to Galia, First Princess of the Lande of Faerie? How indeed?

I pushed her away, jumped over the hedge, and ran.

Half an hour later, after taking what I hoped was a Wessox-proof, circuitous route back to the hall, I charged down to James's quarters.

I was just about to knock on the door when I heard from the other side a female voice say, "Oh, come on now. You can't possibly know it's him." The door opened and Molly the lady's maid stood there, her eyes suddenly widening so much that I thought their whites would reach to her mop cap.

"Oh, beggin' your pardon, sir," she said, her face blushing deep crimson. She curtsied and ran off down the hall.

I stepped in. There were two glasses and a bottle of Madeira on the table.

"Did it go well, sir?"

"I—"

The door flung open behind me and in charged Flippy, who nearly ran me over. "I've just had the most remarkable conversation with Serena. She's broken our engagement. And it didn't even require me dropping a few guineas on a waistcoat. Checkered or not. However did you accomplish it, Reggie?"

"It's all very simple," I said. "Now Serena wants to marry *me!*"

Flippy positively beamed. "Well, that solves my problem." He turned to James. "Your plan worked like a dream. Good job, old man!"

"That wasn't his plan!" I turned to James. "Was it?"

"Not *per se*, sir. However this outcome was part of a back-up strategy of mine related to your mutual predicaments."

I stood there, my mouth agape. "Meaning?" I managed to stammer.

"Recalling your previous entanglement with Miss Wessox, a shift of affections was a possibility."

"But there are still two engagements to be broken. Only now they're both to me."

Flippy said, "But don't you see, Reggie, James has simplified the battle. Now there's only one front to fight on instead of two."

"I don't care if this is exactly the sort of tactic Napoleon would have used. It hasn't helped me."

James said, "If you will simply take two of your visiting cards, sir, and write on the back of both of them, 'Meet me in the rose garden at four PM,' I believe that will be sufficient."

"Sufficient for what?"

"To solve your dilemma," said James. "Leave everything to me."

James, Flippy, and I crouched behind the south end of the rose garden, well-obscured by bushes in bloom. Serena had arrived five minutes early and was pacing. We three watched James's pocket watch as the seconds ticked away until at exactly four o'clock.

"Who are you?" asked Serena.

We looked up and through some that which by any other name would smell as sweet to find that Galia had arrived.

"I'm Reggie's fiancée," said Galia. "Have you seen him? He was to meet me here."

"But *I'm* Reggie's fiancée," said Serena. "He was to meet— He's already engaged?"

"He's already engaged?"

"Why, that rat! It's off!"

"That weasel! It's off!"

"That ferret!"

"That . . . ooooo!" Galia's face turned positively vermillion with rage. "That scoundrel! That charlatan! I'll have him torn to shreds!" She fell to her knees in rage. "I'll call upon Herne the Hunter to loose the stags of—"

"No, no, my dear," said Serena, reaching out and patting Galia's shoulder. "It really isn't Reggie's fault."

"It isn't?"

"No. He's weak, you know. All men are. He really can't be held accountable for the way nature made him: flighty and capricious."

"But he deceived us both." Galia stood up and thrust her fists into the air. "We must wreak vengeance upon him!"

"Sweet Reggie? No, no my dear . . . Some day he will marry and then he'll settle down. Until then, he is to be pitied."

"He is?"

"Oh, my dear, you are still innocent and romantic, aren't you?" Taking Galia's arm, Serena led her towards the folly. "When you've been around as long as I have . . ."

They set off chatting quite companionably. Only when they had disappeared over the hill did I exhale and turn to James.

"*That* was your plan? To get them to hate me?"

"And thus to exercise a woman's prerogative to change her mind. Yes, sir."

"But Galia was about to exercise it by turning me into a pin-cushion for golden stag horns!"

"There is always a calculated risk with any plan, sir."

Flippy said, "James, I know Molly took the note to Serena, but how did Galia get her's?"

"Also Miss Margaret, sir. Her family has lived in these parts for ten generations. As such, they have a certain affinity for the land and its mysteries."

"Good grief," I said. "She's not a . . . Gentry, is she?"

"No, sir. But she has an aunt who is the seventh daughter of a seventh daughter. I believe she keeps a finch which can travel to and from the Lande."

Flippy said, "I suppose you two better hot-foot it out of here. Despite the happy ending Reggie's going to be *persona non grata* in these parts for some time."

I looked at James.

"The two-seater is already packed, sir."

"Will you be all right, Flippy?" I asked.

"Oh, of course, Reggie. Remember, Serena broke it off with me — and for one of my best friends! No, she'll be off on the next train, you can be sure. And I know better than to save any girl I meet with pointed ears."

"Cheerio then."

"Cheerio."

We parted and I asked James, "What was that ditty about the fellow who gets engaged, but then never actually has to marry the gal?"

"Perhaps you are thinking of 'Evangeline,' by Henry Wadsworth Longfellow, sir."

"That's the one. Great stuff. 'This is the forest primeval' and all that."

"If you will recall, sir, the prospective bridegroom, one Gabriel, son of the blacksmith, is parted forcefully from his affianced before their nuptials and does not see her again until many decades later, just before he dies of a pestilence."

"Ah, but dies unmarried."

"If that was any consolation to him, sir, the poet did not record it."

"Still, James, there's no denying that it's a course of action worth examining."

"As you say, sir."

Radon's Daughter

By Julie Jansen

Detective Amerika Weatherford's entrance drew unwanted attention from a few haggard faces that would normally be content staring into their drinks on a Wednesday afternoon. Heads turned not only because the wind slammed the bar's front door shut behind her, or because of the private detective's beauty, or the fact she held a sleeping baby girl in her arms. With the detective's arrival, the power that had been out all over town surged, causing an otherwise dark pinball machine in the corner to spring to life with a light and whistle show rivaling a fireworks display on the Fourth of July.

Weatherford didn't notice the men eyeing her. She was fascinated by the arcade game. It was like nothing she'd ever seen before. There was too much detail in the hand-painted artwork to be anything modern. A female astronaut floated in space surrounded by stars and colorful geometric swirls like a sci-fi drawing from the 1940's. Only part of the astronaut's face was visible, the rest of the picture folded at an odd angle and continued over the side facing the wall. Other than the lighted maze in the glass covered playfield, the only mechanical part of the machine was at the top center, carved into the wood. It was the astronaut's oversized, heavily made-up eye. The pupil contracted and dilated as it focused on Weatherford and her child.

The sudden noise caused six month old Baby Weatherford to wake up. The child kept quiet, but clutched tightly to her mother. Detective Weatherford shifted Baby Weatherford on her hip and the child buried her face in her mother's long brown hair.

The detective stood like a swimsuit model about to dive into a stagnant watering hole inhabited by drunken crocodiles. With her attention still on the machine, she stepped down toward the tables. As she did, the eye closed and the machine went dark. The men's heads turned to focus on their drinks.

The power was out again, the minute long surge just a tease. Without the pinball machine, the place was silent except for the wind that howled past the windows and nibbled at the shingles on the roof. The storm that raged through town brought hurricane force winds and too many inches of rain. Torrents of water coursed through the street and dribbles managed to sneak through cracks in the ceiling. Weatherford side-stepped a bucket full of rain water as she made her way toward Bartender Betty, at work behind the counter.

Weatherford imagined herself in a crypt rather than a drinking establishment. The faces she saw were like the ghosts of men long since passed. Candles flickered in bell jars and cast elongated human-like shadows on the walls. The dim light also illuminated a cloud of smoke that hung like a blanket of fog over the tables.

As Detective Weatherford pushed a chair out of her way, she bumped into a man. The man looked at her with glazed eyes and smiled, showing a mouth full of rotted teeth.

"Mama," the little girl said, afraid of the look of him. She snuggled herself as deep as she could into her mother's chest.

"Excuse me," Detective Weatherford said to the man as she calmed the girl by bouncing her gently.

"She called you. Ain't you gonna play?" the man asked before going into a coughing fit that about knocked him out of his chair. The man hacked. He spit up a glistening ball of what appeared to be mercury that split into several pieces and danced on the table like ball bearings. They fell to the floor where the detective lost sight of them.

She was too engrossed in what had come out of the man to remember he'd asked her a question. Instead she told him, "Mister, you really should get that cough checked out."

Betty's voice called out from behind the bar. "Young lady, this ain't no place to bring a baby! I don't care what kind of wind shoved you through our door. The air in here's not a thing for virgin lungs."

A look crossed the detective's face, a cocktail of emotions the seasoned bartender recognized right away. If the drink had a name it would have been single-mother-struggles-to-make-it-in-a-man's-world. The bartender had mixed it for herself on many occasions and knew it was a hard drink to swallow. As Betty warmed to the detective, she set down the pint glass she was drying and reached out a hand.

"You must be Betty." Detective Weatherford stretched one of her lanky legs over a barstool. "I'm Detective Amerika Weatherford."

Now that Weatherford was close to Betty she saw the right side of the woman's face was badly scarred, perhaps burned in a fire. The other side was weathered and wrinkled. Each wrinkle had smaller ones branching off here and there like tributaries of a river.

After shaking the woman's hand, Weatherford reached into the breast pocket of her blouse and slid out a cigarette.

At the sound of the word "detective," concern crossed Betty's face. At the sight of the cigarette, the woman's look turned to horror. She nodded in the direction of the child as she reached out a liver spotted hand to snatch the cigarette from the detective's mouth.

But it was the little girl's hand that intercepted Betty's and knocked the cigarette from her mother's lips.

A well-dressed man in his forties seated at the barstool next to her bent down to pick it up. "I have to agree with Betty," his deep voice said. As he set the cigarette on the counter, the detective saw his smooth slender fingers had perfectly manicured nails. "A beautiful child like that should be left at home. And a beautiful woman like you shouldn't be smoking."

The detective turned to the man and he got a good look at her eyes: one brown, one blue. He was distracted by them, unable to focus on both at the same time. He tried to look at just one, and chose blue, but the depth of it made him dizzy. He then settled on the brown, the color of a copper penny, and at once his head stopped spinning.

"Thank you for the advice, Mr.?" She reached out a hand which the man took eagerly.

"Bodrov. Elton Bodrov. Friends call me Elton."

The little girl fussed and the detective pulled her hand back to brush downy hair away from the child's eyes.

"She on the bottle?" Betty asked.

Weatherford nodded and pulled a small one from a pouch at her waist. The bottle contained powder but no liquid.

"Fill her up with water not too warm?" Betty took the bottle and the women shared an understanding smile. Betty walked to the sink.

"I lost my husband not too long ago, Elton. Plan was to stay at home with my girl. My plan changed a little," she said, matter of fact.

"Things don't always work out the way we plan," Betty chimed in as she handed the filled bottle to the detective. "We both know that, don't we, Elton?"

At this Elton sipped amber liquid from his glass, swished it around in his mouth, swallowed, and sighed.

Weatherford gave the bottle to the child who grabbed it and settled back into her arms.

"I'll get to the reason I'm here. I'm looking for a man who cashed a check belonging to my client," the detective said. "Happened two nights ago."

"Bah!" Elton exclaimed. "You been hired by that Sam Swank?" The man clucked his tongue to the roof of his mouth.

"There's been no crime committed here, Detective Weatherford. You're sticking your nose in business best left alone. You should hurry your pretty self home," Betty said.

"I'd love to, Betty. But I've got a little mouth to feed and a client who'll pay me decent money to get to the bottom of what I think is a simple case." She pulled a lighter from her pocket, reached for the cigarette on the counter, lit it, and took a deep drag.

"You don't know what you're getting yourself into, Miss Weatherford." At this the woman grabbed a rag and walked away.

The detective turned to Elton. "Mind telling me where you were Monday night?"

"Here." Elton sighed. "But that story's like the trails of smoke you see in here. Following the trails won't show you anything. They only blend together and get mixed up after a while."

A smoke ring rose from Amerika's lips. Elton reached out with his right hand and stuck a finger through it, then flashed a wicked smile. "Had to do that before it disappeared. I made a wish. Ever try?"

"I used to wish," Detective Weatherford said looking down at her baby who stared wide-eyed at Elton while she sucked on the bottle.

"Our machine over there wants you to play." Elton slurred his speech. He lifted his glass to take another sip, until he realized the glass was empty. "When she calls you to play, she'll take you places you never dreamed you'd go."

"My current predicament is a place I never dreamed I'd go. But here I am. And I don't mean to be rude, Elton, but I'm not interested in pinball," she said as she watched the man she bumped into earlier bend over and retch onto the floor.

Weatherford noticed Betty was now at the pinball machine, collecting money from the coin box. "I'll head over and talk to Betty. Information about the person that cashed Swank's check is all I need."

At this the man only laughed.

Weatherford put out her cigarette, slid off the barstool, and walked toward Betty.

The bartender held a box filled with pennies.

"Did those pennies come out of the pinball machine?"

"Yup," Betty replied. "This machine's from Russia, so they say. Should take Russian coins, but our pennies do the trick." Betty picked up a penny, studied it for a moment, then set it back in the box. "Old thing's been with us about twenty years. The owner of this place picked her up at an estate sale. She's never needed not even one repair," Betty paused. "Although there's been many a time I've thought about bustin' her up, myself. Even tried once." Betty shuddered at the memory.

"What happened when you did that?" Weatherford asked.

Betty touched the scar on her face. "I don't like to talk about it in front of her," Betty said and gave a quick glance in the machine's direction.

"Can I try?" Weatherford asked and reached for the box of pennies.

Betty slid the box away from Weatherford's reach.

The pinball machine lit up. The eye opened and shifted its focus back and forth between the women as if listening to their conversation.

Weatherford took a step back. "The power's still out. Why's the machine on?"

Betty frowned as the detective pulled a penny from her pocket and faced the machine. "When she calls someone, she

144

uses her own power. She doesn't need ours." Betty grabbed the detective's wrist, looked into her eyes, and pleaded, "Miss Weatherford, it's best you not play."

A zap of electricity emerged from the machine and hit Betty in the leg. She cried out in pain and rubbed the spot as smoke rose and a hole formed in her pants.

"Betty!" The detective moved toward the bartender.

"I'm fine. Don't worry about me." Betty backed away. She limped toward the bar counter.

An eerie robotic cackle erupted from the pinball machine. It sent a shiver down Amerika's spine and caused Baby Weatherford to cry.

When faced with difficult situations, Amerika Weatherford wasn't the kind of woman to run. Her theory was whatever was out to get you would catch up to you eventually, so why not face it up front and get it over with. The way the machine struck Betty and now laughed at the detective, was no computer program or electrical phenomenon. Weatherford felt in her gut challenged by the pinball machine, as crazy as it seemed. The detective repositioned the baby on her hip and glared into the machine's eye.

"So you want me to play, do you?" Amerika asked it. The detective held the coin, ready to push it into the slot. She hesitated as she watched the metal balls, and found the balls weren't metal at all. It was the futuristic liquid, the same stuff she'd watched the drunken man cough up when she first walked into the bar.

The liquid balls danced on the playfield and bounced off the walls of the targets. The targets were labeled not with numbers, but with Cyrillic letters the detective didn't understand. Before her eyes the letters, made of the same liquid, reformed so that each target spelled "Peter here."

The pinball machine, in a cicada-like female voice, whispered the phrase with a heavy Russian accent.

At the sound of her husband's name, the detective gasped. Baby Weatherford pointed at the eye and whimpered. Detective

Weatherford stared, intensely curious, and came up with several spur of the moment theories: whether within it lived a family of genetically altered lab mice with super powers, or an extraterrestrial being, or if the machine was actually a high-tech robot. She also wondered if it involved her client. He and his drunken buddies could have all pitched in to come up with her two hundred dollar fee and used the smoke and mirrors in the bar to play some sick joke. But she'd never told her client her husband's name and hadn't been in this town long enough for most to know the story.

The machine repeated the phrase, louder this time. The detective stared in awe, hoping the right synapses in her brain would fire and form a logical explanation for this thing. The game started the same type of light show Amerika and Baby Weatherford saw when they first walked into the bar.

"I don't know about this, little one," Amerika said to her child. She placed the penny on top of the glass case and held the child tight as she backed away.

Detective Weatherford felt as if someone pushed her from behind, shoved her toward the game, until she realized that a lasso of electricity originating from the machine looped around her waist. Another snaked out and grabbed her right wrist, forcing her fingers to grab hold of the penny and move the coin toward the slot.

"Let me go!" She looked at the eye, shouted at it, but still it drew her forward.

Baby Weatherford fussed with her feet and knocked the bottle from her mother's belt. A thin stream of formula dribbled across the electric rope and caused it to sizzle and die. The child's foot kicked her mother's hand and the penny dropped to the floor, where it rolled until it came to rest under the pinball machine.

Weatherford shielded her child from the machine and hurried a few steps away only to be caught in another electric beam. It drew her back and turned her to face it. Weatherford felt a penny between her thumb and index finger and couldn't reason how it got there, nor could she reason why her hand inched toward the coin slot. Before she could protest, she had inserted the penny and the pinball machine's flippers seemed to clap as they batted liquid balls around the game's maze.

Out of nowhere, Betty slid in front of the detective just as a blob of the strange mercury-like goop shot from the machine. It would have been on a straight course for Weatherford's mouth but entered Betty's instead.

Weatherford held her baby close as she stepped to the side and out of immediate danger.

Betty coughed and gagged. She began to seizure. Weatherford watched the liquid blacken Betty's eyes like the woman's body was a bottle and the liquid was filling it. Then, one moment the woman was there and the next she simply disappeared.

"Wh-where'd she go?" The detective looked around thinking the woman must be somewhere close by.

Even Baby Weatherford raised her head from her mother's chest and scanned the bar.

Footsteps approached. It was Elton. "She's not gonna be happy."

"I wouldn't be happy either if I was choking on a mouthful of whatever that is."

Elton held his drink, refilled with liquor, and shook it so that the ice clinked against the glass. "Not Betty, my dear. The machine. I have to admit I wish she hadn't missed. It's been a while since we've had anyone new."

The detective glared at him. "I don't know what sick kind of parlor trick you've got going in this place, but I'm not in the mood for games."

"The only game is the one she plays." Elton nodded toward the machine as he pulled up a chair. "That machine may look a little primitive on the outside, but she's an exquisite piece of engineering."

The pinball machine rattled off a few more phrases in robotic Russian, as if mumbling to itself.

"What is it?" Amerika positioned herself behind a wooden beam to block anymore electric shocks that might come her way.

"Good question. I found her many years ago. She called to me. I accepted her game. I've been studying her ever since. Your client, Mr. Swank, he's a newbie as far as players go."

"What does this have to do with Swank's check?"

Elton took a serious tone. "Sam cashed that check himself. He just doesn't remember it because it was so long ago."

"We're talking about an incident he said happened two days ago," the detective was getting frustrated.

"Swank's getting two periods of his life mixed up," Elton explained.

"You gonna start into that physics mumbo jumbo again, Professor?" It was Betty. She'd returned.

When she got over the shock of the bartender's reappearance, the second shock regarding Elton's title set in. "Did she call you professor?" Amerika asked.

"He ain't told you he used to be a professor at the university?"

"No he didn't."

"I hide it well, don't I?" Elton smiled, looking a little bit like a mongoose about to raid a termite hill.

Detective Weatherford wondered what would come next.

"I watch what happens to those she calls and who can't resist poking a token into her slot." Elton glanced in the machine's direction and winked at it as though it were a stripper spinning around a pole.

"What happens when people play pinball?" Detective Weatherford asked, deciding to take the man seriously and see where his answer led.

"She gives you some of this," Elton said and pulled a small jar out of a pocket. Inside was the same substance the man had coughed up earlier.

"What is it?" The detective moved to grab it.

Elton pulled the jar away and placed it back in his pocket. "It's a radioactive byproduct."

"Like radon or polonium?"

He shook his head. "Yeah. But not deadly like those." He stopped, deep in thought. "Like radon is a byproduct of uranium, our element is born from radon, a child of it. A radon daughter as it's known in the field."

"Surely some scientist must know about it."

"Bah!" He exclaimed. "Not one who didn't want countries battling over it!"

"You've lost me, Elton."

"It was on July 16, 1945 that $E=mc^2$ was proven."

"Einstein's Theory of Relativity?"

"A little explosion in Alamogordo, New Mexico was caused by a chain reaction in the uranium atom. It was the dawn of the atomic age. Not long after, this little beauty of a pinball machine was made."

Amerika looked over and saw the machine's mechanical eye blink.

Baby Weatherford cocked her head to the side like a curious puppy trying to make sense of the thing.

"A woman was on the team of scientists testing atom bombs back then, Shirley Hanson. A Russian born scientist too, Vlad Bodrov. The two of them fell in love. When they found this special little radioactive byproduct, Vlad called it Bodrovium, they hid it, so no one would ever find it."

"Your last name's Bodrov."

Elton smiled and pointed a finger at her as if to say "bingo". "Einstein believed in the continuity of time and space. So'd my grandma, Shirley, and my grandfather, Vlad. Grandpa's hobby was building his own table games. Together they built this special container for the Bodrovium they happened upon during one of their experiments, figuring it'd be safe in there. But the element was at a different stage of decay than she is now. Our element isn't a child anymore. She's like a teenager."

"Radon's daughter, an adolescent element. And just like a human her hormones seem to be raging. She's oozing out of the machine and into people. You know how to keep her pants on, Elton?"

"A humorous analogy from our beautiful detective." Elton pulled a small leather bound journal from his jacket and waved it at the detective. "Radioactive elements are very unstable. We don't really know for a fact how they all decay. The microscopic bursts of energy Bodrovium put off were supposed to be contained within this wicked little minx of a pinball machine. But it's like the element has a mind of its own, like it's evolved. It comes and goes as it pleases. Kind of like the people who ingest it, only the coming and going isn't always in the same dimension you and I are now in."

"Time travel?"

"Yup."

"So simply put, that stuff is causing people to slip back and forth in time?" the detective asked.

"Or times," Elton replied.

"Did you plant the machine in this bar as an experiment? I hope you're aware experimenting on subjects who haven't given their consent is highly illegal."

"I've done no such thing! The machine was built in Russia. My grandparents returned there when they got fed up with working for our corrupt government." He chuckled.

"Real funny," the detective looked at him with disgust.

"Eventually Grandpa died. Grandma came back to the states. She hauled the pinball machine with her. When she passed away my mother sold the machine. But not Grandpa's journals. Grandma left those to me. Wasn't until grad school I decided to take a peek. By then the machine was long gone. Took me many a year, but I eventually found her."

Betty, half-listening to the conversation but concentrating more on loud creaks coming from the ceiling as the violent wind fought to make its way inside, raised an eyebrow in response to Amerika's question. "What Elton says is all Chinese to me. What I do know though is that in this place, time's a little unique."

A clap of thunder rattled the light fixtures and caused the detective to jump. Baby Weatherford only stared with curiosity, undisturbed by the storm's foreboding presence.

Elton took on an academic air. "Does that man sitting over there near the jukebox look familiar to you?"

Detective Weatherford glanced over and saw a man similar to Sam Swank, but much older, sitting at a table, nursing a beer and blowing smoke out his nose like a dragon about to spit fire. "Excuse me a moment," she said and stood up, taking Baby Weatherford into her arms.

The man watched the mother and child approach and twisted his lips into a perverted sort of Cheshire smile. "Hey good lookin," he said. "That baby part of the package?"

The voice was more familiar than the face. Amerika met the man's eyes with a bold penetrating glare. He flinched and moved back from the table as she sat down across from him. "I need to ask you some questions, sir. Let's start with your name."

"My name? That's fine, sugar," the man said.

Amerika remained collected, holding the man's stare.

"You're a tough broad. The little one as tough as you?" He glanced at the child gripping her mother's blouse. The girl stared at him cruelly. "Name's Sam Swank," he said and looked in Elton's direction touching two fingers to his forehead in a kind of salute.

"You're not the Swank I remember."

"I on the other hand couldn't very well forget a peach like you, Miss Weatherford."

While perplexing, there was something about the oddness of the situation that was beginning to make perfect sense.

Swank laughed and took another sip of his beer. "I hired you because of my check. A check it turns out was mine and rightly cashed by me. I shouldn't ever have troubled you. I said

I was sorry. You nearly split my lip when you slapped me over somethin' I said after that."

"What would that have been?" Amerika asked, more and more intrigued.

"Somethin' to do with the two hundred dollars I owe you. But I'd rather not go there again," Swank said and as soon as he said it one rusty screw and then another fell onto the table. They bounced and spun before dropping to the floor.

A loud creak and shudder like a tree giving up the ghost and crashing to the ground echoed through the bar. Amerika heard Betty cry out, "Under the tables! Everyone get under the tables!" Which is what Amerika and Baby Weatherford did in the nick of time. A light fixture above the table weighing several hundred pounds broke loose along with several ceiling beams and crashed to the floor.

Unfortunately Sam Swank didn't move fast enough to escape the falling light fixture. The detective shielded Baby Weatherford's eyes as she watched from underneath the table. Swank's left leg twitched a *post mortem* jig and a large red stain began to spread from his waist to his thigh. From the pool of blood, the unknown element separated and formed into liquid pinballs. They darted this way and that, scrambling over broken tables and chairs to get back to the pinball machine.

"Sam Swank!" Detective Weatherford heard Betty's voice. "Swank! Can you hear me?"

Amerika and Baby Weatherford crawled out from under the table and over a large ceiling joist.

An ambulance had already pulled to the curb, its lights flashing through the broken front windows. The pinball machine blazed to life with red and blue sparkles that mimicked the vehicle outside. The detective looked back at it. Elton was there, surveying whether it had sustained any damage. The mechanical eye opened and closed, focusing on Detective Weatherford and her child.

The detective and the baby girl continued toward the front door. Elton saw them and rushed over.

"Wait!" He called to them.

Amerika stopped.

"Your eyes are incredible," Elton said.

As the detective looked into Elton's eyes she saw the whites darken as the element inside him moved across the globes like a black cloud across a stormy sky. "I could say the same of yours."

The detective kept walking with Elton at her heels. As the door opened to the world outside, the sun poked through a few scattered clouds.

Detective Amerika Weatherford squinted at Elton and hugged Baby Weatherford tight.

"You know what they say about weather like this?"

"No," the detective said and had a feeling she knew where this was going. She pulled out a cigarette, lit it, and breathed in deep.

"You're supposed to close your eyes and make a wish," Elton said. "The game in there, you should give her another chance. Play her and she'll grant you a wish."

Detective Weatherford smiled and shook Elton's hand. She noticed Elton's smooth slender fingers were covered with bristly blonde wool. The same kind of hair grew from his ears and nose, like white fluffy extensions of the red spider veins that wove across his cheeks. Elton appeared to have aged twenty years in the course of an afternoon. He coughed, reached into his pocket for a handkerchief, and spit the metallic mercury-like liquid into the cloth. It spilled onto the pavement and approached the detective's feet. It hovered near them, then retreated and ran back toward the bar.

"We've been through this before, Professor Bodrov. Like I told you last time, I don't play games. But you never know, maybe we'll see each other in the future."

"Or in the past," he said.

The detective winked at him, closing her brown eye to flash the one that was blue. She adjusted the baby girl on her hip, turned, and walked down the street toward home. What she thought was a simple case of fraud had taken a multi-dimensional twist that left her short two hundred dollars. It'd be a week she'd barely scrape by. But there'd be another client tomorrow and maybe one more the day after that. Detective Amerika Weatherford wouldn't worry about it too much at the moment. All she knew was that she was ready to concentrate on her own daughter and leave radon's behind.

The Ball

By C Griffith Knowles

"And try to be charming," Felix said, adjusting the shoulder straps on Samantha's dress. "And ladylike. I know that's asking a lot."

"I remember my etiquette perfectly well, thank you. And I'll have you know that before we met, I spent most of my life in an all-girls' school. I couldn't forget how to be ladylike if I tried." Samantha's eyes scanned the floor to her left as she tried not to dwell on her childhood.

"Really? Because I'm pretty sure I can count the number of times I've seen you behave like a *lady* on one hand."

Samantha slapped Felix's wandering digits away from her shoulder.

He withdrew his hand and folded his arms, standing back to admire the finished ensemble. Behind her Rex appeared unusually focused, his fingers darting about working her hair into braids. Felix continued, "Last time you wore something this fancy was our wedding, and I honestly have a hard time imagining you more uncomfortable than you looked in that dress. Of course, your mood changed once I got you out of it . . ." Felix trailed off, his eyes mirroring the wandering of his mind as a moronic grin crept over his face.

The three of them stood in the middle of the main room of the captain's cabin of the ship, Felix having recently commissioned the creation of the vessel in preparation for the turmoil on the horizon. The room was a semi-circle, following the lines of the rear of the ship, decorated with what Felix felt best suited the captain of an airship: dark colors, wood paneling, and a series of cabinets installed in the curved wall, leading into the bar which saw more use by his crewmen. The left half of the room's curvature hosted a long table, matching the shape of a circle, a parody of the fabled Round Table, where Felix always insisted on sitting at the head.

Samantha scowled at him in mock disapproval, placing her hands on her hips. "Are you done yet? There's an idiot in front of me who needs to be slapped." She struggled against the anchor Rex provided, his hands still woven into her gingered roots.

"Please, I'm *creating*," Rex said, continuing to manipulate her increasingly intricate new look.

Returning to reality, Felix added, "It really did turn out quite nicely for a last minute job."

Samantha's outfit had been cobbled together on the fly, but nonetheless was staggering in its completed glory. The black lace of the dress's shoulder straps stood in stark contrast to her pale skin, making her complexion seem almost vibrant in the filtered daylight of the cabin's main room. A ruffled trim crowned the torso of her dress, obscuring what little cleavage she had. A V-shaped swath of flowing indigo fabric hung over the black satin corset which she wore loose in protest, claiming she couldn't breathe otherwise. Stubborn or not, Felix thought, her hips are broad enough that she hardly needs the emphasis. The floral pattern of the lace continued down the shoulderless bodice before reaching more of the same indigo, which flowed from the torso into a long gown. A second tier of black velvet continued from the bottom of the blue cloth at her shins, covering her feet. Without the high heeled shoes, which she had tossed aside as soon as she knew they would fit, she was noticeably short, struggling to reach even five feet.

Behind her, Rex was making the final adjustments to her detailed coiffure. Her shocking orange locks had been braided into vertical rows and drawn back to a central point, leaving her bangs to hang free, framing her lightly freckled features.

"Alright, let's go over your cover for this shindig," Felix said, peering over his conspicuously thick spectacles.

"My name is Moira Reed," Samantha said, "and I'm here for . . ."

"With the accent," Felix interjected.

"And I'm here," she continued, her vowels developing a distinct draw and twang, and R's becoming exaggerated and fluid, "for his highness Prince Sigismund's thirtieth birthday."

"Good, good. 'Bairthdeh,' I like it. The Captain himself would think you're just another bonnie lass from the hills of Scotland." Felix nodded in approval, leaning in periodically to shift tiny elements on the evening gown. "Remember, if anyone asks, you're Lord Andrew Harrington's niece. That guy owes us a favor for bailing his daughter Emilia out of some stuff a couple years ago. If anyone actually follows up on it, he'll confirm that you're just another Britton aristocrat."

"Got it," Samantha said with a nod.

"Now, during the ball, try to show *casual* interest in politics when you talk to this guy. If you make it too obvious, you'll scare him off, and we *need* to know what Alexandre's up to."

From the right side of the room, the door to Felix's private quarters swung open. "How do we even know this guy will have the sort of information we want?" Sa'id asked, stretching the ends of his bow tie as he emerged from the recently opened portal. For the evening he had foregone his usual turban and instead wore his incredibly long black hair in a French braid, which stretched nearly to the coattails of his tuxedo. His beard was drawn into a single braid as usual, completely obscuring the tie with which he struggled, but as much of his moustache as he could wrangle had been waxed and curled upward.

"Wow . . . uh, sir," Rex said with a raised eyebrow, glancing up for a moment from his own efforts on Samantha's braids.

"Because he's part of the Prussian royal family," Felix said, turning to address his colossal companion. "He's the youngest, so he really doesn't have any political sway, which is why they haven't arranged a marriage for him yet, but he hears about what goes on in the big meetings just like anyone else."

"And you think second-hand from a figurehead noble is re-liable enough to work with?" Sa'id had moved across the room and was settling into one of the large armchairs Felix kept near the end of the cabinetry.

"Honestly? We don't have anything else," Felix said with a shrug. "I only heard about this event a few days ago and I fig-ured we might as well capitalize on the opportunity. We have no idea what Alexandre's next move is, and without access to his inner circle, we're left twiddling our thumbs while everyone we know are rounded up like cattle."

"It's the best we've got," Sa'id said, turning his head to look out the window.

"It's the best we've got." Felix looked down, as if searching for a better explanation of his choices. "Anyway, we need to fin-ish getting ready." He walked past Samantha and Rex into his private quarters and shut the door behind him.

Rex moved to collect his own suit, which hung over the back of the armchair opposite Sa'id, then exited the captain's cabin and climbed down the ladder outside to the crew quarters. Sa-mantha lifted her lengthy dress in bunches, shuffled over to the seat next to Sa'id and fell into it unceremoniously.

"Well Sam," Sa'id said, turning back from the window, "you're the star of tonight's show. You ready?"

"It's been a while since I've been to a formal occasion, but I think I remember which spoon is for which kind of soup."

Sa'id chuckled. "There's a bit more at stake here than embarrassing yourself in the company of the social elite. There's a war coming, Sam, and if we can't figure out how to stop Alexandre, we don't stand a chance."

"I know. I feel bad for this guy though. He's just the spare meat from a prestigious family, and tonight I'm supposed to make him believe I could be the wife he's looking for."

"Since when have you ever been concerned with the moral ramifications of lying?" Sa'id asked, leaning in with an eyebrow raised.

"It's just so . . . personal," Samantha said, leaning back in her chair.

"More personal than boosting coin purses in a crowded market?"

Samantha looked down and brushed some dust from the arm of her chair.

"Anyway, try not to dwell on it. He may not be responsible for what's going on, but he's still on the wrong side. Now," Sa'id shifted his weight and sat upright, "are you prepared for things to go wrong?"

"I've got a Derringer strapped to my right thigh and a pocket knife to my left. I'm good to go." Samantha patted each of her legs in turn.

"Not bad," Sa'id said, grinning, "but take this." He leaned over and handed her a small vial full of a clear, viscous liquid. "Just in case."

"What is this?" Samantha asked, leaning forward to take the vile and examine it.

"Your exit strategy." Sa'id gave her a knowing wink, lifted himself out of the armchair and walked out of the room toward the bridge.

Samantha held the vial up to the light with a sideways look, then slipped it down the front of her dress and leaned back in her seat with a sigh.

The sun was just setting as the four lined up on the steps of the banquet hall preparing to enter, the three men of the party all wearing an identical make of black tuxedo.

"Alright," Felix said, staring up at the illuminated building. "Sam, you're the main attraction. Rex, you're her escort. Me and Sa'id will be on the periphery as backup. We go in, we mingle, Sam works her magic, we get some information, we get out. Any questions?"

"I have one," Rex said, looking over to Felix. "What's my alias?"

"You don't need one."

"What? Why not?" His brows furrowed in dismay.

"Well, sorry, but you're not really on anyone's watch list. Just don't draw too much attention and you'll be fine."

"What if Sigismund asks about him?" Samantha asked, still staring up at the pillars of the massive structure.

"Tell him the truth," Felix said, shrugging.

Sa'id, Rex, and Samantha all turned to look at Felix.

"Well, not the *whole* truth," he said turning to look at them. "Just the important part, he's here as your friend. Don't want to scare the eligible bachelor off . . ."

Samantha took a deep breath, then extended her arm toward Rex. He hooked his elbow out in response and they made their way up the steps to the massive doors of the hall.

When they were out of earshot, Sa'id turned from the spectacle to look down at his comrade. "You still haven't thought this through yet, have you?"

"What do you mean?" Felix looked up, puzzled.

"*Your* wife. *Our* Sam. Getting information from a prince in Alexandre's inner circle. By *seducing him.*"

"Yeah? So what? She's great at this covert stuff."

"And you're comfortable with this idea. Her. With another guy. *Intentionally.*" Sa'id raised an eyebrow.

Felix paid his first mate little heed, watching intently as Samantha and Rex approached the attendant at the doors to the hall. "That's it, just smile and enter with confidence," he whispered to himself, squinting. Ahead, the attendant drew his finger across a long piece of parchment, checking for the name

Samantha had apparently just supplied. With a nod, he gestured inside and the pair continued through the massive doors. Felix smiled as his hasty preparations paid off.

Sa'id snapped his fingers in front of Felix. "Back to reality, bub."

Felix shook his head rapidly. "What? Oh right, Sam seducing some guy, yeah, that's the plan."

"You haven't been listening to a word I've said, have you."

Felix's shoulders sank as he sighed. "Look, *bub*, I'm an adult. I've thought this through."

"Are you sure about that?"

"Gods, Charlie, what do you think I'm missing here?"

"I think you're overlooking the only word I can think to describe you in relationships. *Jealous.*"

"What? I'm not *jealous.*" Felix squinted angrily.

Sa'id blinked slowly and stared at Felix, his expression blank.

"When have I ever been jealous over a woman?"

"Oh you do not want to start down this path. Shall I go in order?" Sa'id stroked his beard and looked up. "Let's see . . . how about when we were twelve and you saw Adelaide Cartwright talking to James Underwood? You brought the Captain's *sword* to school the next day. They made *me* do lines because they figured your only friend had to have something to do with it."

Felix's eyes strained upward, recalling the event.

"Or how about that fiasco with Jennifer McQuage's mother when we were sixteen? And what happened with her sister the next school year."

Felix's brow furrowed as his lips pursed to one side. His eyes followed the direction of his mouth, avoiding the truth of Sa'id's accusations.

"And don't even get me *started* on Morrigan. That whole can of worms is so messed up, I don't even . . ."

"Fine!" Felix interjected. "I get it. I do dumb things when women are involved."

Sa'id's arms were still in midair, his exasperation cut short.

"But this is all we've got."

Sa'id lowered his arms and leveled his gaze.

"So just . . . trust me for tonight. Okay?"

Sa'id's expression changed to one of reluctant acceptance. "Fine. We're already in too deep to back out now."

With a nod, Felix started up the stairs to the banquet hall. Sa'id adjusted his jacket, took one last look at the evening sky, then followed after.

Inside, dozens of individuals mulled about the immaculate inlaid marble of the dance floor, the entire hall alive with their chatter. Encircling the area were massive pillars of identical stone, stretching up to the domed ceiling, the gold finish filling the entire hall with a vibrant amber hue. A balcony followed the outline of the dome along the outer walls, leading into a pair of magnificent, red-carpeted staircases, descending down to the first floor. At the back of the main area, a small stage was recessed into the wall, where a symphonic ensemble played for the guests, its music a blend of traditional compositions of Europa, with an emphasis on wind instruments to convey a distinctly jazz-inspired modern sound. From the edges of the main ballroom, hallways stretched back to the staff areas and service rooms. A small bar had been erected against one wall, supplying the attendees' drinks while servants darted through the crowds carrying trays of hors d'oeuvres.

"Wow," Rex gasped, brushing stray hairs from his brow. His pomade-lacquered brown shag was fighting to stay in place amidst his awe. "I've never been to a spot this fancy before."

"Well be sure to take it all in, we won't be back for quite some time," Samantha said, glancing around the room looking for entrances and exits. The male guests all wore a similar cut of the "black tie" formal wear which had become popular in the last few decades, while the women in the crowd sported varying degrees of formality in their evening attire, from the traditional petticoat inflated dress to a more formfitting gown like the one Samantha was trussed up in. Occasionally she spotted military uniforms adorned with medals and badges, honorary titles bestowed on aristocratic generals who stood as upright as they could for their considerable ages. Some of the more extravagantly dressed women bore tiaras, likely nobility themselves, some clinging to the arms of older men, some clearly here as potential candidates for the Prince's affections.

Behind her, Felix and Sa'id entered the ballroom and immediately went in opposite directions, attempting to blend into the crowd as much as possible. Samantha couldn't help but laugh as she watched them go through identical motions, snatching appetizers from the nomadic trays, attempting to look stately and well-mannered. It was easier to keep track of Sa'id's movements as he towered over the majority of the guests. Meanwhile, Felix drifted toward the nearest staircase in order to get a better view of the proceedings from the balcony.

Over the next half hour, Samantha and Rex took in the sights of the upper crust, occasionally leaning in to comment to one another about the absurdity of some hairstyle or conjecture whether the girl hanging on an older man's arm was his daughter or mistress.

When the final piece of the band's suite had concluded, several white-gloved servants lined the edges of the eastern staircase. The hush that fell over the crowd was punctuated by a potent fanfare unleashed by the brass of the ensemble.

Several expensively dressed couples made their way down the steps, every individual wearing a diagonal red sash lined with medals and adornments. As soon as the final pair had reached the ground floor, Samantha heard someone behind her whisper, "Showtime," and turned around just in time to see Felix taking a few steps back, drifting into the crowd.

Still applauding, Rex leaned over and whispered, "Is that the guy?"

"That's the guy," Samantha said. The man in question wore a similar cut of tuxedo to the men of the audience, but bore a heavy white cravat in place of the standard black bow tie. His black hair was a conservative length, parted on one side. He appeared to be in his early thirties, his features angular and the shade of his cheeks discolored by the regular shaving of what would have been dark facial hair. He and his older female companion, likely his mother or aunt, kissed each other's cheeks and parted ways. As he drifted through the crowd, he smiled and shook hands with numerous guests, laughing merrily.

Samantha and Rex stood to the side of the swath he was cutting through the party goers, arms still interlocked. As he passed them, still greeting the attendees, he paused for a moment and glanced at Samantha. She smiled politely and curtsied. He continued on through the crowd, occasionally thanking someone for coming.

"Well, got his attention right off the bat. That's a good sign, right?" Samantha looked up at Rex who was still watching as Sigismund waded through the mass of guests. He glanced down at her and shrugged.

The music began again and Samantha watched as Sigismund spent a solid ten minutes greeting guests before finally settling into conversation with a small group. Periodically young women would approach him and make an introduction. Some would stay to chat for awhile, others would leave, blushing, unable to feign polite conversation with a young celebrity. After the stream of debutantes dwindled, Samantha took a deep breath and shifted toward the royal entourage, trying not to trip over her own dress. As she drew closer, she could see Sigismund eyeing her in his peripheral vision. The nearer she got, the more his grin broadened. Finally, she stopped just outside their conversation and attempted to look involved in a neighboring discussion.

Sigismund approached Samantha from behind, the expressions of the people near her letting her know when the baited trap had captured its prey. She turned and looked up at him.

"I don't believe we've been introduced," he said in a deep baritone, taking her hand. "Prince Franz Friedrich Sigismund of Prussia." He kissed her hand lightly as she curtsied.

"Moira Reed," she responded, replicating the accent she had been taught to use.

"Reed. Is that Scottish?" He released his soft grip on her hand while his eyes took in the entirety of her outfit.

"Aye. I mean, yes, your highness." Samantha feigned embarrassment as Sigismund laughed softly.

"Please," he said, "you may call me Sig."

Around the room, Samantha's three cohorts had taken up posts to monitor the event. From the balcony, Felix smirked as he admired the mastery of Samantha's rehearsed charade.

"I noticed you were accompanied by a gentleman earlier," Sig said.

Samantha glanced back at Rex who was attempting to join in another conversation.

Sig followed her gaze. "Are you and he . . ."

"Who, Rex? Oh no, we're not *together*. We may even be competing for the same man by the end of the night, if you follow my meaning." She turned back to Sig with a raised eyebrow.

"Ah so he's . . ."

Samantha nodded.

"Well I must admit, that news comes as a relief, for you look absolutely ravishing, and I'd hate to find out that you were spoken for."

Samantha looked away and waved her hand in modest dismissal.

"You're so . . . exotic," Sig continued. "That gorgeous red hair, your almond shaped eyes. So blue, so vibrant." He was now staring directly into her eyes. "They look almost violet in the light."

Samantha blushed in earnest.

Upstairs, Felix shifted his weight while watching the exchange.

"Would you care to dance?" Sig asked, his hand outstretched.

Samantha placed her hand in his and they made their way out to the center of the marble floor. The guests all looked on as the pair moved in time with the waltz that played up as the conductor hastily turned to accommodate the man of the hour.

After the first tune ended, the crowd applauded and several couples moved out into the center of the ballroom to join in the festivities.

Upstairs, Felix's brow furrowed as he looked away.

By the third song, many more guests had joined the growing crowd of dancers. The men and women separated into concentric circles, the inner ring moving clockwise while the outer moved to counter. In turn, each pair split, and a new couple formed as the song played in a rhythm of six. Felix drifted down the massive staircase and slipped into the ring of dancers a few dancers away from Samantha.

When the rings lined up to pair them together, Samantha twirled into Felix's waiting arms.

"Having fun?" he asked as they stepped in time.

"It's working perfectly, he's all over me." Samantha threw her head back and laughed.

"Well uh, good," Felix stammered as he unfurled one arm to spin Samantha outward. She reached the end of his grasp and sprang back, rolling off his chest and into the next partner on the downbeat of the next bar.

Samantha watched as Felix shifted out of the circle of dancers and walked over to Sa'id as she continued to move.

When the dance ended, Samantha returned to Sig, breathless.

"It's been a while since I had a good dance," he said, taking deep breaths himself. "Thank you for that."

"Oh please," she said, waving aside his compliment, "it was just as much fun for me."

Sig laughed softly. "Would you care to join us for the evening?"

Samantha nodded and took his outstretched hand. Over the course of the next hour, she sat through polite conversation as relatives and guests stopped by to wish Sig a happy birthday and make various offhand comments about the latest news or some pointless, high-minded drivel. Samantha continued to keep an eye on the uniformed officers in the room, hoping that one might come by and mention something of substance, but by the second hour there had been no such luck.

From across the room, Felix watched and waited as time passed, Samantha's conversation with Sigismund growing ever more casual until he eventually put his arm around her. Felix looked away and began circling the room, hoping to pick up on any conversation that might contain vital information.

After the third hour, a young woman in her mid-twenties bounded over to the royal entourage, calling, "Ziggy!" as she approached. She immediately took Sig's hand and started pulling him onto the dance floor. "Why don't you ever ask me to dance?" she asked as she dragged him along. Sig looked back at Samantha and shrugged, trying to hold up a hand to explain.

Samantha chuckled softly and turned, glad to have a respite from the incessant and aimless banter. When she looked up, Felix appeared in front of her, staring out over her at the members of the royal entourage.

"Oh, hi. Didn't see you come up," she said.

"Anything yet?" Felix asked, still peering over the top of her head.

"Not yet. Sig hasn't really mentioned anything important. I mean, it *is* his birthday. No one really wants to discuss business on their birthday."

"*Sig?*" Felix looked down at Samantha, incredulous.

"What?"

"Look, you've got a job to do. We didn't come here to fraternize with the enemy."

"I'm doing my job." Samantha plucked a small hors d'oeuvre from a wandering tray. "I've been watching the uniformed guys," she said, her mouth full. "I figure eventually one of them is bound to come over and say something. Sig's talked to just about everyone in here."

Felix turned to look at Sigismund upon hearing "Sig" again.

"Are you okay?" Samantha asked, looking up at Felix's vacant stare.

"I'm fine," he said, turning his gaze back on Samantha. "Just stay on task. We need this guy."

"Sure thing," she said, her eyes narrowing as Felix turned to leave. She squinted for a moment, as if trying to make out some indiscernible detail on Felix's person before shaking her head and returning to the small crowd of Sig's close companions.

After a few minutes, Sig stumbled back gasping, his eyes rolling. "Sorry, that's my cousin Viktoria. She's uh . . . well."

"Family, huh? I know what you mean. My cousin Emilia is always trying to talk me into crazy situations."

"Ehh," Sig said, his gaze shifting, "it's probably easier for you. Your cousin probably isn't trying to uh . . . Let's just say Viktoria thinks the royal blood line should be kept as pure as possible."

Samantha raised an eyebrow.

"You know. By . . . keeping it all in the family?"

Samantha's eyes widened. "Ohh." Her expression of surprise turned to a grimace as she squinted. "Eww."

"Yes. It's . . .very uncomfortable." Sig straightened the lines of his jacket and pulled his sash back into place.

"Well, if she comes back, I'll just tell her you're spoken for," Samantha said, grinning up at him.

Sig looked down and smiled.

From upstairs, Sa'id had a clear view of the entire ballroom. Near the band, Samantha and Sigismund were in conversation, periodically laughing. He would occasionally put his arm around her shoulders as they talked to other members of the party. Across the floor, Rex was attempting to blend in with a crowd, his efforts generally going unnoticed. Sa'id smirked. Better to be ignored than to make an ass of yourself like that fellow over at the bar.

Sa'id looked toward the bar again, his gaze lingering on the double take.

That ass was Felix. At the bar? Felix should *not* be at the bar.

Sa'id hurried downstairs and shuffled through the crowd along the edges of the dance floor, the majority of the attendees hurrying to get out of his way as he lumbered over to the refreshment stand.

Felix had a glass of dark amber liquid in one hand, muttering to himself.

"Are you *drunk*?" Sa'id asked, his stare intent but unbelieving.

"Yes I'm drunk, *mother*," Felix said, sarcasm dripping from his mouth like fine brandy as he rolled his eyes.

"What the hell? You don't drink. Whatever happened to 'alcohol dulls the wits, and I need to be on top of my game?'"

"Well maybe the game is playing itself tonight. Maybe the game doesn't need my wits. Maybe I can afford to sit back and have a few drinks while the *game* dances around the room with some *prince,* with his pointy nose and his fancy sash and his stupid *face.*" Felix swung his glass about to emphasize his rapidly slurring speech.

"Oh good gods, of all the ways I expected you to act out, this is the last thing I would've seen coming. Get it together, this was *your idea.*"

"Well maybe my ideas are *terrible.*"

"No one ever said they weren't."

"Well aren't you the master planner, mister *hair.* And how do you think we should go about stopping a megalomaniac from locking people up and taking over the whole . . . global . . . socioeconomic . . . oh boy." Felix set his glass on the bar and leaned over, his hands on his knees.

"Keep your voice down. In case you've forgotten, we're surrounded by that 'megalomaniac's' supporters."

From across the room, Rex watched the exchange and rushed over when it became apparent that Felix had lost his leadership competence.

"Is he drunk?" he asked, moving to place a hand on Felix's shoulder. "I've never seen him drunk."

"There's a reason for that. He really can't hold his booze. We need to get him to a toilet or something." Sa'id looked around the ballroom for some sign of the necessary facilities.

With Felix's arms draped over their shoulders, Sa'id and Rex hustled down the western hallway, past apathetic party guests and nervous attendants. Sa'id bellowed at one of the many servants lining the wall, "Toilet!"

"Through that door, sir," the attendant said as they hurried past, his hand shaking as he pointed.

On the ballroom floor, Samantha caught the trio rushing off out of the corner of her eye. She turned to Sigismund and his guests. "If you'll excuse me, I need to go . . . powder . . . something." Grabbing the sides of her gown in bunches, she hurried off the dance floor and down the hallway, just as Sa'id, Felix and Rex entered a side door. As she rushed to the portal trying not to lose footing in her heels, the attendant waiting outside the room raised a hand and said, "I'm sorry Madame this is the men's . . . lavatory," but she had already slipped inside.

Once in, she followed the sound of voices to the only occupied stall.

"What the hell is *this*?!" Samantha threw open the stall door to find Felix huddled over the commode, Sa'id standing to one side, and Rex bent over with a hand on Felix's shoulder.

"Uh oh," Felix slurred, turning to look at Samantha. "Mom's here, guess the party's over. Heh heh huh . . . huh-oh." In a flash his head was once again hovering over the toilet. All three witnesses grimaced and looked away as he expelled the contents of his stomach into the porcelain bowl.

"Is he *drunk*?" Samantha demanded, her fiery gaze piercing into Sa'id. "I've never even seen him drink."

"We've been over it."

"What's the backup plan for something as catastrophically *stupid* as this?"

"There isn't one. You just get back out there and charm Prince what's-his-face into telling you about the guy trying to take over the world while I deal with the idiot I made the mistake of calling my best friend for the last fifteen years."

Samantha stared intensely at the tiled wall of the lavatory, trying to wrap her mind around the insanity of the present situation. "Will he be alright?"

"Pff," Felix snorted, the sound echoing off the inside of the commode. "I'm better than fine, I'm downright *sharp*." His intoxicated laughter resounded off the ceramic bowl.

"I didn't say fine, I said alright," Samantha said, her eyes narrowing on the inebriate in front of her.

"Well *excuse* me," Felix said, his head still hanging over the edge of the toilet. "I guess we can't all be as sophisticated and charming as Prince I-wear-a-sash-to-my-birthday."

"Right, I'm going back out then."

"No, wait," Felix muttered, his face colliding with the edge of the bowl as he tried to turn.

Samantha stopped.

"I don't want you to go," Felix slurred, looking back at her as she prepared to exit the lavatory. "I just . . . because . . . I . . . ugh." Felix's head lolled to the side, landing on the edge of the toilet.

Samantha's expression changed from one of outrage to genuine concern as she turned and knelt next to Felix.

His head still resting on the edge of the bowl, he managed to express a few random moans before his eyes closed and audible snores filled the room. Samantha grimaced as the foul odor of Felix's breath hit her. She stood and looked up at Sa'id.

"I can't just leave him like this."

"He'll be fine. You've got a job to do, the job *he* planned for you. Just get back out there."

Samantha looked back down at Felix, unconscious and completely exhausted, then back up at Sa'id. He nodded solemnly then gestured out of the stall. Samantha gathered up the sides of her gown once more and moved to the door of the stall, then took one last look at the stall before exiting the lavatory.

Rex knelt next to Felix and looked up at Sa'id, who simply shook his head and pulled the chain hanging from the toilet's reservoir. He sighed as the sound of rushing water filled the room.

Back outside, Samantha rejoined the royal entourage, several older gentlemen in military garb having entered into the conversation with Sigismund.

"Apologies, I believe one of the hors d'oeuvres might have been a bit undercooked." Samantha squinted as she realized how undignified her excuse sounded once spoken aloud.

"Oh, I'm sorry to hear that," Sig said with a slight grimace. He lowered his voice to address her personally, "You didn't miss anything. These men were just discussing some boring military stratagem."

Samantha's eyes widened as the evening's goal finally presented itself.

Across the room, Sa'id and Rex emerged from the hallway carrying Felix between them, his feet dragging across the marble as he attempted to drunkenly move in step with his comrades.

"I suppose someone had a bit too much fun this evening," Sig said, laughing to himself. The other members of the entourage laughed as well, but Samantha looked on the pathetic sight, torn between Felix and the mission Felix intended for her to accomplish. "Listen, Moira dear," Sig continued, leaning in close, "the discussion seems to be shifting toward some sensitive topics, so . . ."

Samantha's eyes grew wide, fearing that the evening's efforts be for nothing if she was simply to be dismissed when the conversation finally became interesting.

"How about we go ahead and make our exit as well? Best to discuss such matters in private." He straightened up, having been leaning in close to speak to Samantha, and continued at a much more audible volume, "Wouldn't want to end up like that fellow over there, eh?"

The royal entourage all turned to look at Felix and laugh. From across the room, the most Felix could make out was the prince leaning in to whisper to Samantha, then gesturing towards him and the crowd of aristocrats nearby, all laughing. Felix's shoulder sank even further as he took one last look at his wife before being dragged out of the ballroom.

Samantha glanced at Felix, then back up at Sig, her expression livid. She could feel the outrage and retort rising in her throat as Felix was escorted out. Her gaze shifted from Sig to Felix, then back again. She swallowed hard and forced a smile.

"Yes," she said, "let's retire, shall we?" The decision tasted foul as the words fell out of her mouth.

Outside, a pair of automobiles resembling carriages with a separate driver's compartments pulled up to the steps of the hall. The chauffeurs hurried around to open the passenger doors as they approached, half of the royal entourage crowding into the second vehicle while Sig, Samantha, and several of the uniformed gentlemen climbed into the first.

Down the street, Rex and Sa'id were attempting to carry Felix away. Samantha couldn't help but watch as the carriages approached them, passed, and continued onward. She'd never seen her mischievous captain look so pathetic as she stared out the window.

Behind her, the conversation began again, and she straightened herself up to listen as the vehicles made their way off into the night.

"I don't see why you're telling *me* these things," Sigismund said while looking out the window of the horseless carriage.

"You're thirty now Sigismund, it's time to start acting like a sovereign." The older man who had said this possessed an immensely bushy moustache, which swished from side to side as he spoke. "Your father certainly thinks so and that's why he asked us to attend your party."

"I'm last in line for the throne. I hardly see how I could act like a sovereign even if I was inclined to do so." Sigismund was now resting his head on his hand, forehead pressed against the glass pane.

"Every member of the royal house is a symbol for the people. You may not wield any real authority, but you can be a leader of men just the same. Alexandre would not trust you with information if he did not see value in your contributions."

Sigismund looked across to Samantha and rolled his eyes. She forced a weak smile while paying attention to the officer's every word.

The carriage rounded another corner and slowed its pace as it began the gradual climb up the slope to a manor at the heart of the city. Though the surroundings were dimly lit in the faint light of the scattered lamps, Samantha had no doubt the exceptionally well-manicured lawn was an oasis in the urban landscape.

When the automobile had reached the front steps of the mansion, the chauffeur scurried out and around to the door, offering a hand up to Samantha as she emerged. Instinctually she hopped down and landed hard on her heels, pausing for a moment after realizing the mistake she had made. Looking back, the men in the cab held their heads at odd angles, brows furrowed.

"Ah . . . must've tripped." She brushed off her dress and looked away, an awkward grin the best she could suffice as explanation.

Sigismund scowled at the driver, who could think to do nothing but hold up his hands, mouth hanging open.

The occupants of the two vehicles all strolled inside, past the attendant at the door and into the manor's parlor. The room was dimly lit by electric lights designed to look like oil lamps, the walls bearing crimson tapestries and massive paintings of various individuals Samantha assumed to be relatives. The floors were a dark brown wood, which produced hard clicks with every step of her uncomfortable heels. Samantha scanned the room, as she was so accustomed to doing now, for entrances and exits, lining up angles and cover should things go awry. One of the older men in military garb walked over to an armchair covered in an aged, but luxurious green velvet and sat down, his beard puffing out as it met his chest.

The first man, who Samantha could only think to refer to as "Stache" looked around the room. "Ladies," he said, "it's getting late. Perhaps you should retire. The gentlemen need to discuss some things that you'd likely not enjoy."

The other women in the room, Sig's aunt, as Samantha had previously guessed, and other siblings and cousins, all smiled politely and moved out of the room, their dresses rustling as they walked. Samantha's eyes grew wide as she bared her lower teeth in dismay.

From across the room, Sig looked over, his head still hanging. He mouthed the word, "Sorry," to Samantha.

"It's a bit . . . early to turn in, isn't it?" she said, scrambling to find an excuse to stay in the vicinity.

From the neighboring room, Sig's aunt leaned in. "Come along, Moira dear. Let the boys have their little chat. We aren't turning in just yet. The girls can have their own fun."

Samantha wrinkled her nose at the prospect and looked to her left. She glanced back at Sig who simply nodded, seeming to have given up on having any more fun this evening. She slowly walked toward the archway where Sig's aunt was still clinging to the frame. She stretched out a hand to Samantha as she drew close. Samantha looked back at the room one last time.

"Come along, love."

Samantha drew her gown up in bunches as she walked hesitantly up the stairs to the mansion's second floor, knowing every step forward was a figurative step back. By the time she reached the second floor landing, she could no longer hear anything from downstairs. Ahead, the women of the entourage were crowding into a sitting room at the end of the hall. As she approached, the older woman adjusted a switch on the wall and the faint light grew brighter as one of the younger girls laid out doilies on the circular coffee table positioned in the center of various sofas and seats. A woman already seated on a sofa of what appeared to be the same green velvet rang a small bell and several butlers emerged from a nearby door, carrying trays of teacups, a kettle, and plates of baked goods.

Samantha sat in an unoccupied seat furthest from the group as a dark-skinned man offered her cookies, while one of the girls placed a cup of tea on the table in front of her. Samantha forced a weak smile as she took the dessert, the butler remaining completely mute and unemotional.

The next ten minutes reminded Samantha of standing too near a bee hive. She knew bees communicated somehow, but to her it was just buzzing and motion, white noise that conveyed no meaning. Her mind raced, searching for an excuse to get back downstairs, knowing that the evening had nearly derailed with Felix's outburst. She had to keep things on track or all the trouble would be for nothing. Without thinking, she stood abruptly.

The older woman who had led her up the stairs turned. "Did you need something, dear?" Her smile seemed sincere enough as she held a small plate in one hand, a tea cup in the other.

"I uh . . ." Samantha struggled. "I think I had a bit too much to drink. Could you tell me where the . . . facilities are?" This would have been easier if she could remember how civilized women talked about answering nature's call. She had been with Felix for less than two years, but the first opportunity to finally throw off the suffocating grip of the corset of civility was all she needed to begin erasing everything her father had wanted her to learn as a child.

"Oh of course, dear." The older woman set down her tea and began to stand up. "Let me show you."

"Oh no, that's alright," Samantha stammered. "You can just tell me, don't want to be a bother. I'm good with directions." Was that the right thing to say? This was rapidly getting out of hand.

"Oh, alright. It's down the hall, second door on the right."

Samantha's eyes lit up. She moved toward the door, which hung open. She gripped the edge and peered down the hall. "Second door on the right?" She asked, clinging to the door as it began to move on its hinges.

"That's right, love."

Samantha nodded and began to move out of the room, the door moving with her. In one fluid, inconspicuous motion, she shut the door, obscuring the prying eyes of the cacophonous hive. She grinned to herself and glanced around the empty hallway. Immediately slipping off her heels, Samantha moved for the staircase, angling her head to the side, trying to hear the discussion downstairs. She slowly tiptoed down the wooden steps, the muffled voices of gruff old men slowly becoming more audible the nearer she crept to the ground floor.

Once on the first floor, Samantha looked around the open entryway, checking for witnesses and a good place to hide. The conversation in the parlor was in earshot, but she had trouble making out the subject of discussion. Samantha crept toward the archway through which Sigismund's aunt had called her away from her duties hardly twenty minutes ago. She pressed her back to the wall, just out of sight of the men in the room, and began to listen.

"And now that he has secured his position in the administration of Home, he plans to track down any remaining undesirables." The voice was one Samantha didn't recognize.

"Yes, they seem to encourage that sort of thing there, don't they." Stache was talking now. "Hardly good business practice for a city run like a corporation."

"I don't know, it seems to work fairly well for them," the first man replied. "The policy is that Home does not expedite and does not respect the warrants of other nations. So long as these *pirates* behave themselves while in the city, the Chief Administrator of Home gives them safe harbor."

"Thorn in our side for far too long," a third voice said.

Samantha could hear the soft pop of someone drawing repeatedly on a cigar as the smell of smoke wafted past her.

"Well he's already corralled some of the important players. That's certainly sent the rabble scrambling. After he captured Gruffydd and some of his children, most pirates went into hiding."

Samantha looked ahead, focusing on something out of view. "He" was definitely referring to Alexandre. Gruffydd, she thought. Uncle Edward. He had been taken in soon after Alexandre infiltrated the governing board at Home. The boys went down with him, and the girls soon after when they tried to free him from prison. Felix didn't talk about it much, but Samantha knew he worried constantly for the well-being of his father and siblings. Felix . . .

Samantha paused.

"What about the young one? K . . . something with a K?"

"Yes, Gruffydd's youngest. He seems particularly frustrated with that one."

Samantha's eyes grew wide, forgetting for a moment that the men in the next room could not actually *hear* her thoughts. They were talking about Felix.

"The plan seems to be to make a public example of the lot of them."

"Execution?"

Samantha heard no response.

An exaggerated sigh punctuated the silence. Sig was clearly out of patience for a discussion he wanted no part of. Samantha heard footsteps moving across the room, growing fainter. One of the unknown voices called after him. "Stache" said, "Let him go."

Samantha moved away from the archway, past the staircase into a part of the manor that remained dark. Looking to her right, she saw a dim light from under a door in the direction the footsteps had traveled. She tiptoed closer and heard the sound of glass against glass, bottles shifting in a cupboard. She slowly turned the knob and pushed the door open, light seeping into the darkened room. Sig stood near a table, a bottle of red wine in one hand, pouring a sizeable amount into a stemmed glass. He took a sip, looked up at the hanging electric lamp and sighed.

Samantha shifted her weight, but immediately regretted the action, as the wooden floor betrayed her with a percussive crack. Sig immediately looked toward the portal.

"Moira? What are you doing down here?" He walked over to the door and opened it wide, illuminating the room. More upholstered furniture populated the darkened den, oriented toward a large fireplace with the mounted head of a bear above its mantle.

Samantha hesitated, unsure of what to say next.

"I thought you'd gone upstairs with the girls." Sig kept his voice low, his need for secrecy very different from Samantha's.

"Well," she said. "I couldn't call it a night without giving you your birthday present, could I?" Samantha did her best to look seductive, batting her eyelashes, placing her hands behind her back, an action which concealed the shoes she still held to avoid excess noise.

Sig smiled and looked back toward the parlor. He looked back at Samantha and held a finger up to his lips, setting down his glass as he began to step out of the electrically illuminated room. Samantha shook her head up at him. His brow furrowed as he cocked his head. Samantha stepped into the light just far enough to grasp the bottle of wine, hold it up level to her head, and shake it back and forth. Sig's eyes lit up as he reached back for his own glass.

The pair hurried as quietly through the second sitting room and up the stairs as possible, continuing up to the third floor where Sig led them into his bedroom. He flipped a switch on the wall and a dim light filled the space. His bed was a four-poster, with a cloth Samantha could not make out in the dark, hanging down from the ceiling around it. Sig stepped back from the wall, opening his arms wide, his glass of wine still in one hand. Samantha tossed her shoes aside and took a swig from the bottle in her other hand before placing it on a nearby dresser.

She moved past Sig and spun on her heel, grasping his jacket and causing him to spin as well. "You're quite the dancer, you know."

"You think?" Sig said, taking another sip from his wine. "I've had lessons." He began to move about the room, imitating the waltz they had shared hours earlier.

Samantha watched as Sig shuffled about the room, his rhythm steady enough. She closed her eyes for a moment and breathed out. Now or never, she thought. She approached Sig as he spun in place, grabbing his cravat as he slowed at her approach. Pulling him down to her height, she kissed him hard, spinning him around toward the bed and pushing him backward onto it. He managed to hold his wine aloft with only minimal spills.

Sig laughed as he fell back on to the mattress. "I knew there was something different about you. I like aggressive women." He brought the glass to his mouth and consumed the remaining red liquid.

Samantha gathered her gown in bunches and hopped up onto the bed, mounting Sig's lap. She began to untie his cravat.

"I always say, the world needs more aggressive women," Sig said, staring up at the ceiling of his covered bed as Samantha pulled the white silk away from his neck.

"You couldn't be more right," Samantha said, tossing the cravat aside. "But you know what we need right now?"

"What's that?"

Samantha lifted the empty glass from Sig's hand. *"More wine."*

Sig laughed as Samantha climbed off his lap and off the bed. He began to unbutton his pressed white shirt as Samantha made her way to the dresser where she had left the bottle. Glancing over her shoulder, she reached down the front of her gown and held the small vial close as she brought the glass around. She emptied the thick, clear contents into the remaining dregs, then proceeded to pour wine into the mixture, enough to fill more than half the glass.

Samantha walked over to the bed, attempting to sway her considerable hips as much as possible as Sig watched, the top few buttons of his shirt hanging open. She handed him the glass and climbed onto the bed next to the unwitting prince.

He took the glass happily and drank, consuming most of what he was presented. Samantha reclined, her elbow pointed out, her head resting on her hand. She smiled as Sig tilted his head back to empty the remainder of the glass.

With a gasp, he looked over at Samantha and smiled broadly. "You know, this really has been the best birthday ev . . . evhuh . . . ugh." He began to blink sluggishly until he fell backward, his chest moving with slow, deep breaths.

"Oh wow," Samantha said, her eyes wide. "That was a lot faster than I expected."

Taking a moment to recover, she slid off the bed and retrieved the glass which Sigismund had dropped as he lost consciousness. She placed it next to the bottle on the dresser and looked around for a piece of parchment. Scrawling a hasty note, which she tucked under the bottle, Samantha looked around the room, raised her eyebrows, then gathered up her shoes before slipping out the bedroom door. She made her way quietly downstairs, pausing briefly on the second floor to roll her eyes at the audible cackles coming from the room full of hens. She reached the front door, opened it silently, and slipped outside.

As she leaned down to put her shoes back on, the doorman looked at her, puzzled. She simply smiled and nodded before hastening down the steps and out to the road at the bottom of the hill. When she had walked far enough that the manor was no longer visible, she lifted her gown and removed the Derringer strapped to her right thigh. She spun the revolver mechanism until reaching a specific chamber, aimed directly upward, and pulled the trigger. A bright flash illuminated the trail of smoke as the flare cartridge sent her signal to Rex. Minutes later, the airship pulled in, hovering low, and a rope ladder descended from the cargo hold. As she climbed upward, she could just make out the shapes of Rex and Sa'id on the bridge.

It might have been her imagination, but it appeared that the taller shape was giving her the thumbs up.

The next morning, Felix awoke to the hum of a dull ache in his head, the dim light seeping into his cabin through shut blinds painful in its muted brilliance. He groaned and tried to pull the covers of his hanging bed over his eyes. From a few feet away he heard high faint laughter.

"How you feeling?" Samantha asked, her arms folded as she leaned against the doorway to the captain's private quarters.

Felix tried to convey as much information as he could in the groan he expelled in response.

"That good, huh?" Samantha strolled over to the hanging wicker basket, the thick black mattress inside forming a cradle for her hungover husband. "You feel like coming up with an explanation for what happened last night?"

From under the covers Felix breathed a sarcastic, "No, I do not."

"You really didn't think out the whole 'set your own wife up with another man to get information' plan, did you."

"No, I did not."

"Well, do you at least want to know if it worked? Or how I got home?"

"No, I do not . . . wait." Felix threw the covers off and sat upright. Unprepared for the dizziness and painful bright of what most would call a dimly lit room, he raised his arms up to protect against the light. With an arm still over his eyes, he continued, "Ugh, yes. I do, actually."

"Sa'id gave me some drug before we landed last night. I let Sigismund talk for a while, let him think he might actually get lucky, then I slipped it in his drink and let him turn in early. Left a note on his dresser thanking him for 'the most incredible night of my life,' then I just walked out the front door. I guess you were already out by then, because Rex brought the ship around and picked me up about a mile away."

"So . . . nothing happened?" Felix was slowly attempting to remove his impromptu shade and squint through fiercely closed eyes.

"I don't know," Samantha said, looking away. "He *was* wearing that sash. I mean, what girl can resist a sash?" Her body swayed as she feigned amorousness.

Had his eyes been open, Felix would have rolled them. "Yeah yeah, enjoy this, because it won't be happening again."

His head bobbed as he spoke, a motion he immediately regretted as he leaned forward and grimaced. "How do people drink all the time? This is *terrible*."

Samantha cocked her head to the side and smiled softly, the sight pathetic, but endearing. She leaned in and pressed her forehead against his, then brought her hands up to the sides of their faces. Felix saw the darkness through closed eyelids and hesitantly peered out to just barely discern the vibrant blue of Samantha's eyes.

"Nothing happened," she said.

Felix managed a weak smile in the artificial dark.

"And," Samantha continued, "I know exactly what Alexandre's next move is."

Felix's hesitant smirk broadened to a massive grin.

A Reversal of His Fortunes

By J Boyer

Muybridge turned up his collar against the chilly London rain. It was every bit a downpour, and he was thinking to himself as he soaked to the skin that there were better ways for a man to make a living than the line he was in. He tugged at the brim of his Donnegal hat until its short brim fully covered his ears. Damn their eyes anyway, the blue bloods just loved playing spy, Muybridge thought. It might as well have been their national pastime.

He was on his way to meet Lord Anthelm at the lord's private club for a five PM supper. To Muybridge's amusement, the lord was one of those very British characters who took themselves more seriously than they really had a right to, and Muybridge might have been more eager to keep the engagement were its occasion only social. Lord Anthelm was widely recognized as a lithe conversationalist as well as a raconteur with many a story to tell of his derring-do amidst webs of intrigue. Muybridge understood he had been during the Second World War a high ranking official of MI5, Britain's legendary intelligence branch, and the lord had never put this behind him, apparently. He was still with cloak and dagger, and he was a character in several other ways as well. The first impression he'd made on Muybridge was of someone who would have been more at ease in trunk hose and a doublet than the bowler he always wore or his Saville Row tailoring, and the image — somehow — stuck. Lord Anthelm had impressed him upon a first meeting as an amusing, patrician fop who was a thousand years removed from his proper place in history, and Muybridge had yet to shake this impression. He might add to it, as he sometimes had in the past two years, having discovered over time that the lord was always freshly shaven, polished, well spoken, ready to pay what he owed, even throw in a bonus. He might take away from it, thinking, as he was thinking at the instant, that the man was a pain in the rectum. But what came to mind first each time the lord wished to contract for his services was of doublets and trunk hose, so fully had this colored his view of the man from the get-go.

Muybridge entered the building with minutes to spare before his five PM supper and he used this time to enjoy his surroundings.

Just as he was about to show himself in, Lord Anthelm, appearing as suddenly as if he'd appeared from the woodwork, said, "There you are, Muybridge, how good of you to come. I thought perhaps we'd lost you."

Right, thought Muybridge. He would not, of course, have been welcome in any of the dining areas without the presence of his host here. He would have been shooed away like a stray dog had he gone it alone. "Good evening, Lord Anthelm," said Muybridge, extending his hand.

When they were seated at a table for two by a steward, Lord Anthelm got right to the point. "I'm told there's a problem. I handpicked you, you realize, Muybridge. You recognize, of course, you're putting egg all over my face?"

Muybridge removed his serviette from a solid sterling collar. "That wasn't my intention. I want to know more about what I'm getting myself into, that's all. I've come to you before. You've heard me out. We've talked."

Lord Anthelm took his linen serviette from the plate before him and spread it neatly across his lap, smoothing its edges as he spoke. "These new heads, Muybridge, they haven't appreciation enough for practical politics, the *Realpolitik*, as it was called in my day. So many of these chaps I run into imagine differences of opinions among longstanding enemies can simply be jawboned away. No sense of bad blood, of how deeply it runs. Too much faith in the wizardry of words."

Muybridge said, "Too little stomach for what needs to be done."

"Precisely," said Lord Anthelm.

So at least they had that much out of the way, thought Muybridge. Someone, somewhere, would have to be assassinated. Thank God it was on the table. He'd been afraid in the taxi this might drag on for hours, late into the night.

Lord Anthelm continued, "All the pleasures of a job well done come from the felicity of the way they phrase things, you see. We've raised a full generation of talkers. Talkers, not doers, as the Americans like to put it."

Lord Anthelm raised his hand. Beckoning for the waiter, Muybridge imagined in passing. Menus, he supposed. Then, as if Muybridge had spoken those words aloud without realizing it, Lord Anthelm said, "I took the liberty of ordering in advance for the two of us, I hope you won't mind. Proscuitto and melon. It's generally rather good." That Muybridge had gotten it wrong seemed to confirm Lord Anthelm's assumption that he would. Lord Anthelm waited for their sommelier to arrive before he continued speaking to Muybridge. It seemed to Muybridge he was savoring the moment this took. "It's one of the advantages to dining here as opposed to a restaurant, ordering off menu, I mean. What's left over from lunch isn't being touted as fresh by some insolent waiter who was only last week a zinc miner in the north."

He debated with Muybridge the merits of two French wines, both of them white, apparently, one of them fruitier than the other, while the sommelier looked on, as of yet unacknowledged. The actual debate was between the sommelier and his host, Muybridge warranted, for the sommelier suggested a red alternative when the final choice was left in his hands, a French bordeaux, a 1981 Chateau Mouton Rothschild, a suggestion he made in a diffident voice.

"Won't that overpower the melon?" asked Lord Anthelm. He was assured that it wouldn't. "Then speak to the chef and make sure our melon is the ripest of the lot, would you be so kind," he instructed the sommelier.

"Very good, Lord Anthelm," responded the sommelier, not quite clicking his heels, Muybridge thought.

Who, Muybridge wondered, would have to be murdered? That's what he wanted to know next. It would be in keeping with what he knew of Lord Anthelm for the man to shift the blame for some snafu to someone else, then have that person killed. He was not above being a scurrilous coward, not when it came to a cock-up. Kill or be killed. Eat or be eaten. One of the higher-ups, Muybridge guessed. Tag, you're it! Bang, you're dead! Yes, that was one alternative, certainly.

"Tell me something, Muybridge. What keeps you at this? It can't be the money. What is it, the intrigue?"

"It's what I do best."

"I thought perhaps it was a matter of principle. You must have some beliefs."

"I have no principles. I can't afford them. I'm straight out of an American Western movie, Lord Anthelm. A hired gun. A gun for hire to the highest bidder. I don't see why you should find that very hard to believe."

Had he been wearing them, Lord Anthelm might have been looking at Muybridge over the top of his demi-lune spectacles, the ones he sometimes wore for reading. "You realize, finding myself in a tight spot, I could have turned to anyone. I chose you in particular. I like to think we understand each other. In fact, I like to think we're cut from much the same cloth."

"You flatter me, Lord Anthelm."

"I don't really think so."

"You've established a reputation for yourself in these matters that will never be equalled, at least not in your life time."

"Now who's flattering whom, Muybridge. Come, come. *Ne penchez pas les chapeau por moi.*"

So that was it, thought Muybridge. A tight spot, was it? It wasn't Muybridge who had distinguished himself from a vast cache of readily available independent contractors. It was the assignment itself that was different. That was not a good sign. What was that expression about the hairs rising on the back of one's neck as an instinctive response to some imminent danger? His own stayed put. But he understood the figure of speech. He had a very good sense of the rum situation. It was every bit a necessity in his line of work.

Two goblets were placed before them by a boy in his teens in an ill-fitting tuxedo shirt too wide at the collar. The sommelier returned with the bottle of bordeaux. Lord Anthelm offered Muybridge the honors, which he was expected to refuse. So expected, he refused and watched with feigned interest the hollow ritual that followed. Yes, it was all a hollow ritual, he thought to himself. The all too early supper. Selecting the wine. Selecting the killer. It was all a deadly but hollow ritual. After sniffing at his goblet and swirling the vintage about, Lord Anthelm glanced at the bottle, which the sommelier had wrapped in a towel while leaving its label exposed. As if there was some reason to question the year, the sommelier said, simply, "1981, Lord Anthelm."

Seeing there was no toast in the offing, Muybridge drank

a full swallow without any such fuss and bother. He looked at Lord Anthelm across the rim of his glass. Yes, thought Muybridge, he wasn't far off the mark, an Arthurian knight. An old knight errant on a grail quest. But no reason to underestimate him. Couldn't assume a Don Quixote. Less quixotic, less comic. A knight wandering on foot through a wasteland — yes, that was closer to it. And having slaughtered his horse for food, there was nothing to do now but look back at its bony remains as he came to terms with starving to death himself or dying of exposure. Muybridge said, "I've been thinking of getting out of the business, actually. I'm beginning to lose my nerve, I think."

Their meals were brought to the table, identical plates of carefully ripened melon and stingy strips of Italian ham. At once gracious but brusque, Lord Anthelm had mastered the art of dealing with servants. He dispatched their servers with nary a thought to their presence. Lord Anthelm spoke with food in his mouth. "Try your prosciutto, Muybridge. Mine's damnably tasty. Is yours as well? Though your kind begin with the melon, I imagine."

They ate a few bites apiece before continuing their talk. Neither seemed to have brought much of an appetite to the table. Still, eating a meal was all part of a thin, social veneer that might explain away the real occasion of their meeting. Muybridge was conscious of the sounds of their cutlery, its clank against the china. Something about this charade made him slightly uneasy, as if it were effeminate. They played with their food the way two little girls might have pretended a tea.

It was common practice to work out the terms of an assassination well before its target was indicated. A name was never proffered before all the terms were settled — it simply wasn't done, at least not among professionals. This was more than common practice. More, too, than good form. Such procedures had about them a kind of transcendental quality that kept the grimy business at hand from soiling one's fingers.

Muybridge took a sip of his wine, holding it in his mouth

before swallowing it down. Lord Anthelm took a sip of his own. When Muybridge smiled, Lord Anthelm smiled woodenly.

He assumed, obviously, that Muybridge was testing the waters for gold. And, in fact, when Muybridge demanded to see him, money was precisely what he had in mind, not background information. But something about the evening thus far struck Muybridge as being slightly off base. It had to do with those hairs on the back of his neck that should have stood up, but didn't. Something here, he thought to himself. Something fishy. For the first time since Muybridge had met him, Lord Anthelm seemed to be showing the ill-effect of his age. Muybridge kept expecting to detect a tremor of his hand, a slight palsy of the head. Something. There was none to be seen. Still, that was the effect this supper was having upon him. It was as if the old boy had suffered a reversal of fortune of late, for Lord Anthelm seemed to be dealing from a position of weakness rather than strength, from shopworn wisdom instead of virility. Or maybe it was something else, a desperation he was unaccustomed to seeing across the table. If so, that was worse. Muybridge did not do business with desperate men. Not if he could help it. At least he did not do business with desperate men unless he very well compensated for the additional risk this entailed to his life and well-being. He decided upon a ploy. He would ask to be told who was to be assassinated before a money amount was agreed upon. Insofar as Lord Anthelm stood his ground, they might yet be in business. If he capitulated, though, the evening was finished. He'd have to stall for time. Ring up a few friends in the morning. Find the back door. Metaphorically speaking, leave by the fire escape. Lord Anthelm would have to be very desperate indeed if he gave him the name. That would be tantamount to contracting for the murder himself. No, he did not do business with desperate men if there was any good way to avoid it, particularly those who fancied themselves as being honorable men, as did Lord Anthelm. Those were the worst of all. If they found your wallet stuffed with pound notes between the cushions of their sofa, they would drive hell to leather in order to return it, refusing to rest until they saw it in your hand again. While at your cottage, however, if they lost a sixpence bet, they would sooner leave England than pay you what was yours.

"I was wondering, Muybridge, do we amuse you, the old uppercrust, I mean? I was watching your face as you were looking around the room, you see. It's quite all right if we do. We amuse the Americans, I know. They think we're quaint. Something straight out of Austen or Thomas Hardy. Or something off of their tele, the educational channels. I won't take offense, I swear."

There was that mocking tone again. "Interest me, perhaps. Not amuse me. I was wondering earlier who would be attending that banquet I saw being set as I arrived, for instance."

Cutting the last of a strip of proscuitto, Lord Anthelm answered, "A duke. A duchess. Your odd baronet. No one very remarkable, really. Something wrong with the melon, is there?"

"Mine's green."

"Mine was rather green as well, actually."

Lord Anthelm made Muybridge uneasy when the man seemed ready to concede a point. It was as if he was giving up too easily what he thought he needed least, it seemed to Muybridge. Lord Anthelm knew how the game was suppose to be played. It was like sacrificing a pawn in a chess game. You had to arrange your pieces far in advance and make the vulnerable pawn seem nothing but an oversight. He would have preferred Lord Anthelm kept reminding him that he wasn't British by birth, insulting him. That would have been preferable to negotiating a contract as if dealing with a dolt. He was in much too big a hurry, Lord Anthelm. Or careless. Or worse, contemptuous of Muybridge, condescending. Yes, that was more likely.

Lord Anthelm signalled for coffees.

Muybridge pushed his plate forward, placing his cutlery atop it in the shape of an X. He wiped his mouth with his napkin. "Where, precisely, do I fit into all this, Lord Anthelm?"

"As you suspect, there is someone who needs to be removed from our consideration."

Their coffees were set before them by a ginger-haired waiter.

Lord Anthelm stirred his coffee with a tiny sterling spoon, held delicately between his forefinger and thumb. Still stirring his coffee to cool it, Lord Anthelm made what amounted to a particularly attractive financial offer without naming a precise figure, though, had the offer been taperecorded, there was no way to prove that. Had the offer been made in any other form, Muybridge would have left the table and walked straight out the door, never to have contact with Lord Anthelm again. "That's our final offer, by the by, though I'm confident you'll find this very generous indeed," said Lord Anthelm.

"I find in myself a kind of impatience which I don't seem to be able to help. I think I'm losing my taste for the way I make my living."

"Impatience breeds carelessness. None of us can afford to be careless. Not in this day and age. Not in any line of work. There are too many pitfalls. What is true for you and I is true for everyone else, simply less so."

"I feel as if I'm waiting on queue for a dowager hunting change in her coin purse. I know when I see her begin counting out her coins that she won't get it right the first time. If impatience breeds carelessness, do you suppose experience breeds impatience?"

Lord Anthelm nodded wisely. "In some of us, no doubt. Personally, I equate experience with wisdom, you see."

"I was thinking of a change of scenery. I've been thinking about a holiday."

"What is it you have in mind, Muybridge?" He took a drink of his coffee. From his expression, it was tepid. "A restorative walking tour in the Lake Country, is it, Muybridge? A chance to clear your cluttered mind by taking in some of England's natural wonders? Would that put your mind to rest?"

Muybridge hated being mocked. He reached across the table and grabbed Lord Anthelm by the wrist. "What would put my mind at rest is to learn who you want killed and how you want it done."

The Lord's face turned purple with pain. Through gritted teeth, he said, "Release me, you fool. Think of where you are. And remember too that you wouldn't know these things had I been less forthcoming. Another man in my position gives your kind a name and a place, and then hands you a pack of notes as if slipping a fee beneath the pillow of a whore. I have been forthcoming, Muybridge, you have to admit that much. Most men in my position would not have dared meet with you this evening at all. The least I have a right to expect from you at this point is civil conduct in public."

The steward who had greeted them as they entered the dining room upon their arrival appeared at their table. "Is everything to your satisfaction, Lord Anthelm?" he asked. Lord Anthelm looked at Muybridge. Muybridge released him.

"Very well, thank you. The melon was delicious. Top-hole that melon this evening."

Lord Anthelm seemed shaken by the way he'd been manhandled. Poor bastard looked to be on the very apoplexy there for a minute, thought Muybridge, trying to stifle a smile. He'd have to be more careful next time, Muybridge reminded himself. He'd meant to jar the man a little, not send him to his grave. Lord Anthelm was rubbing his wrist like someone who'd felt their capillaries swell at the onset of a stroke.

"I'm very pleased to hear that, Lord Anthelm," said the steward. He went back to his duties.

Lord Anthelm said, "I'm simply trying to clarify my position."

"You've made yourself clear enough. I want time to think this over, Lord Anthelm. I want to be certain of what I'm getting myself into."

"What can I do to improve our relationship? How can I sweeten the offer?"

"At least give me time to think it over. Several days."

"I can't do that. Events are already underway. Things have to go forward." He finished his coffee.

Lord Anthelm adopted an avuncular tone, a Dutch uncle offering a lesson. He said, "If we continue this discussion this evening, we will soon be at loggerheads, the worst possible point to reach, can't you see?"

Muybridge began straightening his necktie, preparing to leave.

Lord Anthelm continued, "Don't do anything you'll live to regret. Sleep on it. Wipe the slate clean. Both of us. We'll be in contact again tomorrow. I can give you a few hours. A few days? That's out of the question."

Why would you want to set me up to be killed, Muybridge wondered. What could that gain you? Who am I to you after all?

Lord Anthelm continued, "You'll give this more thought then? If we don't speak before tomorrow night? Here again? You owe me that. You owe me that much and more."

"The same drill?" said Muybridge, pushing himself away from the table.

"We can eliminate the taxis if you like. I know that gets on your nerves."

He was simply too old for this now, Lord Anthelm. He'd passed the point of effectiveness. A reversal of fortunes. The first sign of a man who suffers a reversal of fortunes is the inability to know when it's time to get out. Muybridge was not looking forward to the aging process himself. He was reaching the stage of life where he needed to be taking better care of his body.

Lord Anthelm continued, "Indulge me, my boy. A man of my years has so few pleasures left. What's a little inconvenience?" Lord Anthelm rose. Taking him by the elbow, Lord Anthelm said, "The port-cochere, old boy. That's where you're to meet your taxi. That's where you went wrong the last time, you see."

The door at the end of the hall opened onto a service lane. At the end of the lane, to his left, Muybridge could see a blue canvas port-cochere beyond which his taxi would soon await him. Lord Anthelm said something to the effect that the rain had finally stopped, thank goodness, dreadful business all these windy storms, which reminded Muybridge that he had forgotten his trenchcoat and rain hat. "Isn't that always the way," said Lord Anthelm. "I've done the same thing myself here, I don't know how many times. Never you worry, dear boy. You go ahead. I'll get your things. It's the least I can do."

He was relieved to be outside. Alone. He'd recently given up cigarettes and he longed for one at the moment. He thought of dragging the smoke into the lining of his lungs with devastating force. The very thought of it was salivary. Lord Anthelm seemed to deflate before his eyes, he thought, pleading his case in that desperate, teary tone. He was afraid the old fool was about to kiss him on both cheeks. Had he heard correctly? An offer to ring him up in the morning? Lord Anthelm was slipping. It was an amusing image. Palms moist, listening for a call that, of course, wasn't coming. Well let him sit there and tremble in exasperation. A dash of humility might do him some good. Give him a taste of what the rest of us go through. The poor bastard was over the hill, wasn't he. The rain had ceased. He took a deep breath. The air was nippy, even bracing, one might say. The dining room, he now realized, had been unbearably stuffy. In fact, that's the last thought he had, those very words, unbearably stuffy.

For before he realized what was happening, Lord Anthelm had come upon him from the rear. He'd slit his throat from ear to ear with a pearl handled razor, an Edwardian affair said to have belonged to the Duke of Windsor, a gift from the late Wallis Simpson, the American divorcée.

The Lone Rider

By Dave P Fisher

Cordel Benedict threw his head back and laughed out loud. Here it was 1910, a whole new century, and rustling cattle was easier now than it had ever been. All he ever heard was how things had changed, the law was more advanced, and there were too many people in the West now to get away with such things anymore. It was a load of bull, talk from men who couldn't make off with a little kid's pet goat, let alone a herd of cattle. He was the best then, he was the best now.

He looked over the backs of the thirty head of good fattened Double Bar D cows and steers and added up the cash they'd bring. He had a buyer who paid cash on the barrelhead, no questions asked as to trivial matters like what brand the animal wore or if he had legal ownership to sell it. This was made all the sweeter by the fact that the Double Bar D had fired him when he was younger. The owner, Vic Ramsey, claimed he was shiftless and lazy. He did feel a bit of gratitude toward Ramsey, though.

After all, it was that firing that inspired him to go into business for himself and it had proven to be a financially good choice. Since then he made sure he included Ramsey in his business by picking off his cattle every chance he got. The thought made him laugh again.

He remembered coming into the Wyoming Territory when he was a young man, two horse lengths ahead of the Missouri law. He wasn't an outlaw then, but he had killed a man who had a brother who was tied into the town owned by the Greene family. Like Judge Greene, Sheriff Greene, horse manure shoveler Greene, the usual backwoods story of inbred yokels. The firing, along with seeing all those cattle grazing by the hundreds in huge expanses of hills and prairie with nary a body to be seen, and, well, he just saw the potential and went with it.

A lot of other men, not as skilled as he was, started jumping into the business and making some stupid moves. They were getting caught and making life hard for men like him and those who knew what they were doing. After a few years things were getting pretty hot for those in his profession. The ranchers were getting sore about the disappearing cattle and kept a closer eye on things.

There had been a lull in his business for a spell when the ranchers formed up vigilante groups and went to hunting down anyone who even appeared to be a cattle thief. They managed to stretch a few necks along the Laramie, but his wasn't one of them. He was laying low down in Brown's Hole.

Then came in that damn manhunter Brant Steele. He was scarier than all the ranchers put together; you never knew where that man would turn up. Steele got a shot off at him one day down in the Hole, and that's when Colorado started looking a whole lot better than Wyoming. He jumped over the border and kept riding. That was ten years ago.

Since then the law had shut down the vigilantes, the power of the big ranchers was broken, and it was with a cheer that he read about Steele being hung in Cheyenne. Denver had proven to be a good place to hide out and he had lived well but the thought of returning to his old profession, now that it was safe to do so, was too appealing. He decided to pack up and return to the Laramie country.

His friends in Denver had told him he was crazy, they were the ones sporting the new century ideas and rustling cattle was a thing of the past. The law was everywhere now and the chances of getting caught and hung were better than ever, but these were city boys who had never ridden the range in their lives, they had no idea how easy it was. Larry and Frank, two other former Wyoming rustlers, saw what he did and decided to join up with him. They had been back in Wyoming for two weeks now and he had been right, pickins were easy.

The four strands of barbed wire were pulled back against the posts, cut dead center. The cut wire had been wrapped off on the stretched strands to get them out of the way. Cattle and elk sometimes broke the wire, but to his knowledge they didn't carry wire cutters and neatly clip dead center between the posts and then wrap it back. It had been years since he had seen this and the cattle tracks mixed with those of shod horses going through the opening spelled one thing, and that was rustlers.

The seventy-five year old eyes of Vic Ramsey studied the churned-up sod and searched the country ahead of him. He glanced up at the sun. A couple hours of daylight remained, he could track until dark and then he'd have to give up. It had been at least a day since the cattle were moved out and chances were good he'd never find them, not with the lead they had on him. That didn't mean he wasn't going to try though.

The times were changing fast and in some ways he welcomed the changes, but in more ways he hated them. There was a time when a man handled his own problems, with a Winchester if need be, but now he had the law warning him not to try such things again. It was as if the politicians making the laws wanted to give the outlaws the upper hand. A man could get in more trouble for shooting, or even stopping a cattle thief, than the thief would get into.

He wished for the old days when he could just hunt these men down and let a bullet put a quick and simple end to the problem. Now, he was supposed to notify the sheriff, who would eventually drag his lazy butt out of his office, take a look around and state the obvious, "Looks like cattle thieves alright." Then he'd make some other equally idiotic comment like, "Well, we'll never catch them now." Not sitting on your butt in your office you won't, but I could have them in my rifle sights in no time at all. He spat angrily on the ground. He hated it.

He had been full into the war with the rustlers, riding with the vigilantes until they hung an innocent man one night; after that he left the group and tried to forget what they had done. Hell, maybe there was something to letting the law do it, but they weren't getting the job done. He wasn't talking about a gang going rustler hunting, just him by himself, one man using his head instead of a mob mentality.

He had started the Double Bar D fifty years ago; a lot of hard work had gone into building it into a productive ranch. He buried his wife and a son in the ground of this land, and it was where he intended to be buried one day as well. His last son and grandsons were on it now and he wasn't about to let some rustlers from out of the past take what he was passing down to them. Law or no law, they needed to be stopped.

In spite of his anger, he smiled at the feeling of excitement that was welling up inside him. This was like the good old days before modern society changed the rules. It was all a part of his history, a time that would never be repeated, and he found himself welcoming the challenge in the face of a rapidly deteriorating way of life.

His thoughts were interrupted by the sounds of horses coming up behind him. Turning, he watched as his two grandsons rode in beside him. "Been trying to find you Grandpa, Pa wanted us to stick with you today and lend whatever hand you needed."

Vic grinned to himself, his son was the best foreman he had ever had on the place, but he worried about his old man too much. He had a tendency to assign the boys to jobs that kept them close to him or he found a way to be helping him, whether he needed help or not. He liked having the boys around, but there was his pride to be kept up, and he couldn't appear weak to them or needing help.

"Boys, your pa worries too dang much. This old man has managed to survive this long without a wet nurse; I guess I can make it another day without him frettin' like an old spinster. But as long as you're here, come and read the sign on this story to me. What do you boys see?"

Mike Ramsey was sixteen, his brother Rafe fourteen. Mike looked around. "Looks like the fence got broke down and some cows got out."

Vic frowned. "Look at that wire, boy. You ever see wire broke down like that? All tied back neat as a picture?"

"No sir, looks pretty neat for getting torn down."

Rafe ventured a question, "Grandpa, if it was broke down wouldn't the posts be pushed down too?" He looked a second longer and then almost jumped out of his saddle. "Hey, it's been cut!"

A smile replaced the old man's frown. "Good eye, Rafe. Now, tell me why."

A light of revelation lit in Mike Ramsey's eyes. "Rustlers! Rustlers cut the wire. Wow, we've got rustlers!"

Rafe instantly became excited. "Are we gonna track 'em down Grandpa and hang 'em? Just like the stories you told us about fighting the rustlers in the old days? We gonna maybe shoot 'em?"

Vic held up a hand. "Pull back on them reins a bit boy, calm down. The law doesn't let us go around hanging people any-more and it wasn't a good thing when we could. We can't shoot anyone either, unless they shoot at us first. But yes, we are going to track them varmints down. Now, quick-like, patch up that fence and let's get on with it."

Vic Ramsey was lean as a corral rail and tougher than barbed wire. He wore a six-gun buckled around his waist, and had a Winchester in the saddle boot as he had done for the last half a century. He was a picture of the past. Some considered him an outdated relic, others an icon, but regardless he was a man who knew how this game was played, and few others did.

He was determined to catch the thieves, but he wondered what he was allowed to do with them when he got to that point. He knew what needed to be done here, but it was the new legal boundaries that had him confused. The politicians and newspapers were calling this the *New West* and the old ways had to go for they were too crude and barbaric. He scowled at the thought; obviously these city bred *New Westerners* had never seen the cold look in an outlaw's eyes just before he shot a man for no good reason. In conclusion, he decided that if they made a fight of it, he'd gun them down and let the chips fall where they may, let the *New West* be damned.

Poking a stick in the fire, Cordel Benedict watched as the sparks and bits of flame shot up into the air and disappeared into the night. It was a simple thing, but something he had missed while living in the city. He leaned back on his saddle and stared into the fire. He could smell the cattle and hear the sounds of the night; it was good to be back in "the wilds", as the city people in Denver called it. He once heard a German refer to the wide open country as the *hinterlands*, whatever that was. All he knew was that it was good to be back.

He appreciated the fact that Jerry and Frank weren't talkers; one thing he hated was someone who just ran his mouth. He always figured that a man said what was important in the first minute and the rest was just so much steer manure. Men like them were solitary for the most part and talking wasn't something they wanted or needed. They outlawed together and that was all; this wasn't a friendship.

He was satisfied with himself that he was once again making off with Vic Ramsey's cattle. Ramsey probably hadn't had a cow taken since he left, he could imagine the old rancher's surprise when he found the fence cut and cattle gone. He wished he could have left a calling card telling the old coot that he was back, maybe draw a face on the card with a big grin on it. He laughed to himself at the thought, but why go and put a rope around his own neck? It was enough to be giving Ramsey a difficult time.

Suddenly something shook him deep in his thoughts, stirring him out of his amused fantasies, a feeling more than anything his physical senses picked up. Then, with a startled jump, he realized that a man was standing across the fire from him. The other two men jumped up pulling their guns at the same time. Startled and breathing heavy, the men stared dumbly at the man who kept his face down and paid them no mind.

The man wore a trail-beaten canvas slicker that had seen better days; his weathered hat was pulled down over his eyes. The firelight reflected off the front of him, but revealed nothing of his face. Without a word he bent his knees and hunkered down toward the fire, picked up a tin cup, and poured it full from the coffee pot. He stayed in this position silently drinking from the cup.

Regaining his voice Benedict demanded, "Where in the hell did you come from?"

The man never attempted to answer; his only movement was the bending of his elbow as he drank.

"What are you, some kind of greenhorn? You can get killed just waltzing into a man's camp like that. We might just shoot you anyway if you don't tell us who you are."

The man held the tin cup in front of his face and studied it, his eyes hidden in the black under his hat brim. "What are you doing back here, Benedict?"

Benedict's mouth dropped open as he fumbled for words. "You know who I am?"

"You bet. I missed you the last time."

The outlaw's eyes cast back and forth wildly as he tried to figure out what this stranger was talking about. The character made him uneasy and for the first time in his life he was scared. Sweat began to trickle down the back of his neck despite the cool night. Something about this whole thing wasn't right.

He glanced over to Jerry and Frank who stood in the same positions they had jumped up into. They held their guns in their hands staring at the hunkered slicker-clad figure, too surprised to shoot. A spark of memory began to ignite in Benedict's mind about the last time he was shot at and missed, but he cast it out as impossible.

Tossing the grinds from the cup into the fire, the stranger stood up. "That was lousy coffee, but that's to be expected from an outlaw. Well, time to get on with business."

With his mind swirling Benedict asked stupidly, "What business do I have with you?"

"No, Benedict, you don't have business with me. I have business with you."

As the man stood to his full height of over six feet he brought a Winchester out from under his slicker. The rifle held Benedict's attention, he wondered at the funny things a man notices when he's confused. The rifle was one of those new 30.30's Winchester had come out with in 1894, but this one had seen some rough use. Most men preferred the .44 or 44.40 Winchesters. He only knew one man who ever carried the '94.

"I've come for you, all three of you." At that the man deliberately lifted his head so the firelight could reflect on his face and give the men a clear view of who he was.

Cordel Benedict stood up slowly as his face twisted in fear. He screamed out, "No, it's impossible." He staggered backwards and fell over his saddle. His panicked scream was cut short by the Winchester's report.

The three Ramseys jerked their heads up and stared at each other over the fire. "Did you hear that, Grandpa?" Mike attempted to peer through the darkness. "Three shots, one right on top of the other."

Standing up, Vic craned his ears into the night. No more shots, just the three, each spaced about the amount of time it took to lever in a new cartridge, and then nothing. He whispered to the boys, "I don't think anyone's hunting, not this time of night. Pretty odd, if you ask me."

Rafe scooted in closer to the fire, "Pretty spooky you mean, Grandpa. Who else is out here besides us?"

Mike answered, "Just them rustlers."

Vic continued to stare into the night as if willing the answer to come in on the breeze. "I doubt it was them, they got to figure on being tracked, I don't see why they'd be giving themselves away like that."

The crickets picked back up, a small night creature scurried through the grass, and off aways a coyote yipped, and then another. Vic settled back down at the fire and refilled his coffee cup. He shook his head and whispered, "Pretty odd, boys, pretty odd."

An hour passed as the three sat in silence, the boys had learned from their grandfather not to be talking unless they had something worthwhile to say. It was the way it had been in the old days and the boys wanted to be like their grandfather. Rafe was the first to notice that the crickets had stopped and he commented on it. On the heel of his words they heard hoof falls coming toward them, but still outside the fire's glow.

Vic slipped the Colt from its holster and stepped back into the darkness. "You boys stay right where you're at." The boys came to full attention and wondered what was happening. Then a voice cut through the darkness. "Hello the camp. Can a man come in?"

Mike looked around and couldn't see his grandfather. He wondered what Vic Ramsey would say at a time like this. He shouted out, "Sure, if you're friendly." He suddenly felt like he had stepped back to his grandfather's time.

The boys watched as a tall man in a dirty canvas slicker stepped into the firelight. His hat was pulled down over his eyes and he carried a Winchester rifle in his right hand, the firelight reflecting off its worn stock and forearm. He looked them over and then hunkered down by the fire.

"Mind if I have a cup?"

Mike nodded. "Sure, help yourself."

The man hunkered down next to the fire with the rifle lying across the top of his thighs. He lifted the battered coffee pot from the edge of the fire and poured the steaming brown liquid into a nearby cup. Lifting the cup he sipped at it and then gestured with his head toward the direction Vic had disappeared. "You can come on in, I ain't hunting trouble."

Moving back into the fire's glow, Vic held the .45 down by the side of his leg and studied the man. The man tipped his hat back and looked up. "Evenin' Vic, how's the cattle biz these days? Been a fair bit of rain, grazing should be good."

The boys looked up at their grandfather and wondered what was wrong with his face. He looked like a man who had just been kicked in the stomach and his face had turned a whitish gray color. He looked sick. He just stood there like a fencepost staring at the man.

"Sorry to hear about your missus, you folks were always good to me. Not like some of the others who threw me to the wolves."

Vic continued to stare at the man who took another sip from the cup and then set it on the ground. Brushing back the front of his slicker he reached into his shirt pocket and pulled out a sack of Bull Durham. Still hunkered down, he creased a paper, sifted tobacco along its length, and then expertly rolled the cigarette. Picking a burning stick out of the fire, he lit the twisted end of the paper and drew in a breath. Dropping the stick back into the fire he exhaled a long stream of smoke.

"Cordel Benedict took your cattle."

Moving forward Vic sat back down across the fire from the man. "Benedict? He hasn't been around for ten years. You see him?"

Taking another drag on the quirley, the man sucked the smoke into his lungs and then blew it back out. "There's some things I just know."

"Benedict used to work for me; the man was worthless, lazy as the day is long. I fired him." Vic thought for a few seconds. "He must be fifty years old by now."

The man nodded. "Something like that."

Silence fell between the two men as the fire crackled emphasizing the heaviness of the quiet. Finally Vic broke the stalemate. "Where'd you come in from? You look done in."

"Someplace you'll never know Vic and be glad for it. You can say I never stop riding anymore."

Vic's eyes were transfixed on the hunkered figure across the fire from him while the two boys watched silently. As one they moved their heads to the right and left, following the conversation between the two men. It was plain to both of them that their grandfather was not looking well. There was something going on here they didn't understand except that it had to do with what the two men knew from the years gone by.

Then Rafe's fourteen year old mind could no longer stand not being part of the conversation and spoke up, "We're hunting them rustlers that stole our cattle. When we catch 'em we're gonna shoot 'em all, just like in Grandpa's day."

Without moving the man spoke, "You know son, killing men over cows ain't a good thing. That sort of thing catches up to a man and what comes after is pretty bad."

The few words hit the boy hard, the stranger was spooky, and it was as if he spoke from someplace other than where they now sat. Rafe fell back to silence.

The man set the cup back on the ground, "Pretty good coffee Vic, not like that slop Benedict washed his socks in. Guess I've stayed long as I can; I need to be moving on. Just wanted to share one more fire with you Vic and let you know you'll find your cattle bunched down by Wolf Springs."

Vic stood up to face him. "We heard some shots coming from that way earlier."

"Wouldn't know anything about that. You go on down and get your cows."

Just as easy as he came the man disappeared. Vic stood staring into the night obviously shaken by the man's visit. Rafe looked at the way his grandfather was staring. "Grandpa, did you notice that we heard his horse coming in, but we never heard it walk out?" He looked up at the old man. "You okay, Grandpa?"

Vic nodded his head. "Yeah, I'm just tired boys. Let's turn in."

Vic kicked dirt over the fire as the boys lay down. Pulling his blanket around his shoulders, Rafe watched his grandfather slowly lie down and pull a blanket over him. The last glow of the fire held the boy's eyes, but his mind was thinking back over their visitor. In a low voice he asked, "Grandpa, that man knew you and Grandma. Did you know him?"

Vic didn't speak right away and then he gave the boy an answer. "Yes son, I knew him. Now go to sleep."

The sun was breaking when the three reached Wolf Springs. The lowing of cattle drew them on in the right direction. As they reached the cattle, they noticed three horses grazing among them. A short distance away was a burned out campfire, three tin cups, and a coffee pot laying on its side with the spilled contents staining the ground under it. Around the charred wood were three saddles and the tack for each. It was clear that three men had camped here, no doubt the rustlers, but there was no sign of them anywhere.

Mike pointed at the ground a few feet from the ash. "Look, three rifle casings, right there by the fire. It *was* them who shot last night."

A visible shiver ran the length of Vic Ramsey's back. "Them, or someone else."

Rafe slid off his horse and looked down at the empty brass casings. Picking them up he looked at the bottoms of the brass. "Grandpa, these are 30.30 shells, you know anyone shoots a 30.30?"

Shifting uneasily in his saddle Mike looked around. "Grandpa, it's like the men just disappeared, like the ground swallowed them up."

"Maybe it did."

"What do you mean by that Grandpa?"

Vic took a deep breath. "You asked if I knew that man last night. Well, I do or did, but it was some time back. At times he stopped at our place and had supper with the crew; your pa'll remember him too. When the law broke up the vigilantes some of the ranchers got together and hired a man who was a professional manhunter. His specialty was killing rustlers that the ranchers couldn't touch because the law was making it too easy for these outlaws to get away with their crimes. We never really knew who was in on hiring him. I wasn't, and no one would own up to it, so we never knew, but we had our suspicions. The man they hired was Brant Steele."

Rafe broke in, "Everyone knows about him, Grandpa."

Vic nodded. "I'm sure you do. He wasn't a bad sort; he was friendly with the ranchers, but death on outlaws. He used to stop by our place when he passed through, so I got to know him pretty well. You couldn't miss him; he was over six feet tall. Finally, the law started asking a lot of questions about dead men out on the prairie. One thing led to another and Steele was arrested."

"And then he was hung," Rafe added.

"That's right, he was hung and no one ever owned up to hiring him so it was all just swept under the rug and forgotten. Forgotten until last night."

Both boys stared at him. "What happened last night, Grandpa?"

"I know this might sound like an old man who's lost his mind, but that man last night was Brant Steele."

The boys looked shocked. Mike spoke as if to calm his grandfather, "Brant Steele is dead, Grandpa."

"Yes, he is or was, but he was alive last night, and I don't understand it a bit."

Mike spoke slowly, "Do you think he took those rustlers with him to Hell or some other place?"

Rafe broke in, "Remember what he said last night, about killing men for cows? That afterwards it can be pretty bad? Maybe it was him, but a ghost. Maybe he goes out at night and kills rustlers like he used to when he was alive. Maybe he does live in Hell."

The three returned to silence listening to the wind blow and the low sounds of the cattle cropping grass. Vic glanced down at the brass in Rafe's hand; Steele was the only man he knew to carry the new 30.30. It was all adding up, even if it didn't make any sense. He had seen a lot of strange things in his life, why not ghosts, why not a manhunter who rides up out of Hell to continue the hunt?

Vic forced a grin. "My eyes ain't what they used to be boys, I'm probably wrong, it was just some drifter who looked like him. Well, these cows ain't getting home by themselves, so let's get to moving 'em."

As they gathered the cattle and began to push them toward home a movement off to Vic's left caught his eye. He looked and briefly saw a man on horseback who waved to him and then disappeared. He no longer doubted. He knew that rider. It was Brant Steele.

Stirrings in Hell

By Davin Kimble

Part 1: The Summons

"The summons to court has come much sooner than expected. This is troublesome."

"Why my Lord, I don't see that there is any reason to fear . . .?"

Asmodeus turned on his aid with a fury born on the winds of Hell. "There is much to fear! It has been five centuries since the liege lords were summoned to court. The crown princes take notice of what we do and I fear we have been lax. I tell you now, this summons bodes ill for all of Hell."

"Yes, my Lord, as you say."

Asmodeus turned from his quaking aid and again surveyed the royal papers. The seals were all there, four glowing sigils, embossed with magic, on a parchment made from the skin off the back of a living male. Asmodeus was certain that the poor soul who provided the scrap of flesh suffered still somewhere in the darkness.

Hell, Asmodeus knew all too well, was not a place reserved for those who had passed on into the spirit world. Satan's Mailed Fist, Lucifer's Black Flame, Belial's Obsidian Pillar, and from Leviathan, the Mark of the Tempest; all glowing still with the mark of evil upon them. It would not do to delay, better to be there first and early, than to straggle in late. Lords could be replaced; in Hell the first thing one learned was that everyone was expendable. Even the name he carried was little more than a title that could be stripped and given to another more worthy. Asmodeus had held his title, and his immortality, for more than a thousand years and he had no intention of giving either up any time soon.

"Summon my transport," Asmodeus said to his waiting aid, "we leave within the hour."

"Yes, my Lord."

Asmodeus traveled with only his aid and a small contingent of demons. The roads through Hell were generally uninhabited; the denizens of Hell were mostly occupied with torture and destruction in the pits and in the darkness. Asmodeus found little need for shows of power and wealth. He'd not held his position through force, but rather through intrigue and knowledge. They traveled a narrow mountain road down from his palace and then across a small barren plain. From the floor of it Asmodeus could see the distant cathedral where the masters of this place held court. It shimmered in the distance, a great building made of stone and blood and bone. He traveled in silence, the monotony broken by the occasional demonic grunt and the whisper of wind across the valley floor.

He arrived at the gates leading to the interior courtyard. They opened at his approach, and he and his retinue continued on. The cathedral sat on the edge of the plain in the foothills of another, smaller mountain. The building was in itself a massive structure spanning at least a square mile of the foothills and rising into the darkened sky. Its peaks and towers rose before him as he climbed and he could feel the power of its rulers even from here. Slowly he climbed until he reached the massive steel doors that marked the entrance. Leaving his transport behind, Asmodeus walked alone into the building.

He climbed into the antechamber of the throne room and found a window overlooking the road. Asmodeus had arrived at the great cathedral in time to watch his siblings' appearances. Each came with a full entourage that Asmodeus knew would be turned away, and bearing gifts that Asmodeus knew would be refused. He had time to study each of them, for there were no refreshments served, and no comforts offered.

First, Behemoth came, fat and slovenly, riding upon a dais carried by twenty-three human slaves. He ate, gorging himself on flesh and bone, and tossed the scraps away to the hungry dire hounds that shadowed his great bulk. Despite his girth, the lord demon alighted from his carrier as if he were a mere slip. The rumbling of the ground beneath his feet spoke of the true weight he carried into the main doors.

Before Behemoth could move his great bulk up the many flights of stairs, Lilith appeared. Consort to Satan, and mother to the legions, she was accorded great respect. She came at the head of a column of succubi also twenty and three in number, the Sisters of Sorrow, Lilith's personal assassins. All wore skin-tight leathers, black save for the red hour glass beneath their heavy breasts. Asmodeus had a special accord with Lilith and her sisters and often visited them in their realm of pleasure and pain. In truth, he was in love with her. They'd been lovers once, millennia ago, and he missed her touch, her taste. He calmly turned to watch Behemoth squeeze his flesh through the door as a cry went up in the courtyard that made the fat demon cringe. Asmodeus smiled at his brother's discomfort.

"You consort with those harpies, don't you, Asmodeus?" he asked.

Asmodeus could smell the rotting meat on the demon's breath from across the room and he turned back to the window to spare himself the sight of him, and the smell. "I do," he replied, "and you would do well to remember that, Fat One. They call for your blood I would think."

Behemoth snorted in disgust and settled in to gnaw on a bone, crunching through it and sucking loudly on the marrow inside. Outside, Asmodeus could see the sisters standing silently facing Behemoth's weary slaves and he thought briefly of telling the fat bastard that he may soon be in danger of walking home. Then, of one accord, the sisters turned and left. Seconds later Lilith passed through the doorway.

"Lover," she said as she approached Asmodeus, completely ignoring Behemoth who took no notice of her anyway. "It has been long since we have had your company in the House of Pleasure."

Asmodeus embraced her deeply, falling as much into her voice as her bosom. She was a beauty the likes of which most would never get to see; her body shapely and firm. "It is regrettable, yes, and I promise I will come see you soon."

"You had better, or I may send someone to come see you."

Asmodeus smiled and turned back to the window. He did so as much to show her he had no fear of her silken threats, as to see who next approached. He was in time to see the sisters come face to face with the Legions of Doom. Satan's personal foot solders, these were led by the dread Lord Abaddon. Armed and girded for battle always, they were a large and menacing sight even when only twenty-three in number. Asmodeus watched as Abaddon passed words with one of the Sisters of Sorrow and for a long moment thought there would be bloodshed. Abaddon reveled in bloodshed of any sort and sought out excuses to kill. The scent of lavender drifted over Asmodeus' shoulder and the sisters parted, though reluctantly, to allow the Legions to pass.

"You are bad, Asmodeus," Lilith scolded him, leaning over his shoulder looking out of the window with him. "Would you allow those who have offered you such a taste of ecstasy be slaughtered before your very eyes?"

"I would."

"As ever my favorite, you would allow the competition to weaken each other."

"I have no competition, my love." Her laugh was a sweet tinkle in his ears.

From below he heard the order to halt and the clash of armor and arms coming to an instantaneous stop. For all their militancy and crassness, Asmodeus had to admit that his brother's forces posed an imposing sight. Abaddon himself was the largest of an already large group of demons and fallen souls, tall and straight as the great sword he carried strapped to his back, and just as sharp and deadly. He removed his helm, exposing features scarred from many battles. Though he had the power to cause them to vanish, he wore these scars as badges of honor, and no doubt reminders to any ambitious underlings of why he was the dread lord. He saluted smartly and turned on his heel to enter the cathedral. His twenty-three turned as one and returned as they came.

"Abaddon comes," he said into the air and was rewarded with a sharp intake of foul breath from Behemoth, who immediately started choking on the food in his mouth. Asmodeus and Lilith both laughed at this.

"Careful, pig, don't choke to death before he has the chance to put that sword of his into your guts."

"Never fear, great beast," Lilith said through chuckles, "he won't kill you here."

"I hate him." Behemoth breathed his rot again into the air.

"Best to keep that rotting maw closed in his presence, Fat One, his hatred for you runs just as deep," Lilith replied.

"And the blade he carries is much sharper than that bone," Asmodeus added.

Again the two laughed, but Asmodeus was intent on the road below. Baphomet had not yet arrived and there was no sign of his coming. Would the self-styled "God of Black Magic" dare refuse a court summons? Asmodeus did not know, and this troubled him. He knew every detail of everything his siblings did and this was his greatest strength. This was why he was given guardianship over the gates between the lords'srealms and the princes'. His observations today were merely to confirm what he already knew of his fellow lords. For beings of such longevity, they were predictable and unchanging. He expected Baphomet to be last, the goat-headed mage coming with an entourage of twenty-three archwizards, hooded and crackling with magic. For long moments there was no sign of the Goat and Asmodeus watched the road, tense breath held deep within his lungs.

The thrice ring of the gong was so unexpected, Asmodeus let out a little yelp. He turned to see Abaddon just striding into the antechamber behind him. That meant they all were here. As the great doors opened and they were allowed into the throne room, Asmodeus felt for the first time something he'd not felt in ages . . . fear. There across the threshold, leering grin on his goat lips, stood Baphomet.

This summons boded ill indeed.

The five lords, for all their power and brash boastfulness amongst one another knew well their places in Hell's hierarchy. As one, they lowered themselves to one knee just inside the threshold as the massive stone doors closed behind them. The reverberations echoed through the chamber for a moment and Lucifer, resplendent on his throne, raised one hand. They fell silent immediately, obedient as they all were. That graceful, long-fingered hand descended, palm up towards the five lords.

"Please, my children, rise and come before us," Lucifer said beckoning them forward with one black talon, "you are all welcome here."

Asmodeus knew this was a formality. He had no illusions that any of them was actually welcome within the realms of the crown princes. But then Baphomet had been here before them all and had been granted a private audience. That was unheard of.

He rose with the rest and approached the large dais which held four huge thrones.

The dais was a deep black trapezoid made of a stone that could only be found in Hell. It radiated a bone-chilling cold, so cold it even sapped the strength of devils. Upon its chill surface rested four thrones, each distinct to its owner, that reached high towards the arched ceiling.

To the far left, Satan rested on a throne made of the bones of men, stained a dark red with living blood. It moaned in torment and Asmodeus had no doubt that the souls of the people there had never been released from their bones. The throne bled because it lived. Satan himself was a tall, well-muscled devil with powerful, cruel features. His eyes bore into the soul with an unforgiving glare that spoke only of wrath. Close at hand was a three-pronged trident, its sharp tines wreathed in flame.

Next to him sat Lucifer upon a throne seemingly formed of a dark light. It cast a heavy glow that put its occupant into a shadow that caused the Light Bringer to glow as if haloed. He was beautiful and regal upon his throne, and Asmodeus knew that anyone who did not know better would mistake him for an Angel of Light. He wore white robes that seemed to reflect his own inner glow, and cradled upon his lap a great book. The book, it was said, was Hell's Bible and its knowledge would be released into the world when the world was ready to receive it.

To his left sat Belial upon a throne that was carved from a great rock. The devil's affinity for the earth was so deep; it caused him to never be far from it. Bare to the waist, he was a massive figure seemingly himself a part of the stone upon which he sat. His eyes were mere flickers of flame within the deep caverns beneath his brow, but even for their strangeness they spoke of a deep, unforgiving wisdom and knowledge of the world and its workings. He carried with him a long, thick whip; its end braded with obsidian.

Finally, at one end sat the great beast of the deep, Leviathan, upon a throne fashioned from living coral. Of them all, he was the most unlike any in appearance. Amphibian, but more at home in the seas than on land, he had two tentacles extending from his back in addition to his huge clawed hands. His feet were large and webbed at the end of powerful scaly legs. His draconian features were sharp and predatory, his eyes seeking out victims even as he sat amongst allies. He carried no items save a globe filled with constantly swirling water. Occasionally, he would peer into it as if seeking council.

The four studied the five, and the five studied the four, each taking the measure of the other. For the first time in five hundred years, the nine had come together in one room to discuss . . . what? This was the question gnawing at Asmodeus as he glanced again at the dark mage. What indeed?

"We have called you four here today to inform you of a decision that has already been made." As Lucifer's deep, melodic voice rang throughout the chamber, Asmodeus could only think that he'd said four, not five. He looked again to Baphomet and wondered how the beast mage had cloaked his actions. Asmodeus would have to slaughter his spies on Baphomet's realm. Unless . . .

"Be silent, Fat One, or be silenced!" Satan's roar brought Asmodeus's mind back to the matters at hand. "You grow complacent and comfortable," Satan continued. "Remember who it is you pledged your loyalty to! You can still be destroyed."

"Allow me," Abaddon said, reaching for his sword. Behemoth took two steps for the door before Lucifer's voice halted them all.

"Be still, my children, there will be plenty of time for bloodshed in the very near future." He paused allowing everyone time to regain his, or her, composure. Then he continued, "We have made a decision and we have called you here to inform you of this decision, so that you may make whatever preparations you deem necessary. We will hear your thoughts, but be wary for we will not be dissuaded."

Of the five only four looked around at each other then, worry apparent on each face. Lilith held her hands balled into tight fists and Asmodeus knew she concealed something sharp and poisoned there. Abaddon stood as tall as ever but his eyes were darting, calculating, and weighing each devil in the room carefully. Behemoth quaked, his considerable bulk moving like an earthquake, which was likely what he was planning to unleash in the room. Asmodeus looked to Baphomet then and saw no worry on his snout, simply pure pleasure at watching the others' discomfort.

"Your distress amuses me," Satan began, bringing them all back to attention, "but if a war between our own was what we wanted, we would not have it begin here."

"And if any of you were to be dismissed," Leviathan's hissing roar interrupted, "you would have found yourself in the pits, not in the Holy Cathedral."

"Cowards, lay about lackeys," Belial's voice grated and shook the room, "use your heads, focus or our plans will change yet again."

Baphomet laughed aloud at this, his mirth finally spilling over into words.

"Remember where you are brothers, this is Hell. We are brutal . . ."

"But we are no fools," Satan interrupted. "Listen well, for your future depends on what you do next. I am releasing the Kith into the world."

"And I am giving the world the Dragon Kin," Leviathan said.

"And I am opening the gates to the Deep Dwellers," Belial said.

"And I am giving them Hell's Bible." With that Lucifer rose from his throne and extended the book he carried to Baphomet. Astonishment was apparent in the gasps Asmodeus heard from his siblings. For his part he only stood and stared.

"Then this means we go to *war!*" Abaddon roared the last word with unrestrained glee.

"It could come to that, yes," Lucifer said.

"The Kith are . . . unpredictable, difficult to control," Asmodeus said. "Who will rule them?"

"Man," Satan said. With that word the room fell into an uneasy silence.

"Man," Abaddon finally repeated the word.

"You cannot be serious," Lilith said.

"Oh, but we are indeed," Leviathan said, hissing through his gill slits. "Your efforts on the world have been lax. Belief in Hell's might is waning and those that do follow us squabble like any other faith. We will bring them together under one banner."

"What of the Muslim?" Behemoth asked, still proud of his words to the desert nomad Mohammed.

"Madmen, fools!" Belial roared. "Their belief in the blood thirsty Allah has only created another force we have to deal with."

"One of your more shining failures," Baphomet said, glancing casually through the book he held. Asmodeus did not miss the ploy to draw attention to his part in this scheme. Neither did Lucifer.

"It is quite a disappointment, Behemoth," Lucifer began.

"But they crush the Zion horde at every turn around the world," the Fat One protested, "and . . ."

"And they do nothing to further our cause, they answer to Allah now, not to you." Satan rose from his throne, the flaring of his trident stood testament to his ire.

Lucifer raised his taloned hand and every devil turned to him. Satan regained his seat, but did not release his grip on his weapon, or the anger that fueled it.

"Man will be our vessel and we will begin with those who already take Satan's name."

With these words Satan's trident flared anew and his throne unleashed a mighty wailing. He was proud that his name bore the hallmark of Hell's might.

"They know well, Baphomet. This is why he was chosen to lead them, and with the wisdom of the book, the monsters and demons from the deep places of the world walking—"

"—or swimming," Leviathan interjected.

"Or swimming free," Lucifer said. "There will be no further doubt from the followers of darkness as to what is, and what is not real."

"This will bring a counterattack from the Light." Asmodeus said the obvious for he knew the others were too wrapped up in what could go wrong, plotting their escapes, while he'd already seen the benefits of this plan.

"Yes, and this is where you three come in," Lucifer continued. "You will have access to the world again."

Lilith laughed her glee at this. Asmodeus knew well the machinations of the Sisters of Sorrow and the suffering they could bring. He smiled at the thought; together they could bring great power to the followers of Hell. He looked to Satan for his approval and he found the Vengeful One smiling, his sharpened teeth gleaming in the raging fire of his trident. Asmodeus gave a subtle bow in obeisance. This would be glorious, no longer would the dire omens of Hell's might go unheeded. The world would know them once again. Abaddon's hounds would roam the land, Lilith's sisters would seduce the unwary, Baphomet's minions, with the support of the mighty Kith would unleash true magic, Behemoth's ghouls would raise the dead and heal the dying, and behind it all Asmodeus would pull the strings of intrigue. There would be war, of course, the Masters of Heaven would rise in righteous anger, but they had mishandled the world for far too long. It would be a war fought not in Heaven or Hell, it would be a war fought in the hearts and minds of men.

"I see you understand," Lucifer said. "You are dismissed."

Part 2: Intrigue

Asmodeus walked the streets of Gomorrah alone. His current mission required stealth and not a small amount of decorum if he were to actually accomplish it. Lilith wouldn't have him marching into and disrupting her city with an entourage. His retainer was nearby, Asmodeus knew, watching over his lord. The soul had been a man once. Asmodeus had plucked him from the tortures of Hell with one command, serve me. The man had served him well for centuries since.

Turning a corner onto a narrow street, Asmodeus ran into a gruesome scene not uncommon on these streets. Two minor devils had a poor soul pinned down on the dirty streets and they were raping her with a passion only the true evil could conjure. The woman, for her part, was handling the brutality as well as could be expected. Being long dead held advantages in Hell. There was little to be done to you that you hadn't already suffered a hundred thousand times before. Asmodeus never faltered in his step, simply continued down the street. Skirting the scene, he pulled his cloak and hood tighter around his body.

"Hey, boy," the demon at the woman's rear spoke to him as he passed. Asmodeus kept walking but the second demon, the one holding the woman's head down, grabbed him by the cloak, tearing the material.

"Did you hear, dog? This one spoke to you."

"I heard him." Asmodeus said stopping, turning to the two foolish demons.

"Well . . ." the first demon stood, his member huge and glistening as he slid from inside the woman. "Maybe I should finish my business with you?" The demon was a massive brute, and though Asmodeus was no small being, he most often took on a human form, preferring the ease of living in the body of a man to the power of living in the body of a Fallen. The creature towered over him, stinking of unwashed demon flesh and fresh womanly scent.

"I have no time for you little demon," Asmodeus rumbled low in his throat, "but as payment for stopping me on my way, I will give you a moment of my time."

The demon laughed and Asmodeus frowned, his eyes narrowing to slits in his already narrow face. In one motion he shed his cloak and the dampening spell that disguised his true power. Too late, the demon realized his mistake and started to turn to flee. Asmodeus reached out, his hand quick as a snake and already covered in an oily purple-black smoke. He grabbed the demon by one thick wrist and the being howled. At the sound, his partner and the woman turned to see. Asmodeus now swirled, barely visible in the cloud of power spreading over him. The demon he held tried to pull away, but it was too late. In one powerful motion, Asmodeus slammed him into the cobblestone street, breaking one horn and both tusks. The demon howled and tried to scramble away in pursuit of his partner and their victim, but Asmodeus' strength was mountainous. He crushed the demon's wrist in his hand and turned the arm, grinding bones, tearing massive muscle, and with one powerful yank, wrenched the demon's arm off. The creature howled anew and lurched to his feet, or he tried to, but Asmodeus was already on him.

"I am Lord Asmodeus of the Great Darkness, Keeper of the Seventh Gate, I am among the first who fell, the greatest warriors of Heaven and the greatest rulers in Hell!" The inky power flowed from him as he spoke, into and over his fallen foe. The demon tried to speak, or maybe scream, but when he opened his mouth the darkness flowed in, stifling him. "Your time is up, *dog*." The darkness filled and crushed the demon at the same time, rendering him a bloody pile of demon flesh and ichor. Asmodeus stood and for a moment his true form showed through the illusion. It was a beautiful creature, tall and stately, dark hair cascading over his powerful shoulders, and black feathered wings stretched across the street. Then the vision was gone and again there stood only a man wrapped in a blood-soaked cloak. He continued on his way.

Seeking out Lilith in Gomorrah wasn't a difficult task. Though she'd dragged the ruined city into Hell after the Holy One's mercenaries destroyed it, she still lived in her palace on the outskirts and rarely ventured into the city of sexual debauchery. It stood in ruins populated only by the damned and the unlucky. He wound his way through a few more streets and found himself breaking from the narrow city into a dead courtyard. Across from him stood a tall wall broken only by a pair of plain metal gates.

She knew he was here, of that he was certain. Yet the gates remained closed to him, which was unusual. He thought to call out to her, but no matter how he toned his voice, she would know he was furious at being kept waiting. After a few minutes standing in the courtyard staring at the closed gates, he turned to the city. His retainer came from the shadows, appearing almost as magically as any creature in this dark place.

"My Lord?"

"What have you seen of the city?"

"Little, my Lord. It is quiet. More so than usual, and I don't believe there is a single sister in its confines."

"Strange . . ." Asmodeus mused.

"Indeed my Lord. You wouldn't think . . ."

"Speak."

"You wouldn't think that she's already gone to the earth?"

"That very well could be."

"That would be a bad portent indeed, my Lord."

"This is Hell, fool." Asmodeus said as he strode back into the dark city streets. "Nothing good happens here."

His retainer stared back at the dark lady's palace before turning and following his master. A cold shiver touched his spine and didn't leave him.

She had never denied him entry before. Lilith stepped back from her seeing stone and turned to the two sisters who awaited her orders.

"He's right," she said to them, "we are going into the world and we will get there first. Have the sisters finished bribing the Goat?"

"He has a great many appetites," one sister replied.

"And they run deep," the other chimed in.

"Prepare the rite." Lilith shed her clothes and took up a dark shift as she spoke. "I will see to it that the beast is satisfied."

"Asmodeus would make a fine ally in the coming chaos, Lady," the first sister said, her eyes pinned to Lilith's exquisite shape.

"And he will still," Lilith snapped, "but we must make it into the world before those brutes and bastards get there. There can be no distractions." She strode from her chambers and down a long, gently curving hallway. The stone floors were well-worn under her bare, dainty feet. Her retainers followed at a close pace until Lilith made a left at an intersection. Without a word they continued on while Lilith went to seek out Baphomet. She hated him; she always had. He was a descendent of a much older deity, a true god, deep and unfathomable, the mother of a thousand young of which Baphomet was said to be the last. His magic flowed from that ancient womb still, his only goal being to bring his mother back into the world. He neither cared for nor catered to the machinations of Hell. Yet, he held Hell's Bible, her only way into the world. Reaching the end of the corridor she stopped before a plain wooden door. Taking a breath, she entered.

The sight before her was atrocious. Two of the three sisters she'd sent in to him were slaughtered, eviscerated and dismembered on the floor. The third dangled from the ceiling in a tangle of rope and chain. Her pain and the strain on her body were obvious as she struggled there. The Goat took no notice. He licked her flesh, his snout a bloody mess, and snorted with delight when she squirmed.

"What are you doing here, beast?" Lilith howled at the sight. "I gave you no leave to slaughter my sisters."

"Ah, Lilith," he said looking over his muscular shoulder at her, "have you come to please me yourself? Now that," he paused, turning from his victim, "would make me very happy indeed."

"Explain yourself, Baphomet!"

"I am only taking my fill," he said, moving towards her across the room. His torso was streaked with blood and gore, the breasts leaking milk, his deep black member erect and pulsing against his hard belly. His hooves clacked on the stone as he lurched forward.

"I will hold my end of the bargain, beautiful." He stopped before her. In spite of herself, his naked form intrigued her. She wanted to quiet him; she wanted to quell his passions and her own. More than that, she wanted him to open the fucking gate.

"Cut that one down. She is mine."

Baphomet waved one hairy clawed hand and the ropes vanished. The sister crashed to the hard stone and didn't move. Baphomet reached out and tore Lilith's shift from her body. He took one firm breast and one solid buttock in his hands and buried his muzzle in Lilith's neck. She giggled in spite of herself and took his penis into her hands.

"Yesss," Baphomet hissed, "you are indeed the greatest of all whores. You please me and you will have your way."

"Stand fast, dogs!" Abaddon bellowed at his troops. "Hold that line!"

The demon horde rushed forward, roaring their battle cries. The ragtag group of demons and lost souls arrayed before them broke and scattered. The last of Behemoth's forces, already weak and ill-trained, fell back before Abaddon's superior troops even though they outnumbered them three to one.

"Kill them all!" Abaddon rushed forward into the fray, his great sword swinging through one torso, a neck, and embedding itself in a tusked pig-like skull. Yanking his sword free, he turned in time to parry a weak blow from a lesser demon. His boot lashed out, the toe spikes catching the sad creature in the gut. The blow was powerful and as Abaddon pulled his foot back, it came with a rush of viscera. This was the last in a series of battles Abaddon had fought against Behemoth's slaves. The foolish fat brute thought to strike without warning in an attempt to assassinate Abaddon. Since the failed attempt, Abaddon had carried on a campaign of complete destruction. Now at the open gates of Behemoth's stronghold, his vengeance was almost complete.

"Destroy everything. The fucking fat beast is *mine!*"

Abaddon smiled as he watched his troops do what they did best. Soon they would be in the world and they would spread destruction there. It was said that there were billions of people on the world. Not nearly enough, Abaddon thought as he slid his sword into the frail chest of a lost soul. He believed that he would be more than capable of taking the entire place with only a handful of his best. Blood rained down from the skies. Hell rejoiced in the slaughter and showed her appreciation by weeping blood onto the battlefield. Abaddon stormed from the downpour and the cacophony of battle, and into the reeking darkness of Behemoth's lair. He met little resistance as he walked, the occasional brave demon or devil attacking him and falling in a brilliant display of violence. Corridor after corridor, door after door left splintered on its hinges, Abaddon searched the place for his enemy. Finally at the end of one wide hall lined with torches set into the upturned skulls of men, he found his quarry. The door to the chamber was stronger than the others, but it too came down under Abaddon's assaults.

Behemoth sat on his massive throne, a leg quarter of some sort held in one hand. Abaddon seethed. Only a few steps, one or two swings, and that great bulk would spill out onto the floor. "Behemoth, now you die!"

"He will do no such thing, warrior." The voice was soft, but the power of it was unmistakable. Abaddon stood in his tracks watching the great devil appear from behind a curtain. Satan approached, his leathery wings blocking out the sight of Abaddon's hated enemy. "I have allowed this to go on because I do admire your wrath. I honor you because of it and I ask you to lead my armies. But you will lead them under my rule and you will destroy only what I tell you to destroy."

"Attack dog on a leash," Behemoth said with a chuckle spewing fat and meat bits from his rotting maw.

"Silence," Satan hissed, "or I will unleash him upon you and find another to fill your shoes. Maybe that poor retainer you keep chained. Is it from fear that you bind him, Fat One? Fear, that given the chance, he would make you suffer for your inequities? You will suffer Behemoth. Remember that and my champion just may be the one to bring you your death.

"This battle is over," Satan said turning back to Abaddon. "Gather your forces, Abaddon. We march into the world."

Abaddon turned from his lord and stalked back through the stronghold and out into the courtyard. Once there he followed his orders.

"Regroup, we march on the earth!"

Part 3: Hell on Earth

Asmodeus stepped from the portal and onto an abandoned street. Well, mostly abandoned. He could feel the lesser demons and their thralls fleeing from his power. He hated that Lilith remained in the world; he hated visiting her here. When this whole thing began, he never would have thought that Hell on earth would be less tolerable than Hell in Hell. The place stunk of death and those who lived here, lived in complete savagery. He was sure that the only reason he hadn't been set upon was because he took little effort to mask himself.

Looking around, he realized it wasn't difficult to spot the building where Lilith now took up residence. It was a tall glass spire, one of the remaining relics of man's rule on earth. Aside from a few broken windows, it seemed to have survived Armageddon unscathed. The remainder of the city, however, was a heap of rubble and only partially intact structures. Lilith preferred to be surrounded by ruined cities. This one she'd left in the world, Gomorrah she'd dragged into Hell.

Asmodeus made his way to the front doors. They were huge, made of glass and steel, but in spite of their size, they swung open easily at his touch. Asmodeus was greeted in the lobby by a gaggle of human women in various states of undress. While most of the fallen that kept humans as pets kept them in a weakened and tortured state, Lilith kept her thralls fit. They swarmed him, offering themselves to him.

"Greetings, my Lord," one said, baring her breasts, "would you like me to take you upstairs?"

"I would," Asmodeus replied. "I wish to see your Mistress."

"I cannot take you so far." She backed away from him, pulling her clothing back up over her chest.

"Then show me to one who can," Asmodeus said to her. She gestured to him to follow her, and she led him down a long corridor and to a small steel door.

"It's a long way up, my Lord." She opened the door. "Seventy-five floors if I remember correctly."

"So you have been up there before?"

"No, never, but I was in this building a time or two," she paused and looked down at the floor trembling slightly, "you know . . . before."

"I see . . ." He reached out and brushed her cheek with his fingertips. She was soft and fragile. His passions didn't run as deeply as many of the other demons of Hell. He would leave her for his business with Lilith; she would find suffering enough without his hand being a part of the deal. He turned from her and climbed the stairs. Suffering. He knew there had to be an easier way to reach Lilith's suites but she reveled in the suffering of others. She forced him to climb these stairs as a way of asserting her dominance in this place. Asmodeus didn't mind it so much. It was a small annoyance and gave him time to think.

The last time he'd been in contact with Lilith had been just after the invasion of the world. She had been in the world for a few years before the hordes arrived and she'd created a massive stronghold on earth. She'd spread her particular brand of debauchery far and wide, and the humans only barely noticed. She'd become a small goddess on earth. Then she told him what her plans for the world were and he'd joined her cause. Instead of destroying and conquering the world, they sought to control and manipulate the humans living on it. It worked for a while and they'd lived in grand style. Then the hellions came and the world fell into a lasting darkness.

Humans were fodder, chattel, and food. Their cultures and deeds wiped out in a matter of months.

Asmodeus arrived at the top floor to find the door open to him. Inside was one long hall that terminated in another doorway. Lilith stood leaning on the frame.

"Asmodeus, how good to see you my love. Please join me." She turned from the doorway and he followed her into her usual lavish surroundings. Plush furniture and expensive fabrics abounded. Lilith surrounded herself with the most beautiful of her sisters and thralls. Asmodeus watched them watch him as he moved through the room behind their mistress. He knew that at the smallest command any one, or all of them, would move to give him all of the pleasure he could handle. But he was not here for that now. Lilith passed through the room and out onto a large balcony. Lilith leaned against the railing there, a light sheer gown clinging to her body in the wind. She was the most beautiful woman Asmodeus had ever seen and he always fell for her. That, he supposed, was her power.

"Do you still live in that hole?" she asked him as he joined her at the railing.

"I am surprised you still live in this one."

"It's a place to live," she said, gesturing to the wasteland beneath them.

"It's a waste," he said.

They stood beside one another for a moment, his wings rustling and her gown clinging in the wind. Each was lost in his own thoughts, but Asmodeus was sure that their thoughts were not all that different.

"What went wrong here?" Asmodeus asked his companion.

"We unleashed Hell on earth, which was all it took. Man was too weak to control the powers of Hell, and too petty and too jealous. Too full of vice and lust and anger. Mankind had begun destroying one another before Hell truly came into the world. The influence alone was too much for them and they subjected and slaughtered one another. One act of violence answered by another; one act of vengeance spawning thousands. Man began to close in on itself. When Hell came . . . there was truly no hope."

"There is no hope for us," he said to her, placing one arm around her waist; his hand rested on the upper curve of her hip.

"There never was, since the Fall we have been damned and they will come for us one day."

"Will they? His creation is in ruins, and still they haven't come."

"It's a waste," she said. "All of this didn't have to die did it? I'd been having so much fun."

"Anger, passion is all we know. It was bound to come to this end, whether by our hand or theirs." He looked over his shoulder into the room at Lilith's thralls. They stood aside from the demons in their midst, even after all these years still uncomfortable in the presence of evil.

"They believed in passion and hope once, too."

"And now, what do they believe?"

"Nothing," she said.

"Have you heard word of the others?"

"I never keep up with those dogs."

Asmodeus knew that this was a lie. He lived in Hell because it was quiet. There he could keep to his own council. He left the ruination of the world to the others. He knew they laughed at him for his folly, but he didn't care. Since they fled into the world, he had little reason to keep them in his eye, little reason to guard the gates, but he did it still. He came onto earth only to see Lilith.

"What would you have of me, wicked woman," he asked her finally.

"I would have you stay here with me. Be my companion in these end times. I would have you love me as you once did, if you can."

"And if I can't?"

"I would have you thrown from these battlements . . . like I did that bitch goat."

"I can fly, love." Asmodeus looked deep into her eyes.

"But he couldn't."

They laughed and he pulled her into his arms. Together they watched the sun set over a damned world.

Weep Not, Fair Freya, for I Will See You in *Niflheim* and We Will All of Us Be Dead

By Robert Penson

> *"It is sated on blood*
> *Of fated men,*
> *Red it paints the halls of power.*
> *Black becomes the sun,*
> *And in summer,*
> *Winter falls in awful hour."*

Her pale face, her cold eyes, they stared straight through him, her gaze never straying.

"Do you still seek to know? And what?"

A sweet voice, more like an echo of one. She spoke in some unknown tongue: a hard, throaty language, ancient, one that he did not know, yet understood.

Her skin glowed white, long golden hair as bright as the sun. Her eyes were cold blue. She was not young, she was not old.

233

She was a beautiful ghost. Her feet hung below her, peeking from under her long white robe. She simply floated, floated in the air, in the blackness. A dreadful void all around, as if all had ceased to exist but her.

She stared, her head nodding gently, almost with a coy flirtation. She carried a taunting smirk across her fair lips.

"I sink now," said the spirit.

The light pierced his eyes, the darkness peeled back, like the blackest veil being drawn to reveal the brightest light from behind. He shut them quickly, turning his head away. But the light was everywhere, inescapable. He groaned as shots of pain darted through his neck. His body ached, stiff and sore. It was as if every muscle groaned with him. "What . . . where . . ." he coughed out; his throat hoarse and dry, his breath sour. His voice seemed muffled, like in a helmet. *Alright, alright. Calm. Get your eyes open,* he ordered himself. *Eyes open.* He slowly and gently pulled back his heavy eyelids, allowing them to adjust.

He turned, remembering again the pain that had overtaken his body. His eyes felt like sandstone. He inspected himself, then his confinement. White padding lined the walls all around him. He was in some small imprisonment. It was a box, or container of some sort, the equivalent size of a coffin. Tubes and wires protruded from all sides of his padded coffin, convening around his body, his limbs, his torso, and his head. He looked forward. Glass. A glass window. But his eyes failed. No, there was just no light. It was just more darkness outside the glass window. Suddenly, a *ping* rang out from unseen speakers in his pod and then a voice. Automated with the pleasant sound of a middle-aged woman, it popped and cracked as a recording does.

"Good morning, Lt. Henriksen. First, you are urged to remain calm and still, for all is well. Surely you are disoriented and a little confused, but be assured that this is normal, and your memory will return to you in time. You have just awoken out of hibernation stasis, according to scheduled rotation, and it is imperative that your body be given the time to recover, as well as your mind. So, sleep now, Lieutenant, all is well. Sleep now."

He took a deep breath, a sigh of relief. It was returning to him. Lars. Lt. Lars Henriksen. "That's right. That's right . . ." his voice croaked. "Hypersleep. I'm on the . . . I'm on the *Niorun* . . . Wanderer class . . . frontier space. Mapping . . ." His eyelids, heavier now, fell as curtains do. Darkness again overcame light. His thoughts echoed in his head. Sleep, once again, overtook him.

Again, the blackness peeled away, allowing the flood of white to rush in. Easier now, the soreness and stiffness had subsided. He glanced down, noticing the wheel at the center of what he now realized to be the door. He took hold of the assist handle and turned until the sound of a seal breaking urged him to push. The large metal hatch lurched open revealing the room before him.

He allowed himself to float out of the pod, gently removing the tubes and sensor nodes. His back was still tight, most likely from the awakening. He was cold. He shivered and rubbed himself for warmth. There was a cold inside him too, he noticed. An anxiety, a feeling of something impending. *Emotional instability is normal when you're waking up*, he noted. *Nothing to worry about.*

He made his way across the room to a series of lockers, each with a personalized plaque. He found the one marked, in official corps lettering, "Lt. Henriksen." He removed the blue, embroidered jumpsuit, pulling it over his cold body. He turned around, zipping up, rubbing his shoulders firmly, aching from hypersleep. Looking at his empty sleep-pod he floated over to close the hatch, taking notice of the other four pods. The other sleepers in their beds. He tried to remember them; an exercise taught to all *sleepwalkers*. There was, of course, the captain. He had sailed with him before; he held him in high enough regard. Asleep next to him was the first officer, a colonel. Through the glass, he glanced into the next pod. A beautiful young girl lay peacefully inside. Lt. Yeoman. Emily when they weren't on duty. The last held P. O. Dallas. *Rick? Richard?* he thought.

But it was his shift now, his watch over the ship. Henriksen could feel himself relaxing a bit, finally, as the memory now poured into his troubled mind, washing away the cold fear that had resided in the tension in his back, in his neck, in his soul ever since waking up.

Do you still seek to know? And what?

The voice echoed to him, deep from his memory. Odd as it was to dream in hypersleep, Henriksen dismissed it as just a rough awakening. He made his way out of what the crew affectionately called "the bedroom" out into the stark white hall.

It was a long white tunnel, brightly lit by the serpent of florescence running its length. On opposite sides were two continuous columns of bright yellow handles, like ladder rungs. He climbed his way forward until it ended at a large, much larger than the others, round hatch door. Above it read "BRIDGE."

The door screeched and groaned as Henriksen pushed his way in. He enjoyed being on the bridge. It was the largest room on the boat, and one of the few with a view. The gigantic bay windows were covered now, their great metal shields extended over them as they always were while the *Niorun* was in stasis conditions. The lights came on automatically now that the ship's mains were online. He floated his way to the conditions station, one of the larger control stations on the bridge. He cranked the lever at the side of it until it locked into place. The hums and beeps of all the control stations filled the room as the bridge awoke from its long slumber.

He looked about the room, a large round chamber, more like a cylinder. A very official white, colored only by the knobs and switches and gauges all around. Gauges. *Where are we, anyway?*

he pondered. He glanced down at the instrument array. He did protocol checks, a quick inspection of all the vitals. Power, fuel, life support . . . and then he glanced at a particular gauge, an analog screen of red lines of light. Above it read "DURATION." He stared at it, waiting for it to clear itself of its own slumberous fog and shine back to life, enlightening him as to how long they had been out. Finally, it glowed awake, filling all the red lines bright before dimming again to cough out its reading:

$$999.999.999.999$$

What? The screen read a maximum reading, which was impossible, of course. They obviously couldn't have been out that long. *Stupid piece of . . .* He moved his eyes down to an identical analog screen. It was just glowing awake itself. Above it read "DISTANCE." *Ok, how far have we gone then?* Already warmed up, it illuminated with the same devilish red:

$$999.999.999.999$$

What? He tapped it with his finger. Maxed out. The tension returned, creeping across his back and shoulders. His heart began to pound. *It's just this instrument display. Must be something wrong with the display.*

He flew over to the navigational station. The memory bank was full. The communications station. Maxed out. Flight control station. Maxed out. All of them. *Why are they all maxed out?* It made no sense. *Nothing goes that far or stays out that long; surely it was a catastrophic instrument malfunction, not the systems. But an equipment failure of that magnitude could prove catastrophic on the systems themselves.*

He thought for some time, staving off the panic. He searched his training and the room for any answer, but none came. He knew that he needed the captain, probably the whole damn crew, awake. Dallas was the equipment specialist, and the others should be awoken for safety purposes, in case there was a systems failure. He swam towards the door, turning back one last time to analyze the situation. His eyes caught a large red handle. It was a lever, the largest in the room. "SHIELDS."

He floated across the chamber taking hold of the handle, pulling it towards him. A great roar of machinery, motors being engaged, the wail and howl of metal sliding on metal as the great bay shields retracted back into their hiding places behind the walls. They parted like curtains, laying the scene.

He started back towards the door, finding the screeching unpleasant. Just before reaching the hatch, a loud *clang* rang out, the machines stopped, the motors rested again. He glanced back to take in a view of the space outside.

His eyes widened, his pupils narrowed. The pounding of his heart could be seen in his temples. Beads of sweat snuck out onto his brow.

There was darkness. Only black. A black like no night he had ever known. There was nothing. There was just an endless . . . endlessness.

"What? Where . . . where are all the stars?"

He couldn't tell if they were in a vast abyss reaching to infinity or if they were buried beneath a great black mass. There was no starlight. There were no suns, no moons, no blue planets or barren rocks. There were no stars.

He flew back over to the nav station. He looked at the glowing green of the RADIS screen. Two rings rotated on opposite axes, pulsating like a heartbeat, beeping with each pass, vanishing and appearing like phantoms. There was nothing. The rings wiped the radiant green, showing nothing, not even debris. The energy detectors only picked up their wake behind them.

He swam for the door, down the tunnel, and to the bedroom.

An hour passed as Henriksen awaited the crew, allowing them to recover. He floated in the center of the great ship's bridge, his arms crossed. His gaze was fixed forward and above, out the windows into the infinite blackness. His eyes were mesmerized by the perfection of it. It was a pure black, no shades, no flaws. It was a gloomy ocean of nothing.

And then he saw something. A dot, tiny. Or at a great distance. Yes, something far out. It seemed to emit a luminescence. And it drew nearer. It came closer. Closer. He could see it now. It was floating towards the ship.

It was her. He could see her now. Glowing white, golden hair, bright like the sun. She drifted towards the ship, towards the window, closer now. She stared at him. Her head nodded gently, her hair floated around her beautiful face. He was at the window now, his palms pressed against the cold glass. A beautiful angel. No, a goddess surrounded by the never-ending void. And oh, how she stared.

Henriksen kicked back from the window, knocking his head on a control panel. He flailed like a drowning swimmer, trying to reach the door. She was at the glass now. He made his way towards the hatch when it suddenly flew open, almost hitting him. The startled crewman let out a shout of surprise.

"What the hell are you doing, Lieutenant?"

Henriksen spun back to the window. Nothing. Nothing but the blackness.

"My god, what . . . Is there something on the glass?" The first officer flew to the RADIS screen that Henriksen motioned to with his finger. "What the hell. Is this what you were going on about, Henriksen? Sir, you better look at this!"

The captain was now floating through the door, followed shortly by Lt. Yeoman. "What the hell . . ." he muttered.

Yeoman responded, "Must be something on the glass."

"Maybe you should look at this," said the first officer.

The captain and Lt. Yeoman floated over to the green screen. Both jerked their heads back to the window. "Where the hell are all the stars, sir?" Yeoman softly asked.

"I'm going to go have a look outboard." The first officer swam out the door, down the hall towards the airlock.

The captain looked up at Henriksen, confusion in his eyes. "What's going on here, Lieutenant?"

"There must have been some sort of malfunction, sir. I'm not too sure. I was hoping Dal could tell us more. But what I do know is . . . we didn't get woken up. So, we must have just kept going . . ." Henriksen said shakingly. "I don't know how. But we must have just kept sailing."

The captain, with a troubled expression, looked back down at the screen, illuminating his face with an otherworldly green.

"I was thinking it was instrumentation at first. But Dal knows more about this stuff. Where is he?" Henriksen asked, looking towards the hallway. The captain and Lt. Yeoman exchanged unsure glances. "Sir? Where's Dallas?" Henriksen asked again.

The captain turned his head, looking Henriksen in the eyes. Yeoman dropped her head, chewing on her lip.

"He didn't make it." The captain's voice cracked as he spoke, like the first words from some one waking from sleep.

"Didn't make it? What does that mean?"

"Something went wrong during the awakening. We're not sure. He never regained consciousness. We performed emergency protocol, but . . ." Yeoman's voice trembled.

Henriksen's heart sank. *Dead? During awakening?*

"There's nothing we can do about it," the captain said abruptly. He was right.

Time passed like waves in a pool and the crew settled in. The captain floated diligently at the bridge, hunched over workstations. Yeoman went about standard protocols: checking equipment, inventorying supplies, going over printed reports. Henriksen took to wandering the halls. He snaked his way through the bright tunnels, climbing the yellow rungs from here to there.

Henriksen traversed the maze like a lab rat. He explored a multitude of identical causeways. All dead ends. Yet he kept wandering, as if there were someway out. He'd pass by the dark engine room, the storage holds, the supply closets. He thought about how they could live, how they could survive for a long time. *But why*, he thought *and to what end? Getting back home? We've been out for so long, everything we ever knew is surely gone. Planets are born and die in the time we've slept. We already died, or might as well have, long ago.* He turned upwards, down a long corridor, exactly like the others. *What's the point? The point in working towards some end, any end? We are as the dead. What I do, what we do, what we want, will have no effect on anything. Our actions will do nothing to influence anything around us, anything anywhere. We are a tree, deep in the forest, and we have fallen. And no one was around to hear it.*

He passed by a glass-walled chamber, stopping to look in. It was the airlock, a red light shown above it, declaring its "in use" status. Closer, he found the first officer inside, busy removing the cumbersome support-suit from his spacewalk.

"Anything, sir?" shouted Henriksen. The first officer gave no response. He drifted up to the glass between them, knocking on it. The first officer did not look up. "I said, did you find anything?"

The first officer shook his head. Saying no more, Henriksen turned to leave.

"It's just like it was. Pitch black. No light. Nothing . . ." the Lieutenant heard as he swam away.

Henriksen grabbed the wall nearest to him, stopping himself. He slowly turned back. The first officer had turned also, facing away. Henriksen carefully floated himself closer. The first officer was muttering now. "Black. Black all around . . ." He struggled to hear the officer's voice. "Just like it was, but . . ." his voice died off.

Henriksen recoiled. The first officer, still facing away, anxiously continued removing the bulky suit. Henriksen floated back before turning to climb onward down the tunnel.

Like a whispered secret passed through a crowd, time became subjective, abstract, obscure, and merely lost in the cluttered mass (or lack thereof). Hours turned to days, days became clouded and blurred. They had no sense of time, as they knew of it anyway. Their clocks were in the same state as most of the electronics: burnt out or malfunctioning. There was no sun to tell the days, no calendar to mark the months. They simply existed out in the abyss.

Henriksen and Yeoman took to maintenance tasks, carrying around their toolboxes and their holstered multi-tools. It helped them feel normal or at least useful. The captain kept watch at the bridge, pining over the instruments, entering information, mapping out a plan of procedure.

The first officer, however, was keeping to himself more and more. He spoke only to direct orders, always avoiding the eyes of the others.

Yeoman talked to Henriksen. She talked a lot, making conversation about anything new or old. He listened and enjoyed the company.

"So, what's with all the spacewalks?" she asked over a blown heating coil.

"You mean the F.O.? Strange, I know." Henriksen floated opposite of her over the exposed wires and heat vapors.

"He goes out there all the time. One time I looked out a port window. He had harnessed himself to the ship and had just let go. He was free floating. I mean meters out. All still and lifeless. It creeped me out."

Henriksen imagined the experience. Being consumed by the blackness, taunting the abyss. No light, no sounds, no smells, nothing at all. No sound, save for the breathing inside the helmet, the pulse of one's heart. *Like the womb.*

"I don't know. Boredom is a hell of a thing. We're all dealing as best we can," his voice strained as they pulled free the coil.

"Still, it's weird . . ."

Nights, days, maybe weeks later, restless and awake, Henriksen wandered the halls. Through lifeless corridors, he pretended he did not know the ship, that this was all new to him. He soon found himself near aft, on the starboard side. Lt. Yeoman's quarters where down the tunnel a few meters. He swam his way through, stopping at the hatch of her room, slightly ajar. He heard something. Crying.

"Knock, knock," he announced.

"Hey," she replied sniffling and wiping her eyes free of the tears that filled them.

"Hey, what's goin' on? What's wrong?"

"Nothing. It's nothing," she said as she dabbed her puffy eyes with the sleeve of her jumpsuit, sniffling again.

"It's got to be something."

"Just stress. What's up? To what do I owe this pleasure?" She spoke in a feigned sarcasm, changing the subject.

"Oh, nothing. Bored I suppose." He swam in a ways, taking position on the wall opposite of her, floating a bit above her.

"There's plenty of that to go around these days." She sniffled again, trying to prove once and for all that she had not been crying. "Hey, so can I ask you a question?"

"Why do you always ask me that? Yes, you always have permission to ask me a question." Henriksen chuckled teasingly, rolling his eyes dramatically, attempting to add some levity.

Yeoman half-heartedly giggled. "Do you . . . do you believe in ghosts?"

His head cocked towards her, his brow constricted. "Why would you ask me that?" he snapped, failing to hide his uneasiness.

"It's just something I ask people sometimes."

Henriksen sighed, lowering his shoulders. "Do you?" he retorted.

"Well, I don't know. I've never seen one. But I suppose most of my life has been spent out in space and there are no ghosts in space."

Henriksen looked away. "Is that so? Well, why do you ask people if they believe in ghosts?"

"Because I think it says a lot about a person."

"How so?"

"Well, to believe in ghosts, you have to believe in having a spirit or something. And you have to believe in an afterlife, right? That says something about a person."

"Yea, I suppose so."

"And, if there is in fact an afterlife, some place that we go, there must be a god to run the whole thing, wouldn't you think? Now you've found out whether that person believes in God or not, and that says a lot to me. That's how I see it anyway."

"That's fair," he replied, staring off into the distance.

"I guess that's what's got me bothered."

"What? Ghosts?"

She giggled again. "No, not ghosts." She fidgeted with her long hair, gazing down into her own lap. He bit his lip and pulled on his pant leg. "You know, I was never really sure what I believed. I mean, I've prayed before, sure, when it counted. If someone was dying or I needed to pass an exam . . ."

Henriksen turned to look at her. She continued, his heartbeat quickening, "But I always wondered if He was even out there." Her voice quivered. "And now . . . now I want to believe that He is. But what if it's too late." She turned, meeting his gaze. "What if . . ." her tears returning now, "what if He can't hear us?" She looked away, trying to suppress the whimpers. "What if He can't hear us out here? Is He even out this far? Did He create this, or is this like . . . like, the end of Creation? The edge? What if we're too far out?" She returned her eyes to his; her's glistening in the florescent light. "Do you think He can hear us? Do you think He comes out this far? Is He even listening?"

Henriksen eyes shut, his hands grabbed and pulled at his jumpsuit.

"WAS HE EVER?" he exploded. "Was He ever fucking listening to us? He sure as hell wasn't listening to me!" Her eyes shot open, startled at the lieutenant's outpour. "We looked for Him. We looked for Him everywhere we knew: the skies, the stars. And He never showed! Nothing but stars, barren planets, and gaseous giants!" Her face was in her hands now, muffling her sobs. "And then, guess what? We ran out of those, too! We turned over the very last rock, and NOTHING!" Droplets floated up and away from her face. "And even if He is out there, I think it's safe to say that He does not see us out here. So my question really is: if He is out there, but can't hear us out here, what good was He in the first place?"

She wept now. Henriksen clenched his teeth together, looking away in disgust at himself. He floated down, taking a place next to her. Her tears danced through the air like little bubbles.

"I'm sorry," she choked out.

"No, don't be. I'm sorry." He paused. "But . . . hey, look at me." He took her chin in his hand and turned her head to face him. "We are out here, okay? We are out here and we are alone. All alone. There is no one listening. There is no one watching. There is nothing but empty space. That's all there was all along, I suppose . . ."

Yeoman forced out another polite giggle through her tears. "You're right. I'm just a little bit of a mess right now."

"No, no, don't apologize. This is hard on all of us . . ." He forced a smile, as did she. He leaned and kissed her wet cheek. They sat there for a time in silence. He breathed in heavily, then turned and floated upwards to leave. Before exiting, he turned to her once more.

"So, you don't think ghosts can haunt a spaceship, huh?"

"Well," she said, looking at him, "I don't know. It's outer space. The way I see it, a ghost can't haunt where nothing died, right? Or ever lived, for that matter." He nodded his head in agreement, idiosyncratically. "I could be wrong, of course," she added, half-joking. He looked at her inquisitively. "Well, the captain's told me a few old seafarer tales, ancient history really. The Norse, I think, had said that they saw ghosts in their dreams while at sea, some even said they saw a goddess." She laughed dismissively.

Henriksen looked her in the eyes, unable to speak. She gave him a concerned look, snapping him back to his senses. "Yeah. Well I'm with you on the first part. A ghost can't haunt where nobody has been before." They shared a delicate smile as he sank back, pulling the hatch door closed behind him.

He paused for a moment outside the door, closing his eyes. *I need sleep*, he relinquished.

"Everything all right?" A gruff voice from behind startled him. It was the first officer.

"Yes, Colonel."

The first officer looked him up and down, his face was sullen. "Best to call it a night. You need sleep, Lieutenant." His words were curt and short.

"Sir." Henriksen turned, starting his way back down the hall. He heard the slam of the first officer's door behind him. *Hell is, truly, other people.*

Back up the corridor. He climbed the never-ending yellow ladder through the narrow white tunnel. *That was rough. I was harsh*, he thought. *But this is rough. She's going to need to toughen up if we're going to make it* . . . His thoughts were interrupted. Passing through an intersection, something caught his eye from the hallway to the side. He stopped himself on the ladder, pushing himself back. It was the airlock. All lights were off.

Dark. Save for a glowing white woman staring back at him.

Henriksen recoiled, hitting the corridor walls. He started to push back, his eyes unable to break from hers. He stopped. She stood. She actually stood on the floor, stood in the absence of gravity. She stood there, burning bright, her head nodding gently.

She simply stared at him. He held his breath, his muscles seized in fear. He forced himself back the way he had come.

Around the corner, he took a moment to catch his breath. *Why does she haunt me? Why only me?* he thought, almost angrily. He quickly made his way back down the direction he had been coming from, too embarrassed to admit to himself that he was afraid to pass the airlock again. He found his way back to Yeoman's quarters.

Pushing the hatch open again, he propelled himself inside. "No! Oh, God! Emily!" he screamed.

He dove towards her floating body. She had pulled a belt around her neck, fastening it tight around her windpipe. Her face was blue; her body lifeless. He cut the belt off with his multi-tool. She had no pulse. He performed emergency protocols, resuscitation from basic training. Nothing. She was gone.

He held her tight, hugging her. He squeezed his eyes closed. Finally, he released her from his arms, letting her float away. He let out a groan. His eyes became blurry with moisture. Then he noticed, out of her breast pocket stuck a crisp, white piece of paper. He leaned in, gently removing it from her jumpsuit. Unfolding it, he read, "I am sorry. I'll let Him know that we've been looking for Him."

Henriksen's heart pounded, his hands balled up into fists. He choked out a wail and tears streamed out of his eyes, saliva from his lips. He wept loudly, beating his fists against the walls around him. His tears danced in the air like little bubbles.

Back on the bridge, the captain wrapped a jacket around Henriksen, taking his shoulders firmly in his grasp. "Don't blame yourself, son. She made her choice," he said to the lieutenant.

"I know, sir."

The captain released his grip and chewed on his own thoughts, searching for the words to say. He hesitated. "It was bound to happen eventually." Henriksen glanced at him before turning away once more. "I didn't think it from her, though. Damn it all." The captain wavered, he floated back behind the lieutenant, studying him. He returned to a workstation, glancing up at him once more before busying himself at the instrument panel.

"I don't know that the colonel even knows yet. Went for a walk again." The captain made conversation without looking up.

"You know about his spacewalks?" he replied, looking out the windows, out into the emptiness.

"I'm the captain aren't I? It is strange though. But what is strange now?"

"Sir?" Henriksen inquired.

"Strange. What does that mean? It means 'different from the normal.' Well, what is normal based upon?"

Henriksen looked at the captain blankly.

"It's based upon the things around us. On what we perceive. Things are only strange when they are different from that frame, wouldn't you agree?"

The lieutenant did not respond. The captain continued, "Well, we have no such luxury. We have no comparison. We have no environs at all. Nothing to hold ourselves up to and thus be judged."

"We have ourselves," the lieutenant replied after a pause.

"Sure, sure. But what are we? Are we not the bound feeding the gagged? Are we not mere droplets hanging in the mist all around? We have no way to gauge our own actions, to gauge ourselves at all. We have no way to tell time, no relation to it. So how do we judge how long ago something was or how soon something will happen? We have nothing to pass, so how can we be sure we are moving forward, or moving at all?"

Henriksen stared into the abyss as he listened. "Perception is reality. If we are not perceived, how are we to know if we exist?" His voice echoed before losing himself in the dark, in the abysmal blackness.

He stared out into oblivion, the captain's voice humming from behind. He felt as if he had closed his eyes, but they were as open as they ever were. He stared out into the sea of nothing.

And there the phantom was, floating bright and clearly in the blackness of eternal dark. She floated as if underwater. Her head nodded coyly; her eyes never moved. Her sweet lips revealed the slightest grin, her golden hair waved around her beautiful face. Henriksen heard the captain's voice, preoccupied with his philosophical recital. He looked back at the lady, the goddess. He tried to allow her light to warm his face, her presence to bring some understanding. But it didn't. It brought nothing but the same cold fear. She stared deeply into his eyes, speaking to him in silent words, with no meaning. She was simply there. Her cold blue eyes fixed on his, until they suddenly shifted, looking behind him.

They were interrupted by the moan of the hatch door opening. He turned to see the first officer making his way in. He jerked back towards the windows, but she was gone. She left nothing but the incessant darkness.

The captain's voice broke the air, startling him.

"What the hell do you think you're doing?! Answer me, officer!" the captain shouted.

Henriksen spun around to see the first officer floating just inside the doorway. In his hand was a black pistol pointed at the captain's head.

"Did you go into my quarters, go through my things? You must have lost your goddamn mind!"

Henriksen floated in the air motionless. He mustered enough to interject, "What's going on, Colonel?"

The first officer floated with one hand against the wall, holding the gun steadily towards the captain. His eyes were wide like two moons, his brow constricted in intensity. Perspiration seeped from his face.

"Tell me, Captain. What has become of us?"

"What the hell do you mean? Why are you waving a gun around?" he answered angrily.

"What has become of us?" he repeated, shouting now.

The captain glared at the first officer. "Same thing I told you before. Ship fucked up, we didn't wake. We kept going. Now we're lost. What do you want me to say?"

"That you are wrong, that's what I want you to say. We've all been wrong this whole time. We're no more lost than we were before waking up," the gunman screamed.

"You're insane," grumbled the captain.

"We are exactly where we are meant to be. We are exactly where she wanted us. We always have been."

She? Henriksen thought to himself. "Who?" he asked, nearly pleading.

The first officer darted his fanatical gaze towards the lieutenant now, eyes agape, before returning to the captain's glare. "The ghost. The goddess, I think. I'm not sure, yet."

Henriksen panicked. The pounding in his head was unbearable, his mouth was dry, his throat closed on him. The first officer again looked at Lt. Henriksen, noticing his expression, his bafflement. His eyes narrowed at the lieutenant.

"You've seen her, haven't you?"

Henriksen was struck dumb. He forced out a whimper, "Who is she?"

The first officer laughed. "A ghost, bringing us rumors of our own doom? The fair Goddess, come to show us to her fields. Perhaps it is Hel herself calling for us!" His voice deepened. "I suppose it doesn't really matter in the end."

"ENOUGH! We're all impressed that you can read and we thank you for the mythology lesson! Son, I'm only going to say this once: give me the goddamn gun right now!" The captain's scream pulled the first officer's maniacal eyes back to him.

A smile crept across the first officer's face, his eyes matched with the captain's. He roared, "HEL HATH HALF OF US! AND NOW SHE CALLS FOR US ALL!"

The captain started, "You've lost your goddamn mind! Give me that FUCKING gun OR . . ."

"Hel hath half of us already! AND NOW THEY AWAIT US IN THE GREAT CORPSE HALL!"

Henriksen was frozen in fear, paralyzed in bewilderment. The first officer returned his gaze once more, looking him in the eye. He turned back towards the captain, his words echoed in the room.

"Fear not, little brother! For I will see you in her fields, where we shall sleep no more . . ."

The shot left a ringing in Henriksen's ears that was deafening. Blood spewed from the captain's head, spilling out into the air like vapor from a ship's thrusters.

Henriksen looked in horror. Quickly looking back at the shooter, he lunged forward. The first officer raised the gun at him, but Henriksen swatted it with the back of his hand, flying forward. He wrapped his legs around the assailant, crashing them both against the wall of gauges. He hooked one arm under his shoulder, locking the gun hand away. With the other arm he reached around his neck, clasping his hands together. He squeezed hard. The first officer struggled wildly, his voice muffled in Henriksen's chest. He tried to punch him and knee him from under. Two shots rang out, striking the walls near the windows. Henriksen squeezed until he felt no more struggle, no more breath. The first officer relaxed, the gun floated out of his hand. Henriksen released the first officer, freeing him. He too free floated back, again to the center of the room.

Henriksen treaded the air now like a seabird atop the water. He floated, staring upwards out the great bridge windows. He stared into the vast abyss, the never-ending void of blackness. The captain's body hung in the air behind him, dancing with the other corpse. His blood danced in the air like little bubbles.

His mind was wild. He closed his eyes, breathing the recycled air deep into his lungs. His mind flowed over Yeoman's face, over the immeasurability of infinity, over the chilly air of a sleepwalker like the *Niorun*. His eyes opened. He looked, again, into the abyss. But the abyss did not look back.

She was not there. No white dot approaching. No beautiful lady. No horrific specter. The black sidearm was cold in his hand.

Is He even out there? Is He even listening?

It would have been a heavy weapon, if there were such a thing as "heavy" out here.

Do you still seek to know? And what?

He waited for her, searched for her in the dark.

But she did not come. He put the gun to his head.

"I sink now," said the spirit.

Darkness, again, overtook him.

> *"It sates itself on blood*
> *Of fated men,*
> *Red it paints the halls of power.*
> *Black becomes the sun,*
> *And in summer,*
> *Winter falls in awful hour.*
>
> *Do you still seek to know? And what?"*

She spoke in a tongue he did not know, yet understood.

The light pierced his eyes, the darkness peeled away, like the blackest veil being drawn back to reveal the brightest light from behind.

Still hungry for more PULP?

Then check out our other installments:

Available through Createspace.com and Amazon.com

ISBN 9780984547715
ISBN 9781453628584

Also available as a digital download through
Amazon.com, BarnesandNoble.com, Kobobooks.com, Sony.com,
Diesel-ebooks.com, Smashwords.com and the Apple iBookstore.